THE
BOOK
OF ASH

THE BOOK OF ASH

A NOVEL

JOHN A MCCAFFREY

BOXFIREPRESS

Published by Boxfire Press.

Printed in the United States of America
17 16 15 14 13   1 2 3 4 5
ISBN 978-1-938191-04-6
ebook ISBN 978-1-938191-15-2

Every attempt has been made to ensure this book is free from typos and errors. We apologize if you do stumble across one and hope it won't hurt your enjoyment of the story. Thanks to changes in technology we can easily correct errors for future readers with your help. Contact us at editorial@boxfirepress.com.

To my wonderful family, my father, mother and sister, for their unconditional love, support and generosity.

And for my beautiful wife, Grace, who is all I will ever need in this life.

ACKNOWLEDGMENTS

Many people helped to make this novel a reality, and I am grateful beyond words. Special thanks to Jill Dearman, my writing coach and friend, who always had faith in the project and kept me going during the tough times. Douglas Light, my colleague from the City College of New York, provided invaluable critiques during the writing and editing process. Mark Kleber, the wisest man I know, always lent a compassionate ear. And my writing students in Hoboken and Queens were a regular source of inspiration and encouragement. Finally, I would like to thank Scott Sparks and the team at Boxfire Press for giving *The Book of Ash* a chance to meet the world.

*B*aldwin Wallace was alone in bed, reading from *The Book of Ash*. He was also anxiously waiting for his wife to return home.

Reading was not helping him to relax or to forget that Nadine was late again. They fought about the issue just the night before. Perhaps "fought" was not the best description for what happened, as it implied a give and take between opposing parties with the mutual intent to harm. Certainly Nadine – with voice and hands – fought with such purpose, but Baldwin, consistent to his careful upbringing and non-aggressive nature, mostly listened...and ducked.

Their disagreement, as he saw it, started with a simple question, which he posed to Nadine while she was unchanging in their bedroom, having finally come home well past the moonrise gong.

"Do you still love me?"

Nadine's response was to throw her clogs at his head, and when they missed, to hurl accusations at him instead. These found their mark. "Controlling," "Needy," and "Suffocating," words said with striking force, knocked him back against the headboard and sent the candle on the adjoining nightstand tumbling to the floor. After the initial shock subsided, he gathered himself to rescue the flame, while Nadine, perhaps to emphasize her claims and give them a visual context, ripped off her shirt and used it to fashion a garrote around her neck. Luckily, he was able to right the candle before it burned out, and by its light untied the knot and removed the garment just as Nadine was beginning to lose consciousness.

Understandably, they talked no more that night, or the next morning, except for Nadine blaming him for her not sleeping well and thus feeling too weak to meet the increasing demands of her utility. In her defense, it was a stressful time in the Circle, a place named not for its rounded shape or curvy topography (the terrain was mostly flat, often sunken, and the borders formed a near-perfect square), but because of the unified commitment of the citizens to be, well, unified. The cause of the current uproar was the looming Day of No Consequence, the lone holiday in the Circle's calendar, when men and women (and children over the age of five) were encouraged to let loose with fury, to release latent hostilities, to reclaim a peaceful mindset through violence and mayhem.

Preparing for this carnage kept everyone busy, but none more than Nadine. As a hygiene counselor, her main duty was to maintain the aesthetic integrity of keratin, the hard protein that constituted the human nail. Most of her clients were women who wanted a simple smoothing of the free edges, or a light polish to fortify the nail plate. But around the Day of No Consequence, their beautification needs grew more mysterious and more complex. Baldwin remembered Nadine telling him about an older lady who asked that each of her toenails be filed into three sections – the center flat, the bordering sides dagger-shaped. It took considerable effort, but when finished, each foot had the capacity to puncture and tear through the toughest flesh. Yet Nadine doubted this possible, given that the woman was quite infirmed, practically immobile because of swollen knees and ankles, and certainly unable to kick anyone with tenacity. Perhaps, she reasoned, the style was selected more as a deterrent than a weapon, a façade to scare away anyone who wanted to do her harm.

While Baldwin did not doubt that Nadine was being overworked, never before in their five years of romantic union had the Day of No Consequence caused her to be this consistently late. He had a feeling something else was involved, some other element that was taking up her time, but he dared not ask what it was, for fear he might reignite her anger and trigger another traumatic scene. But holding everything in was killing him. His nerves, erratic during the best of times, were shot, and the loneliness he felt was compounded by the idea that he was not supposed to feel lonely. It was something his life counselor, Harold, often said in sessions, that loneliness is most felt by those who are not alone. Baldwin never fully understood the meaning of this before, but he did now, feeling that he was in a relationship without having one.

This was probably why he had sought out affirmation—"Do you still love me?"—the night before. He hoped Nadine did. Not because of any great happiness he derived from their union, but because he could not endure an even greater unhappiness from it. His only hope was that Nadine might change, or at least go back to the way she was, early on, when she seemed content with domestic predictability, enjoying with him the intimate rituals of a couple, such as sharing the evening's edibles bag, discussing their utilities and the people they disliked, kissing each other with eyes open when the moon was waxing, and with eyes closed when it was waning.

Perhaps the Day of No Consequence would help. While Baldwin had never partaken in the frenzy, he did value the holiday's ability to create closeness, the fear of attack often encouraging friends, couples, families, even strangers, to come together, to work together, to hide together, to unite under one common, powerful purpose: survival. While violence ruled the open spaces, love often bloomed in the hidden ones, and after each holiday stories came forth of new romances forged and old romances repaired.

Baldwin took a moment to visualize this happening with Nadine. He imagined spending the day alone with her, barricaded inside their unit, talking through problems, reconnecting and reigniting passions, kissing freely (whatever the moon phase) and, finally, making love. The thought triggered an erection. He watched as the section of the sheet covering his waist rose. He savored the moment. It felt good to think of Nadine this way – to connect her with pleasure, and not just pain. But the feeling was fleeting. The sheet began to descend, and with it his mood.

Finally, he turned his attention back to *The Book of Ash*. He had completed the last of the text's 100 Encouragements the night prior, right before Nadine had come home. Now, as he was trained to do by his stepfather, he backtracked to the beginning, to work through the list anew. But a tinge of rebellion caught him by surprise, and after a quick glance around the room to make sure no one was watching, he sifted through the pages until he stopped somewhere near the middle. Still feeling paranoid about jumping ahead, and also a little guilty, he began to read just as the Circle encouraged…one word at a time.

ENCOURAGEMENT 44−CULTIVATE REJECTION

Strive for success and you strive for failure. While this may seem illogical, if you truly contemplate the result of success on your life, you will find the axiom has merit. Take work, for example. To secure employment, or gain promotion once hired, you usually must beat out someone for the job. Your win will be their loss. While victory is pleasing to the victor, the feeling holds no lasting value. The practice of competition for reward isolates the spirit, encourages selfishness, and gives rise to narcissism. Once an inner-focused mindset takes hold, it is difficult to see beyond the boundaries of one's flesh, and with each passing day the quest for individual satisfaction over-whelms any other desire. Losing the ability to be empathic, it is easy to grow paranoid and suspicious, to devolve into a bitter, angry, untrusting person – in other words, a failure.

To avoid this fate you must treat success as the enemy and excise its dangerous pull from your mind. A simple way to accomplish this is to cultivate rejection. For instance, never marry someone you desire or who desires you. Better to bond with a person who finds you unappealing, and who you find unappealing. Fueled by dissatisfaction, you will work hard to find interests outside your relationship to occupy your time, becoming in the process a more complete person, a more autonomous individual, someone whose emotional health is not tethered to the whims of their partner. Thus, what might be perceived as failure – spending time with someone you hate – will ultimately lead you to a rich and fulfilling life. You will be a success.

Reaction Step: The next time someone compliments you, explain why you don't deserve the praise, how their words threaten your attainment of a balanced and enlightened spirit. Then punch them.

1 SNAKE SKIN

*T*he punch, four knuckles and a chubby thumb, came at his forehead. It was delivered by Simon, who lived down the hall, in the only other unit on the floor. His neighbor, as usual, was wearing only underwear, a sequined blue thong that squeezed tight against his wide waist and plump thighs. He also had on matching heels, giving him just enough height not to appear short.

"Sorry about that," Simon said, lowering his hand to his side. "It appears you caught me at mid-knock."

Baldwin tried to regain his composure.

"It's my fault for opening the door without looking through the peephole. I should know better."

Simon swept away an uneven row of red curls from his tiny, close-set eyes. Although appearing to squeeze against his nose, their unique turquoise color made them the best feature in his otherwise plain, fleshy face.

"Anyway, I'm grateful to see you," Simon said.

"Likewise."

"Don't lie."

"I'm not."

But he was. While it was encouraged in the Circle to "greet with gratitude," Baldwin found the practice tiring, even duplicitous, never quite believing people were as appreciative as they said they were. He certainly wasn't pleased to see Simon, who he found cloying and tiresome.

"If you have a moment," Simon said, "I have a favor to ask."

"Can it wait? I'm in a rush to the miracle office."

"I won't hold you up long."

Baldwin was in no mood to talk even for a moment, having suffered a torturous sleep and a worse morning, waking with the sunrise gong (longer and higher-pitched than its midnight counterpart) to an empty bed. Nadine's absence was as upsetting as it was mysterious. He was not sure if she had slipped in beside him during the night, if she slept in another part of the unit, or if she slept in the unit at all. He was certain, however, that she came home at some point, as the past evening's edibles bag, which he left half-full on the kitchen table, was now empty, folded neatly on a table near the front door for him to leave outside.

"Are you sure it can't wait?"

"Yes."

"You mean we can talk later?"

"No," Simon said, dragging out the word, "I'm sure it can't wait."

Baldwin already felt drained. But perhaps it was best to get it over with.

"What's the favor?"

"Did I say favor?' Simon returned. "I misspoke. I do that sometime with 'f' words. I meant to say *opportunity*."

"So what's the opportunity?"

"First tell me what you got last night?"

"Excuse me?"

"In your edibles bag? What did you get?"

Baldwin had forgotten he was holding the bag. He quickly laid it on the tiled hallway floor, careful not to lose the crease in the burlap. He reminded himself that he needed to slip a chit (the Circle's monetary denomination) into it before the Day of No Consequence, an annual gift of gratitude to the nutritional counselor who came each evening to pick up the empty bag and replace it with a filled one.

He straightened and shook his head.

"Nothing special. Just the usual plant matter and protein."

Ordinarily, Baldwin would have been delighted by the meal provided the night before – a handful of dried green beans, two overripe tomatoes still connected to the vine, a stick of squirrel jerky, and, a real treat, a honey-ball wrapped inside birch bark – but his appetite had faltered, his stomach always reacting poorly to stress, and he had only managed a few nibbles and licks before giving up and going to bed.

Simon eyed the bag on the ground.

"It's terrible what the Circle thinks of our stomachs," he said. "Last night I got three apples, two green olives, and one smoked garter snake. There's no way to make a coherent meal from that combination. Plus I hate when I get six items. I always get indigestion when I eat that number."

"Well, they say food distribution is a random process."

"They say it," Simon said, "but they don't mean it. "I wish nutrition counselors would just admit they play favorites. I know for a fact that ours hates me."

"I'm sure he doesn't hate you."

"You never think anyone hates anyone."

Simon was right, sort of. Baldwin believed hate existed, just not inside of him. It was his mother's doing. Not only did she encourage him not to hate anyone growing up, she forbade him to utter the word in her presence, insisting he use "dislike" if he felt the need to affix a negative description to another person.

"Simon, I really have to get going."

His neighbor frowned.

"You're too concerned about your utility. I never let a job dictate my day – that is, when I had one. Besides, you look terrible. I bet it's because you're working too hard. Or maybe it's your jeans. They make your legs look too short, and that makes your torso look too long. You look all out of balance. You should wear briefs instead of pants. If you like" – Simon tapped the front of his thong – "I have another pair in this style, except it's red with emerald sequins in the back. I'll trade it to you for a pair of knee socks, preferably egg yolk yellow or aqua blue."

Baldwin wiggled his toes, exceptionally long, almost like fingers.

"Sorry, I never wear anything on my feet."

"What about Nadine?"

Baldwin thought about her recent tantrum, her clogs whistling by his head.

"She wears shoes, but not socks."

"So it's a sockless union," Simon said wearily. "Well, what do you have in your closet?"

"Only what I need. Which is what the Circle encourages everyone to have when it comes to non-essential items. So I'm satisfied."

It was another half-truth. Baldwin wished he had more clothes, but did not like the laborious process (and sometimes underhanded means) needed to procure them. At the moment, what he owned was what he was wearing: a pair of shin-length denim pants, a white button shirt with the right sleeve missing, and, because it was encouraged by the Circle to wear an item of clothing (or accessory) associated with the opposite sex, a pink scarf made of silk that once belonged to his mother.

"You think clothing isn't essential?" Simon asked.

"Don't you? You seem to wear very little of it."

Baldwin immediately regretted the snide remark, but Simon did not appear ruffled by the comment or aware that it was meant to belittle. In fact, he smiled proudly.

"I'm lucky to have a body that begs to be seen. But you shouldn't be shy. You're reasonably fit and you still have your hair. I don't even see any gray in it, and you're what, in your late 40's?"

"I'm thirty-three."

"Really? You dress like someone past the age of counting. Please, let me get the thong. We don't even have to trade. I'll share it with you."

Baldwin had enough.

"I'm comfortable in my own pants, thank you."

He made a move to push past, but Simon held up a hand to stop him.

"Okay, don't be upset. I won't ask again. You probably don't have the legs and hips to pull off a thong anyway."

Simon paused, glanced up and down the hallway, and then leaned forward.

"But here's something you can't pass up," he whispered, his stale breath tickling Baldwin's nostrils. "I found a timehole last night—took a step into some soft soil and plunged right through."

His eyes widened to nearly normal size.

"I've never seen anything like it. It's absolutely loaded."

Searching for timeholes was a side-utility for many in the Circle. But it was a dangerous business, as most people died upon finding one, sustaining fatal injuries after crashing through the earth and falling into an antiquated past. Those who managed to survive the descent (and climb out) had the opportunity to glean the bounty inside – at least until the Circle became aware of the hole and sent in conflict counselors to confiscate the goods for public distribution.

"It must have been a couple's dressing room," Simon continued, leaning back and losing the whisper. "It's full of clothes and shoes and sexy stuff."

"Sexy stuff?"

"You know what I'm talking about."

"No."

"The kind of stuff people use in bed to make them think they're not alone...or that they're with someone else."

"Oh."

"If I don't go back tonight, someone else will find it for sure. That's where you come in. I need you to be the rope man. All you have to do is lower me into the hole and then pull me out."

Baldwin eyed his neighbor with some doubt.

"Don't worry," Simon said, "I won't eat today so I'll be extra light. I just need you to catch what I throw up."

"Excuse me?"

"From the timehole. I'll throw everything up and we'll bring it back here to sort."

"So that's the favor?"

"I thought I already corrected myself. It's an *opportunity*. If you help me, I'll help you. Meaning you get to keep one item for every three we bring back – except, of course, knee socks."

Baldwin thought a moment. He wasn't entirely uninterested in the offer, but the reward Simon was offering did not seem worth the risk.

"I'm sorry, but I'll pass," he said. "I'm sure you can find someone else to help."

"It has to be you. And it has to be tonight."

Baldwin was startled by Simon's desperation.

"Why?"

Simon's lips twisted in thought.

"Because it has to."

"That's not a reason."

"Well, you should do it because I'm your neighbor and I'm asking you a favor."

"You just said it was an opportunity, not a favor."

"I'm still your neighbor."

"Simon, I have to go."

"Okay. You want to know the real reason I'm asking you?"

Simon paused.

"I'll tell you if you really want me to."

"It's up to you."

"Alright," Simon said, "since you're dying to know. The real reason is that you're my only friend. I have no one else to ask."

"I am?"

"At least you talk to me."

Baldwin began to feel sorry for his neighbor, but he still could not imagine trudging off to a timehole with him that evening.

"I'm sorry again, but I just can't."

Simon blinked hard at Baldwin. His cheeks reddened, but not from embarrassment. His neighbor's voice took on a crude tone.

"I imagine the sexy stuff in that hole would perk up any romantic union, especially if it needed perking. Get what I'm saying?"

Baldwin blushed.

"I bet Nadine would not be pleased to find out you passed on an easy chance to fill up her closet," Simon continued. "I know I wouldn't."

"Who would ever tell her?"

"Things get around in the Circle," Simon said flatly.

Baldwin blinked. The thought of alienating Nadine even further was troubling. The thought of renewing their sex life was even more powerful.

"Where's the timehole?"

"No, no," Simon said, shaking his head. "I tell you now and you'll mention it to someone else and before you know it a hundred people will be cleaning the place out before lunch. Better you meet me after utility and we'll go together."

"I just want to be sure I'll be home before Nadine. That way I can surprise her."

"I wouldn't worry."

Baldwin wasn't sure if Simon was reassuring him that their trip to the timehole would be brief, or if he knew about Nadine's increasingly late hours.

"Just meet me at Big Birch before the sunset gong," Simon continued. "We'll walk from there."

"You're positive no one else knows about it? I don't want to go and find an empty hole or a conflict counselor waiting for us."

"Believe me, as long as we go tonight, it will be all ours."

"I guess I have to trust you."

Simon smiled widely. Baldwin hadn't noticed it before, but something green, perhaps a leave-behind from the olives or the snakeskin, was wedged between his neighbor's front teeth.

"As it says in *The Book of Ash*," Simon said, his tongue darting over the morsel. "Encouragement 22: 'Trust is a thing best learned, not earned.' Don't you agree?"

Baldwin didn't, but he had no more time to talk, let alone disagree. And besides, Simon was already walking back to his unit.

2 LOOK OUT

*B*aldwin was having a difficult time getting to his utility. In addition to being delayed by Simon, he was now held up by a rustball, which emitted a terrifying, tinny whine, as it spun, somersaulted and bounced along the white cement path he was walking. Finally, a gust of wind encouraged it to roll off the pavement and into a bordering thicket of thorn bushes, which shredded the mass into a benign, but beautiful looking, orange mist.

The sight caused Baldwin to think of Nadine. Early in their union they had made a pact to kiss whenever they saw a rustball, a silly, somewhat superstitious ritual to reinforce their intimacy. They even played the game inside their unit, holding hands and looking out the window, waiting for a streak of orange filament to pass by, and if it did, touching lips for a few seconds before resuming their watch. But that closeness between them had eroded, and now the only memory he connected to rust was pain.

It was two years almost to the day, almost a full ten seasons, not long after his mother died, and he was returning home from utility. It was a comfortable evening, the sun was setting, and he had taken a moment to watch its descent, relating its fall with the loss of his mother, hoping the symbolism would help him weep and release his sadness, something he had been unable to accomplish since her passing. But as the sun vanished below the horizon, he sensed something rising behind him. He turned to see a rust ball, larger than any he had ever seen before, angling toward him, moving through the air like a rolling flame. And directly under it ran a deer, its massive head crowned by a spray of horns, its eyes large and dark and violent. The impact with the deer spun him into the air, into the heart of the rust ball, and when he fell to the ground his skin was stained orange, his collarbone and two ribs shattered, his mouth filled with blood. He waited a few moments to die, and when he didn't he struggled to his feet and staggered home, whereupon seeing Nadine he did, finally, cry.

Since the "connection," the word Harold encouraged him to use when retelling the incident, Baldwin had worked hard in sessions to address his feelings of panic whenever he saw a rustball. He thought he had made good progress in this regard, which is why he was surprised, that morning, to feel the familiar twinge of anxiety biting at him: a numbness in his toes and fingertips, a tightening around his chest, the desire to flee. He had made the decision to follow the last impulse when he heard his name called out. Emerging from behind the thicket and piercing through the lingering mist that was once the rustball was his stepfather, Leonard Living.

"Baldwin, wait a moment."

Leonard's gait was smooth and steady for a man who had eclipsed by many sunrises the age of keeping count of age. He was wearing his "browns" – dark khaki shorts, a matching short-sleeve button shirt, and ankle-length rubber boots the color of wet mud. Looped around his left wrist was a jade bracelet, its murky green stones settling nicely with Leonard's deep tan. Like the scarf Baldwin was wearing, the bracelet once belonged to his mother.

Leonard waved with his left hand as he approached, the right being occupied with holding *The Book of Ash*, something his stepfather never left home without. Over the years, Baldwin had taken to thinking the book a living extension of Leonard's right arm, an elongated appendage that he used to expert advantage.

"I'm grateful you heard me," Leonard said, catching his breath and tapping Baldwin on the shoulder with the book. "Of course, I'm also grateful to see you."

"Likewise."

"Thank you Baldwin. Your gratitude reminds me so much of what I lost when you moved out and then your mother passed."

"My mother died long after I left."

"Yes, I suppose so. But I still have difficulty disconnecting the two events. Ash, I believe, says it best." Leonard raised the book so that it shielded Baldwin's eyes from the sun. "Encouragement 74, paragraph three, line two: 'Details are death to emotion.'"

Leonard gave the book a quick kiss and then lowered it.

"You see. I don't want to ever think too clearly when it comes to you and your mother. It's too painful."

Baldwin felt a tinge of sympathy for his stepfather. He also could not help but admire how well Leonard looked. He had always been a

handsome man, possessing a firm jaw line, good solid cheekbone structure, and symmetrical nose and eyes, but now his face also possessed
a wizened aesthetic, the unique beauty created by natural erosion, like
a rock face chiseled and smoothed by wind and rain, or a dead tree
transformed into a pile of finely milled pulp.

"Anyway," Leonard said, blowing out his cheeks. "How are you? You
seem somewhat anxious."

"I'm fine, just late for utility."

"You are at that. I don't mean to add to your upset, but it's a terrible
thing to be tardy. I'd hoped you might take after me in regards to punctuality, but I doubt very little of the positive behavior I modeled during
your youth guides your subconscious as an adult."

Baldwin's panic, first brought on by the rust ball, intensified. Perhaps
it was a reminder of the 12 years he spent enduring Leonard's over-
bearing approach to parenting – from the age of eight, when he and his
mother first entered Leonard's trailer, to twenty, when he completed
school and moved out. Or it could be that his stepfather, as Mentor of
Self Esteem, was one of the most powerful and influential individuals
in the Circle. Either way, Leonard scared him.

"I can still beat the utility gong if I hurry," Baldwin said.

"I doubt it," Leonard returned. "But maybe we can turn your de-
linquency into something useful. We haven't seen each other in some
time. Let's take a moment to catch up. How are you, really?"

"Like I said, I'm fine, other than being late."

"Forget about that. Concentrate on the moment. Be here, with me.
Focus on the present, not the past, not the future."

"I'm sorry."

"And don't apologize. 'Sorry' is a wasted word. It never feels good
saying it or hearing it. If I was the Mentor of Expression I'd remove it
immediately from the Circle's encouraged vernacular."

Baldwin suppressed the urge to apologize again.

"I must say I doubt that you're fine," Leonard continued. "Your eyes,
your skin, your lack of energy. To be honest, you look worn and worn
out."

Baldwin's anxiety was peaking. He wished he could float away, im-
itate the rust ball and disintegrate into the thicket. But Leonard had
the ability to immobilize him. He was trapped until let go.

"So what's the problem?" Leonard continued. "It must be something."

"I don't know. I'm not sleeping well lately."

"Well, the secret to a sound sleep is a sound mind. And the secret to a sound mind is a strong sense of self-esteem. By the look of you, I'd say your confidence is lacking. Let's work on that. Let's find something to boost your morale."

Leonard snapped his fingers.

"Your hair still holds its natural color. You've no gray."

"I'm only 33."

"So what. Age has nothing to do with aging. I was younger than you when I first started to show some white. But then again, my thinking has always been mature. I never had the opportunity to be frivolous. Even as a child I was forced to concern myself with adult matters. And as an adult I'm forced to concern myself with childish matters."

"I'm not a child anymore."

"Put aside your narcissism, Baldwin. I was speaking about my utility."

"I'm not a narcissist."

Leonard shook his head as if amused.

"I always forget your contrarian nature. If I say you're stupid, you'll say you're smart. And if I say you're smart, you'll say you're stupid. Am I right?"

"If I answer, I prove your point."

"Exactly."

"But admit you hate me, at least own up to that."

"I don't hate anyone."

"Your mother's dead, Baldwin. You don't need to pretend anymore that you're nice."

"I'm not pretending."

"Then you're lying. And you shouldn't. It's good that you hate me. A son should always hate his father while the father is alive. That way he can love him when he's dead."

"You're not my father."

"I raised you."

"Not all the way."

Leonard nodded sympathetically.

"I understand your misguided resentment. Did I ever tell you my father made me sleep with a rock in each hand when I was a child? Not a pebble, not a stone, but a heavy, jagged rock. He thought it would make me emotionally hard and impenetrable. He blamed his own lack of happiness on his compassion and inability to withstand suffering in others. Sometimes he even put rocks in my pillow to ratchet up the lesson."

"That's horrible."

"That's what I thought," Leonard said, "for more seasons than I care to admit. But a day doesn't go by now that I don't thank my father for his harshness. The only reason I'm as effective as I am at helping people reach their full potential is because I can accept that some of them can't. Thanks to my father I don't feel sorry for people or get caught up trying to save lost causes…even when it's family."

"Are you saying I'm a lost cause?"

"There's that narcissism again. I was thinking of someone else, but I do fear you're at a point in your life where you're closer to being lost than found."

"I told you I'm fine. You don't need to worry about me."

Leonard bowed his head a moment. When he looked up, there was the faintest trace of a frown crinkling his lips.

"Actually, I do. I hate to tell you this, but a person came to me yesterday and told me of their intention to kill you on the Day of No Consequence. I imagine they thought it best to give me forewarning, considering our familial connection. But while I appreciated the thoughtfulness, I resented the difficult situation it put me in. As you know, it's my utility to encourage people to undertake activities that will improve their self-esteem, but this activity will end your breathing. So I made a decision to discourage the venture, meaning you have nothing to fear that day, at least not from this person."

Baldwin thought fast of the people in his life who might harbor enough resentment to try and kill him. There were several difficult miracle cases he had decided against over the year, much to the dismay of the claimants, but he did not think any of them capable of such a dramatic revenge. His mind could not lock on to anyone else or a possible motive.

"I see you're troubled by this," Leonard continued. "Don't be. I must have had hundreds of people wanting me dead over the years, and as you can see, I'm still taking in air by the mouthful."

"That's because you hide on the Day of No Consequence."

"I don't *hide*," Leonard corrected. "I isolate. I need to be alone so I can contemplate the significance of the holiday. I am in charge of it, you know."

"I know."

"Then you also know if I tell you not to worry, you shouldn't worry."

"I can't help it. It's scary."

Leonard clicked his tongue with dismay.

"I should have made you sleep with rocks. One threat and you unravel. It's your mother's fault. She shielded you too much. An overprotective mother denies a boy the opportunity to gain toughness through abuse. I remember being bullied by another boy nearly every day growing up. He was a heartless young man blessed with an early puberty. His body was all muscle and cystic acne. I suspect he took out his malformed sexual urges with punches to my genitals. But like my father, I'm grateful he did what he did, because it made me hard."

Leonard smiled peacefully.

"Forgive my momentary nostalgia, but he's the only person I ever killed on a Day of No Consequence. That might change, of course, but right now he's my first. And so it's special. It was right before I met your mother. I caught him walking alone near my trailer and I ran and got a kitchen knife and hacked off his head. The human neck is much tougher and more resilient than you think. It was messy business, but I did it all with a smile, and not a trace of bitterness."

"I don't want to die."

"And you won't. At least not until your mind is ready to give up on your body."

"But this person—"

"Please," Leonard interrupted, "let's not waste any more time on this. I told you I encouraged this individual not to kill you. And as you know, even the most crazed maniac steps in line when I encourage them."

Leonard cleared his throat.

"By the way, does a man, first name Simon, live in your building?"

"He's my neighbor. Why do you ask?"

"No reason."

"There must be a reason for you to bring him up."

"Don't be paranoid, Baldwin. It's just that I heard from someone that this Simon might need help with his self-esteem, and I thought I might see if I can help."

"Well, he's inside. I just spoke to him."

"And how did he seem?"

"Fine, I guess."

"That's good enough for me. You've saved me a trip."

Leonard paused. Baldwin thought he saw a brief flash of insecurity in his stepfather's eyes.

"And may I ask on Nadine? How are you two getting on of late?"

"Fine," Baldwin lied, knowing he would never confide his personal problems with Leonard.

"Isn't that glorious. It's important to keep romantic unions vibrant. Always remember that. Please share that thought with her. Will you do that?"

"Sure," Baldwin said absently.

"Then we're done," Leonard said. "I encourage you to forget about what I said before and put in a good day judging miracles."

"I'll try."

"And, Baldwin?"

"Yes."

"That scarf doesn't match your shirt."

With that Leonard turned and followed the path of the rust ball, disappearing behind the thicket just as the utility gong rang out.

3 HEAD LOCK

The fit was a bad one. Manu had coached Baldwin many times over the years on what to do and what not to do if he had a spell. It was quite simple: Baldwin was to make sure Manu's head didn't bang into anything sharp or hard, and nothing else. Manu particularly warned Baldwin not to go near his mouth or put anything inside it to keep it open. He told him how he once nearly severed a woman's finger when she tried to clear his throat while he lay stricken. He also had several chipped molars to show for people who jammed sticks, once even a rock, between his teeth to keep his airway open. Manu assured Baldwin that other than protecting his head, there was nothing that could be done but wait for him to come out of it, which, he assured him, he always did.

Baldwin made good time getting to the miracle office after leaving Leonard, widening his stride and pumping his arms (it was not encouraged in the Circle to run, unless it was done in place), to add speed to his regular pace. But the extra exertion resulted in a heavy, itching sweat around his neck and under his arms, and rather than add to this problem by climbing up stairs (the office was on the tenth and top floor), he decided to cool down a moment in a shaded alcove around the corner. There he found Manu, his partner at the miracle office, lying face-up in the gravel, his arms and legs moving in opposing rhythms to the rest of his twisting body.

Baldwin's first response was to retch, but when he opened his mouth the only thing that spilled out was a glob of golden saliva, a remnant of the small bit of honey he had ingested the night before. His stomach clenching, he wiped his lips and concentrated on doing what Manu encouraged. It was not easy to take hold of his friend's head amidst his frenetic gyrations, and even harder to hold on, as the smooth skin around the skull (Manu was bald by choice) was slick and slippery with sweat. There was also the issue of conduction: the extreme heat coursing through Manu's convulsing flesh into his own hands was excruciating. But Baldwin, working himself into a seated position, was able to draw Manu's head into his lap, spreading his legs wide so that his inner thighs provided extra stabilizing support to his friend's shoulders.

He was about to re-grip Manu's head when he felt a sharp rap atop his own.

"What are you doing?"

Baldwin looked up. A tall, broad-shouldered man was looking down. The man's craggy face was softened by purple eyeliner and lipstick. A learning stick, wrapped in birch bark and half the length of the man's long leg, dangled from his right hand. The makeup, and the stick, indicated that the man served the Circle as a conflict counselor.

"My friend's having a seizure."

Manu's eyes were far back in their sockets. His teeth clicked wickedly as his mouth snapped closed. An acidic smelling, yellowish foam oozed from his taught lips.

"I can see that. But what are *you* doing?"

"Securing his head."

"I can see that too," the conflict counselor said.

"I need help. I think he's dying."

The conflict counselor looked annoyed, even bored, as he slipped the stick through a loop on his belt and knelt down beside Baldwin.

"What's your friend's name?"

"Manu."

The conflict counselor leaned over, cupped his hands over his mouth and shouted:

"I'm grateful to meet you, Manu."

The spasms wracking Manu's body intensified. More of the vile yellow foam leaked from his vice-like mouth.

"I guess he's not grateful to meet me," the conflict counselor said matter-of-factly. "Perhaps we should just leave him alone."

"No. Please. Don't give up."

"Who said I was?"

The conflict counselor blew hard on his right palm. Then he pressed it over Manu's nose and mouth, creating a tight seal.

"What are you doing? He can't breathe."

"That's the point."

"Stop it, you're killing him."

"Not quite."

Manu's spasms halted. For a moment, Baldwin thought his friend had indeed perished, but then he saw a slight rise and fall of his chest, a loosening of the mouth, a twitching of the eyelids, and then the eyes themselves rolling forward in tandem, stopping with a bounce into their rightful place in the sockets, ready to resume their utility as soon as the rest of Manu's body, if not his mind, caught up.

4 SICK BED

With Baldwin's help, Manu had pushed up on his elbows and noticed the conflict counselor standing a few feet away. Now that the crisis had passed, Baldwin took a moment to examine the man, saw that he was wearing heavy, black-leather boots, the laces untied, each tongue flap hanging down as if panting from the heat. A single purple stud, matching the makeup on his face, gleamed from his left earlobe. Like Simon, he was shirtless, but that is where the similarity ended: the conflict counselor's chest was heavily muscled, his stomach toned and taught, his waistline narrowing nicely into a pair of black leggings a perfect match to his boots. Along with his close-cropped sandy hair, he looked streamlined and dangerous, but also, at least to Baldwin, a tad absurd.

And who might you be?"

"I'm the one who encouraged you to give up the fit," the conflict counselor answered Manu's question.

"Then I'm encouraged to give you my gratitude."

"No need. It's my utility to end conflict. Your mind was in conflict with your body, so I ended it."

"May I ask how?"

"By trying to kill you."

Baldwin regretted the statement immediately. It was never wise to question a conflict counselor's actions, even worse to ridicule them.

"I'm sorry," he said, hoping to sound more conciliatory than he felt. "I didn't know what you were doing."

"I'm surprised by that. It's rather a simple survival technique. I merely cut off his breath to convince his mind that he was in grave danger. Basically, the threat of death often ends it."

"I'd rather not talk about this anymore," Manu interjected, crossing his arms and hugging them tight to his torso as if cold. "Whatever you did, I'm quite satisfied with the result, so let's move on."

"Who says I already haven't?" the conflict counselor snapped back. "I just need your name for the report."

"I'm Manu."

"So your friend already told me. What's your second name?"

Manu batted his eyelids.

"I only give that out to friends and lovers."

"Just give me the name."

"Make me."

The conflict counselor began to knead the top of his learning stick with his fingertips.

"I will if you want."

"I want if you will."

"Reynolds," Baldwin spoke up, knowing that Manu was flirting, but not sure about the conflict counselor. Either way he didn't like where it was heading. "His name is Manu Reynolds."

"Is that true?"

"Why would I lie?" Baldwin asked.

"You tell me."

This time it was Manu who cut in.

"That's my name. Manu Reynolds. Although I wish my second name was different, something starting with an M. There's something sleek and sexy when the two initials match, don't you think?" Manu batted his eyelids. "I bet your initials match."

"They do."

"Tell me."

"Conflict Counselor."

Manu clapped his hands. "I like that. Conflict Counselor. Can I call you Cee-Cee?"

"No."

"Of course not," Manu giggled. "I was just teasing. But what's your name, really? I want to know so I can send you a chit of gratitude." Manu paused. "Or even two."

"Don't do that," Baldwin said, keeping his voice low. "He was only doing his utility. You don't owe him anything but verbal gratitude."

"Who said I even want that?" the conflict counselor asked. "I don't work for praise."

"Of course you don't," Manu spoke up. "Baldwin was teasing as well. He's quite funny when you get to know him. But please, give me your name and I promise to give you something else."

The conflict counselor spat, the saliva landing with a plop to the right of Manu's left knee.

"In my experience," he said, "the only people who break promises are the ones who make them." He spat again, this time barely missing Manu's other knee. "And I don't like those people."

"Don't worry. I never break a promise. Ask Baldwin if you don't believe me. We're miracle counselors. So you know we don't lie. Isn't that right Baldwin?"

Baldwin nodded his head. "He doesn't lie."

The conflict counselor made a motion to spit again, but this time he swallowed. He had a pronounced Adam's apple that took its time to settle.

"Franklin Ramson," he finally said. "You can drop off any chits at the conflict office in Section 4."

Manu exhaled as if punched in the stomach. He patted his heart with both hands. "Franklin Ramson. I can't believe it. This is so amazing. My father's name was Fenton Reynolds. You have the same initials—F.R. And guess what? You're not going to believe this, but four is my favorite number. Ask Baldwin if you don't believe me."

Baldwin nodded again.

"He likes four."

"See," Manu said, "it's a miracle."

"It's not a miracle," Baldwin said, shaking his head.

The conflict counselor, Ramson, rocked on the balls of his clunky boots.

"And why is that?"

"It just isn't," Baldwin said.

"That explains things," Ramson mocked. "But if it isn't a miracle, what is it?"

"A coincidence."

"And the difference?"

"A coincidence doesn't always improve your life, a miracle does."

"Then let's hope it's a coincidence," Ramson said, "because I like my life the way it is."

Manu struggled to his feet.

"Remember me: the person who almost died? Perhaps we can concentrate on the miracle that I'm still breathing and not this nonsense."

Baldwin stood as well. His knees cracked as he rose, the joints stiff from constriction and tension.

"I'm sorry," he said, taking Manu by the elbow. "Let me help you to the office."

Manu shook his head.

"I'm going home. There's no way I can climb those stairs. The Circle won't mind if I perform my utility from bed today. There's a claim from yesterday I can contemplate just as well on a mattress as a desk."

Manu smiled suggestively at Ransom.

"I wouldn't mind a helping hand to get home. I still feel weak and these stupid fits sometimes come in clumps."

Baldwin pulled Manu close.

"I'll do it. And I'll stay with you."

Ramson stepped forward. Took hold of Manu's other elbow.

"He meant me."

Baldwin gripped Manu tighter.

"That's okay, I can do it."

Manu smiled happily, his head turning back and forth between the two men. Finally, he settled on Baldwin.

"I'll be safe with the conflict counselor. And you know we can't leave the office unattended a whole day without losing our chits...or worse."

"Are you sure?"

"Of course. You know how the Circle is about people not doing their utility."

"I mean about my not taking you home. I'm worried."

"That's sweet, but you're being overprotective. Wasn't that what you disliked about your mother?"

Baldwin let go.

"At least send a message counselor back to let me know you made it home and you're okay," he said.

"I'll make sure he does," Ramson said. Then added with a smile, "Mom."

Baldwin watched them walk away. He almost chased after Manu when he saw his friend stumble rounding the corner. But Ramson caught him before the fall. The sight looked surprising tender and he suddenly thought of Nadine. He wondered where she was and what she was doing. Perhaps she was filing some old woman's toenails into daggers. Or maybe she was also thinking about their union and how to repair it. If Manu could find love from a fit, then there might be hope for them as well. Anything was possible he reasoned, be it a miracle, or a coincidence.

5 EAR MARK

*B*aldwin's legs gave out on the sixth floor. He had been taking the stairs two-at-a-time, hoping that by exhausting his body he might also exhaust his mind. He did not want to think anymore, not about Nadine, not about Leonard, and not about what just happened with Manu. But all three began an assault on his thoughts as he rested, and so with clenched teeth he resumed his ascent.

By the time he reached the tenth floor he was sweating and out of breath. He allowed himself to calm down before opening the office door.

"Hello."

For a moment, Baldwin thought he had the wrong office, as a beautiful woman he had never seen before was sitting behind a desk. But then he remembered the miracle office took up the entire floor, and that the desk she was sitting behind was his.

He stepped inside, cleared his throat, and closed the door behind him.

"Hello," he returned.

"I took the liberty of letting myself in," she said. "I hope that's okay."

"It's fine. I'm sorry to be late."

"Perhaps I came too early," she said, smiling so that the tip of her tongue poked out from her rouged lips. "One should never force punctuality on another person."

Baldwin wiped perspiration from his forehead as he took in the woman. She was classically attractive, with clear olive skin, a long, feminine neck, angular face with pointed cheekbones, slim nose and full lips, moist blue eyes with purple tints, all framed in a luscious cascade of blonde hair. Yet there was something absent in her beauty, a missing ingredient to pull it all together into a comfortable congruence. Looking at her he felt both aroused and frustrated to find out what she was lacking.

"Sorry," he said, loosening his scarf to cool down. "Usually there are two of us here, but my utility partner is sick."

"Should I come back another time?"

"No. Please stay. I mean I can take care of you. I just mentioned about my partner" – he shook his head – "I don't know why I mentioned it."

"Perhaps you're worried?"

"I am."

"What's your partner's name?"

"Manu."

"I like that name. But I'm not sure if it works best for a man or a woman?"

"Well, he's a man."

"What's he like?"

Baldwin rarely took time to consider the personality makeup of the people closest to him. He assumed he enjoyed Manu's company because he was witty and unique in his dissection of life in the Circle.

"He's funny."

"I imagine that's a relief in the kind of work you do," she said. "I don't know if I could move through a day after hearing so many amazing and emotional stories. It must be nice to have someone to laugh with."

"It is."

"I can send Manu a positive message if you like."

"A positive message?"

"Like a suggestion, to help him feel better."

Baldwin thought the intention odd, but he was drawn in by her sincerity.

"Okay. If you don't mind."

"It works best if I close my eyes and concentrate. And you can't ask me after about the message. If I tell you, it won't reach him."

She closed her eyes and leaned forward, giving Baldwin a glimpse of her full breasts, which hung loosely underneath her light pink dress.

She leaned back, opened her eyes and smiled.

"Done."

Baldwin looked up fast, concentrating his gaze on her forehead.

"Excuse me."

"The positive message. It was delivered."

"Thank you."

"So what now?"

Baldwin hesitated. He thought he might tell her that she was in his chair, but decided it did not matter on what side of the desk he sat to listen to a miracle.

"I assume you are here to put in a miracle claim?"

Baldwin wormed himself into the chair, which was slightly smaller and less comfortable than his.

"Why don't we start with your name, utility, and where you live?"

"In that order?"

"Whatever you like."

The woman took a moment to pull back her hair. Baldwin was startled to see a patch of mottled skin where her left ear should have been.

"I'm Hetta Earnest. I'm a tactile touch counselor. I live in Unit 2, Building 4, Section 4."

Baldwin forced his attention away from her missing ear, finding safe ground by concentrating on her forehead.

"So tell me about your experience."

"You mean my miracle?" she said, letting her hair fall back in place.

"Yes." Baldwin smiled apologetically. "But I'm not encouraged to call it that until I verify it really is that."

She blushed, blotches of red appearing on her cheeks and her neck.

"I don't know where to begin."

"It sometimes helps people to start at the end and work their way back to the beginning," Baldwin suggested, feeling it safe again to look into her eyes. "But it's entirely up to you…Hetta."

Baldwin was surprised he said her name. He was trained not to be friendly with people putting in a claim, to be aloof, even cold, as it helped when rejecting them.

"Okay. Last night…" She closed her eyes again. But this time when she opened them they were moist with tears. "I don't know why this is so hard?"

"That's okay," Baldwin soothed, wishing he was on the other side of the desk, as he kept in the top drawer a hand towel for people to use when a claim got emotional. "Take your time. I'm not in a hurry."

"Thank you for saying that," she said, wiping her eyes and smiling. "You're very kind…."

"Baldwin."

"I like that name even better than Manu," she said.

This time Baldwin blushed.

"Just begin when you're ready. Last night…"

"I had an orgasm." She finished the sentence and smiled proudly.

"Last night I had the first orgasm of my life. I never thought I could have one, so when it came I knew it was something special…something miraculous."

Baldwin tried not to show surprise or excitement. He scratched at his right eyelid and said as nonchalantly as possible, "Go on."

"It happened in my kitchen. I was sitting alone, waiting for my husband to come home. He's always late, by the way. So I was waiting and waiting and finally fell asleep, right at the table, and I had a dream where a woman came to me and…"

She paused, winced as if in pain.

"I hope this isn't boring. My husband says I take too long to tell a story."

"No, don't stop." Baldwin forced himself to take a breath to calm down. "Besides, this is a miracle…I mean a claim for a miracle. Not a story. It demands details. So please, continue with the dream."

"Are you sure?"

"Tell me everything."

"Okay. Like I said, a woman came to me in the dream. She was sweet and her skin was soft and she smelled like a cherry tree right before it blooms. She asked me to lie down and spread my legs. Then she told me to touch myself. She stayed with me the entire time, coaxing me to enjoy the pleasure I was giving myself, willing me to open my mind to the possibility. And I had an orgasm, the first of my life."

Baldwin had been taught from his first day of utility never to approve a miracle that occurred in a dream. In the Circle, dreams fell under the realm of the subconscious. And since the subconscious, individually and collectively, was considered the absolute ruler in the Circle, any attempt to provide mastery over it was not only discouraged, it was grounds for a fast trip to a gratitude farm for a period of "emotional reorganization."

He hesitated a moment, wanting to choose his words carefully.

"My concern is that the orgasm occurred while you were sleeping." He coughed into his hand and cleared his throat. "Are you sure it was a dream?"

"Yes. Why?"

"It's just that dreams are ethereal by nature. I mean, what happens in them isn't real."

"So you think I faked the orgasm?"

"Certainly not."

"Then you must think I'm after chits. I don't care about compensation. The only reason I'm here is because the woman in the dream encouraged me to come."

"I know...the orgasm."

"I mean *come here*. She was very clear. She told me to 'give voice to the miracle and free him.'"

"Free him?"

"Yes."

"Who do you think the 'him' is?"

"You, of course."

"Me?"

"The woman told me to voice my miracle. Who else would I voice my miracle to but a miracle counselor?"

"There are other miracle offices," Baldwin returned. "You might have gone to any one of them."

"I didn't. I chose this one."

She looked hard at him.

"Don't you want to be free...of something or someone?"

Baldwin studied his hands. The skin around his knuckles was chapped, his fingernails frayed at the ends and cloudy in color.

"I'm sorry," Hetta continued. "I've made you uncomfortable. I shouldn't ask such things. I'm probably just projecting my own problems onto you. Anyway, I'm sure I'm taking up too much time. What happens now?"

Baldwin looked up.

"I decide on your miracle, meaning I give you two chits if it is one, or take two from you if it isn't."

Her face fell.

"I didn't think coming here would cost me anything. I can't afford to lose anymore."

Baldwin and Manu heard this lament often. People came to the office, told their miracles, and if it wasn't a miracle, claimed ignorance on the penalty. While Manu had no trouble taking their chits anyway, Baldwin found this part of the utility difficult. The problem was that the chits the office took in were the same ones they gave out. So if they didn't reject miracles, they couldn't reward them. It was similar to the Circle's policy concerning children: a family had to have a member die before a new one could be conceived. Sometimes, when the office's chit count was low, Manu would go "prospecting," walking about the Circle and talking to himself in a booming, boastful voice about the "mountain of chits" he had made by claiming the most mundane experiences in his life as miracles. But Baldwin was incapable of such coercion, and often would drop a chit or two of his own into the office pot to provide a worthy miracle claimant with their reward.

"So what's your decision?" she asked.

Baldwin knew Manu would reject the claim without pause. While their decisions did not help or harm the Circle chit-wise, it was important to strike a fair and consistent balance between why a miracle was approved and why it was rejected. It was not uncommon for the Circle to encourage a person to claim a miracle they knew should be rejected, just to see if it was rejected, or send in a person to claim a miracle they knew should be approved, just to see if it was approved. Manu and Baldwin both knew miracle counselors from other offices who had been caught making "unhealthy" miracle decisions and were remanded to gratitude farms. It was a frightening possibility, and so the two them had developed a variety of criteria to judge a miracle's veracity, and miracles that occurred in dreams, as Baldwin had hinted, were summarily rejected.

Baldwin glanced at Hetta. There might be the possibility she was a plant sent in by the Circle to judge him, but there was a part of him that did not care if she was. And while her beauty and vulnerability were factors in his inclination to trust her, they had a greater effect on his desire for her to like him.

"Can you excuse me a moment?"

He rose from the chair and headed to the back of the office. He opened a closet door and stepped inside. It was a large closet and he was hidden from Hetta's view as he opened a small tin box. Inside was a single blue chit. He reached into his pocket and pulled out a matching one.

"Congratulations," he said, handing Hetta both chits when he returned. "Your miracle is approved."

"So you believe me? You believe my orgasm was a miracle?"

Baldwin hesitated. He realized he did not want to lie to this woman.

"I believe in your belief," he said.

Hetta held the chits close to her face.

"One feels warm," she said, "and one is cold."

"That's strange."

"Maybe it's another miracle."

They were silent a moment.

"You know," Hetta said, "your scarf is beautiful. The color matches my dress."

"Thank you. It was my mother's."

"She has good taste."

"She did."

"Your mother's no longer breathing?"

"Yes, she passed a few years ago."

Hetta took in a deep breath, and then exhaled, letting the air out it in slow slips, as if she was blowing bubbles.

"Can I tell you something?" she asked.

"Sure."

"As you can see, I'm not wearing anything masculine. It's not because I'm rebellious, or hate the encouragement, it's just that when I wear something on my body that once was a man's it makes me want to hate them. And I don't want to hate men. I don't want to hate anyone. Do you understand?"

"I do."

"So you understand me?"

"Yes," Baldwin said. I think I do."

"Can I say something else?"

"Of course."

"I notice you didn't greet me with gratitude when you came in."

She saw remorse on Baldwin's face and held up her hand.

"I'm not upset about it. In fact, I'm glad you didn't. Perhaps it's just me, but I always think greeting in such a way puts distance between people right from the start. Like setting a tone when you don't know how the conversation will go or what might happen with the other person. It's controlling, don't you think?"

Baldwin remembered Nadine's stinging words two nights earlier, when she went on a tirade after he questioned her lateness, her accusation that he was "controlling."

He looked down at his hands and said:

"I think sometimes being grateful is helpful, and sometimes it isn't."

"I'm sure you're right. Anyway, I don't know why I'm telling you all this. What does it say again in The *Book of Ash*? – 'Don't offer an opinion if you want to keep it.'"

"Don't *give* an opinion," Baldwin gently corrected. "Not offer."

"That's right. I haven't been keeping up with my reading of late. Although I think I prefer my version, even if it's wrong."

"I was taught there is no right or wrong when it comes to *The Book of Ash*, just as long as you know the difference."

"I suppose that makes sense. You sound devoted to the text."

"No. My stepfather."

"Oh."

She left a short time after. He was alone the rest of the morning. Right before the mid-day gong, the nutritional counselor arrived with the lunch bag. It contained two cucumbers, two carrots, and a pair of smoked pigeon feet. Despite Simon's warning about the danger of eating six items, Baldwin, with Manu absent, consumed the entire portion. As he sucked meat off the last foot, he thought about Hetta, wondering if the strong connection he felt toward her was the result of his feeling so disconnected to Nadine. Or perhaps it was just the stark eroticism of her miracle claim that attracted him. Regardless, he was tired from the morning and the meal and laid his head on the desk, hoping not just to fall asleep, but to also meet a woman in his dreams.

6 MIDDLE MAN

*B*aldwin woke with a start. Standing in front of his desk was a young man with soft brown eyes and thick eyelashes that shaded them. The young man was wearing high-topped sneakers and fishnet stockings up to his waist. He was skinny and shirtless. A rubber band held his brown hair in a vertical ponytail.

"I'm grateful to meet you."

Baldwin's eyes had dried from sleep and he blinked moisture back into them.

"Likewise."

"I'm here to see Baldwin Wallace."

"I'm Baldwin. Are you here for a claim?"

The young man shook his head, causing the ponytail to sway side-to-side.

"I'm a message counselor. Manu Reynolds requested my utility. He said you would pay for it."

"I thought messages were free?"

"Not anymore." He looked around the office. "What do people claim here anyway?"

"Miracles."

"What's the payout?"

"Two chits."

"It used to be three."

Baldwin shrugged.

"Anyway, it's one chit for the message – two if I sing it."

"Just say it…please."

The young man readjusted the rubber band. When the ponytail was upright again he said:

"I'm refreshed. I'm renewed. I'm in love. I'm Manu."

"Is that it?"

"That's all he told me. I can repeat it if you want, but that will cost another chit."

"No, that's fine."

"So you owe me a chit."

Baldwin realized he had given his last chit to Hetta.

"Will you accept a promise as payment?"

"When will it be fulfilled?"

"The next day of utility."

"That's too long. We have to hand in our chits by sunset. If I'm short, they extract it from my allotment."

Baldwin did not like to do it, but he knew Manu always stashed some chits for emergency purposes. He went to Manu's desk and opened the bottom right hand drawer, found a small square tin, pried open the lid with his thumbnail, and emptied the contents, four red chits, into his palm. He snapped the lid back on and returned the tin to the drawer and closed it.

He handed over two chits and sat back down.

"I can't take it," the young man said, angrily tossing one of the chits onto the desk. "I'm only allowed to accept verbal gratitude."

Baldwin pushed the chit back.

"No, it's for a new message. For Nadine Wallace. She works at the hygiene office across from the charred woods. Do you know where that is?"

The young man wrinkled his nose.

"Doesn't everyone."

"Good. Are you ready for the message?"

He reached for the chit with reluctance.

"I'm listening."

"Tell her Baldwin would like to talk tonight over dinner, no matter how late she comes home."

"It's better if you rhyme it?"

"Why?"

"Because it's easier for the receiver to remember a message that rhymes," he said in a bored monotone.

"It's not that complicated a message."

"I've seen simpler forgotten. And then I get blamed."

"Can you do it for me?" Baldwin asked. "I'm not good at rhymes."

"I can. But that will cost another chit."

"Everything costs extra."

"Take it up with the Mentor of Communication. He sets all the message fees."

Baldwin bowed his head and thought hard, playing out lines in his head, nodding as he tried to find the right rhythm. Finally, he said:

"Nadine, my wife, my partner in life, let's dine tonight, let's make things right." He looked up.

"How's that?"

"I've delivered worse."

"Thanks."

"I'm just being truthful," the message counselor snapped. "You don't need to be sarcastic."

"I'm sorry."

"Sure you are. Everyone thinks my utility is so easy, that all I have to do is repeat what I'm told to repeat. But no one realizes how difficult people are, how many times I've been accused of giving the wrong message when I gave the right one. The problem is people only hear what they want to hear. I never misspeak, but plenty of people mishear, especially when the message doesn't fit their needs."

Baldwin began to feel bad for the young man.

"I really am sorry," he said. "I appreciate what you do."

"Forget it."

"I mean it, I'm grateful."

The message counselor studied Baldwin. His gaze had a furtive quality, as if he distrusted the answers to questions he had not yet asked.

"Are you grateful enough to approve a miracle?"

"Did you have one?"

"Only like every day."

Baldwin pointed at the empty chair in front of him.

"Sit down and tell me."

"You probably think I'll make something up."

"Why would I think that?"

"Because everyone does."

Baldwin sensed that the young man was debating in his mind whether he should sit down or not. Finally, he said:

"I'm not going to waste my time. I can see you're the type not to believe anything incredible."

Baldwin was happy when the young man finally left.

The rest of the afternoon saw no one else come through the door, odd, as they were usually quite busy with the approaching holiday. All in all it was dull going. Worse, Baldwin fell to brooding, alternating between thoughts of Nadine and what Leonard had told him about the threat on his life. He did not see any connection between the two, not that he was looking for it, but it seemed unusual that his life should be spinning toward such a dismal direction.

Nadine, in particular, confused him. When they first met, she had been the one in dogged pursuit of his affections. Her zeal wore him down and he grudgingly accepted her opinion that they should form a romantic union. But with that binding connection began a change in their relationship, imperceptible at first, like a bud that seemingly blossoms into a flower overnight. With each passing year, the balance of power in the relationship swung toward Nadine. And then it became Baldwin who pined, begging for attention and affirmations of love from her ever-hardening mouth.

Baldwin knew his neediness was not helping, that the worst thing he could do as Nadine pulled away was to try and pull back. But it was hard for him to let go and hope for the best, as Harold suggested. He was also not ready to do as Manu urged, which was to petition the Circle to break up the union. Manu, who he often confided in, was adamant that the relationship was terminal, not holding back his belief that Nadine was spending time with another man – even many men. Baldwin was not angry with Manu for the accusation, but he did argue passionately against it. Quite simply, if Nadine had taken up with another man or more, she certainly wouldn't be discreet. She was too explicit in her needs, too honestly selfish, too pragmatic in her actions to put in the extra effort to maintain a covert affair when it was easier to conduct it out in the open. Besides, the Circle encouraged romances outside a romantic union, a quick and effective way to rectify a faulty relationship. The general idea was that illicit sex held no staying power for the parties involved, and that eventually they would tire of the enterprise and return renewed and refreshed to their original partners. Baldwin, however, was not built to stray. He was loyal, fiercely so. And he was avoidant of change. The combination made it difficult for him to give up on things, be it a favorite shirt or Nadine.

Like the night before, he felt a surge of optimism: his message to Nadine would find fertile ground, she would come home at a reasonable time, they would share the edibles bag, they would talk, and they would resolve their problems. There was also the promise of gifts from the timehole, the "sexy things" Simon spoke of. And it was a full moon. Surely all these elements might spark romance. He visualized how it might play out: the two of them undressing and getting into bed, him, sliding a hand over to discretely fondle Nadine's small, firm breasts, and if not rebuffed, bringing his mouth into the picture, moving under the covers and licking his way down her shapely legs, waiting patiently until she encouraged him to use something else to penetrate her, and once that was accomplished, engaging his hips to perform a series of quick, even thrusts until completion. It all seemed possible except one troubling thing, which he realized as he walked away from his desk and out the door, with Manu's two chits clicking in his pocket. He was not excited.

7 SUN BURN

*S*imon was waiting for him at Big Birch. It was the largest tree in the Circle, with egg-white bark that flaked off in long curled strips at the end of each growing season. The event brought out many to watch and more to wait under its flush of cricket-green leaves, people jostling for position and scrambling to catch falling pieces of bark, which they turned into anklets, necklaces, headbands...or, as he saw with Ramson, covering for a learning stick.

Pale as he was, Simon stood out like a patch of mud leaning against the gleaming white trunk. His neighbor was still wearing the blue thong, but had added a lacy woman's brassiere on top, the front of the two cups cut out to reveal his bright orange nipples. He had also changed out of the heels and into a pair of black flats with silver buckles.

"I'm grateful to see you," Simon said.

"Likewise."

Baldwin stretched his arms and yawned.

"Tough day?"

"More like a long one," Baldwin said.

Simon scratched absently under his armpit.

"I'm glad I haven't been assigned a new utility. It seems to take the life out of people."

"What did you do again?"

Simon sniffed his fingertips.

"I worked with vines, mostly grapes, but also some decorative ivy. My job was to make sure the vines covered the trellises or fences or whatever artificial construct they were suppose to grow around. My official title was Direction Counselor, although I don't think you can influence a vine to go anyway it doesn't want to. It's probably why I got taken off the duty. I couldn't bring myself to lift a hand to help something that doesn't want help."

Baldwin began to regret his decision to meet Simon.

"Should we get going?"

"Not yet. I want to wait until after sunset. It will be hard for anyone to follow us in the dark."

"Who's going to follow us?"

"You would be surprised how many people trail me," Simon said. "They know I have a talent for finding timeholes. All they have to do is find me – meaning, I take the fall and they get the reward."

Baldwin looked around. He did not see anyone who looked like they might be interested in either of them.

"I thought we could wait at a warm wash," Simon continued. "I heard about a place nearby that charges only a chit to get in. It's supposed to have the best touch counselor in the Circle. Do you know Morris, from our building?"

"No."

"Morris Martin. He lives two floors above us."

Unlike Baldwin, Simon seemed to know everyone in the building.

"I never heard of him."

"You must not follow running in place then."

"I don't."

"Because Morris is the best. He's never been beaten. I heard he once split open a stone stage during a match. That takes an enormous amount of stomping power."

"Or rotten rock."

"Whatever. Morris told me about this woman at the warm wash who worked a miracle on his feet. He said that after a few minutes of rubbing he felt as if he was curled up on a cloud."

Baldwin thought of Hetta, her utility, her blonde hair and pink nipples that matched her dress.

"Did he give you her name?"

"Morris asked but she wouldn't tell him. I guess she has to be careful not to let clients get too close. You know how easily some men fall in love. I'm not like that. I know the only reason a touch counselor touches me is because it's their utility. As long as they pretend to like me, that's good enough. I don't expect anything more."

"So how will you know which counselor to ask for?"

"Morris said she's missing an ear."

Baldwin blinked. It had to be Hetta. The idea of seeing her again thrilled him, and that made him feel guilty.

"I really don't have time to go to a warm wash and the timehole," he said. "I was hoping the whole thing wouldn't take long."

"How come?"

"Because I need to get home."

"So you can wait around for Nadine?" Simon nodded knowingly. "Don't look surprised. Your door is thin. I hear what's going on…and what's not going on."

"That's really not your business."

"Don't get mad. I imagine the same thing happens to all romantic unions eventually: the sex dies and so does the connection. I used to hear the two of you make love, but not anymore."

"You shouldn't eavesdrop."

"Who has to? The whole building can hear the screaming and crying coming from your unit.'

Baldwin flushed, feeling more embarrassed than defensive.

"It's just that Nadine's been working hard lately," he said. "She's under a lot of stress with the Day of No Consequence coming. Filing and trimming nails is a very exacting utility. She's very dedicated to it. Besides, you shouldn't spread rumors or make things up. Nadine, for a fact, never cries."

"Then I guess it's you."

Baldwin pretended to ignore the comment, peering at the sun, wishing it would hurry and set, so that they might get on with it and he could get home.

"And I only say this to help you," Simon continued, "but you're completely delusional. Women will also always put a man over a mission. If Nadine's not coming home, it's because she doesn't want to."

Baldwin continued to stare at the sun, even though doing so hurt his eyes. He wondered what encouraged it to rise and fall each day. It couldn't be as free as it seemed.

"That's just your opinion."

"Okay. Go home and see if I'm right."

Baldwin lowered his gaze. Perhaps it was the prospect of seeing Hetta, but he realized how unbearable it would feel to be alone again in the unit, waiting with his thoughts and a bag of uneaten edibles for Nadine to arrive.

"Okay," he said, "I'll go. But just for something to eat. I'm not going to get touched."

Simon readjusted the bra so it rode higher on his chest.

"You say that now," he said, "but wait until you meet this woman. Morris said that even without the ear she's beautiful. I bet you'll change your mind about getting touched once you see her."

"You're wrong."

But Baldwin was not sure, was not sure if Simon was right or wrong, was not sure why the sun rose in the morning or fell at night, was not sure why he was attracted to Hetta but still pined for Nadine. Perhaps, like *The Book of Ash*, it didn't make a difference, if he was sure or not, at least when it came to right or wrong, just as long as he knew the difference. But he was not sure if he did or didn't.

8 PIPE DREAM

*B*aldwin and Simon each dropped a chit into a tin pail held by a grizzled counting counselor looking to be far past the age of counting. The old man narrowed his wrinkled eyes before taking one precise step away from the opening of a large corroded pipe.

"Head down and don't stop," he said, his voice as weathered as his face. "It's exactly fifty-two paces to the other side. Don't panic if you have trouble breathing. There's more than enough air to keep you alive."

Baldwin followed Simon into the pipe. It was wide and tall enough to move freely, but spider webs and fungi coated the ceiling and sides, enough inducement for them to walk in single file…and stooped over.

"Fifty two."

It was Simon. He had been counting aloud his steps. He stopped abruptly, causing Baldwin to bump into his backside.

"The old man lied to us," he said, panicked. "We should be there already."

"Why would he lie?"

"To trap us. We pass out and he comes in and picks the chits out of our pockets."

"That's ridiculous. Just keep walking."

"My lungs feel tight."

Baldwin pushed at Simon's back.

"You're fine. Keep moving."

"We're going to die in here."

Baldwin was never comfortable taking charge, but he had found, over the years, that he did have the capacity for clear thought in moments of crisis. Perhaps it was the result of living with Nadine, of the necessity to keep calm and focused during her tantrums. Without hesitation, he grabbed Simon's hand and pushed past. It took a few yanks to get his neighbor's thick body moving again. After a few steps a flicker of light could be seen up ahead. A few more and they were finally out of the pipe.

"We're here."

"Don't lie," Simon said, breathing raggedly.

"Look for yourself."

Simon released Baldwin's hand and stood up straight. Small groups of men and women, naked or partially clothed, were scattered about inside the oval bright blue walls, talking and laughing and nibbling on edibles set out on folding trays.

"It fantastic," Simon said, tearing off his thong and bra but leaving on the flats. "I feel like I'm back in the womb."

Baldwin made a more detailed study of the area. Rimming the oval were a series of closed doors. One suddenly opened and Hetta emerged. She was also naked.

"Simon," he said. "I'm leaving."

"Why?"

Baldwin did not answer. Hetta had spotted him. She waved happily.

"You know her?" Simon asked.

"She put in for a miracle today."

"I hope you approved it."

Baldwin did not answer.

"She's coming over." Simon punched Baldwin excitedly on the shoulder. "Quick, my shoes – on or off?"

"What does it matter?"

"Okay, I'll leave them on."

Baldwin lowered his head as Hetta got closer. It was not just that he felt shy to see her again, particularly in these circumstances, but public nudity, although common in the Circle, made him extremely uncomfortable. Like his aversion to hate, it was most likely his mother's fault. She herself would never leave their home without being fully clothed, never, even on the hottest day, shedding an item she considered "acceptable" for a woman over thirty – blouse, slacks, and high heels. The only concession she made was to remove her shoes if on a long walk, particularly if the surface was uneven, rutty or chipped. But even then she doffed them with a sigh of defeat, telling Baldwin that "comfort never translates into class."

Simon spoke first.

"I'm grateful to meet you."

"Likewise."

Baldwin looked up, surprised by Hetta's greeting.

"I'm honored and happy you came to see me," she continued. "Is this your first time here?"

"Yes," Simon said. "But we were referred."

"That's sweet. But I was actually asking your companion."

Baldwin kept his head raised, but trained his gaze several feet over Hetta's right shoulder to avoid eye contact or seeing anything below her neck.

"I've never been here," he said. "We actually just came for a snack."

Simon thumped Baldwin again on the shoulder.

"That's not true. I want to be touched."

"And what's your name?"

"Simon."

"And how do you two know each other?"

"I'm his best friend."

"Neighbor," Baldwin corrected. "We live in the same building."

"And the same floor," Simon added. "Actually, another person in our building recommended we come and see a woman with one ear. Do you know her?"

"I like to think so."

Hetta pulled back her hair to reveal the deformity.

"You're her," Simon said. "I want to touch you."

"No one touches me." She let her hair fall back over the scar tissue. "I touch them."

"Okay," Simon said. "I want you to touch me."

"That's not possible. I've already a person scheduled for this time."

"So I'll wait?"

"That won't help."

Simon's face fell.

"Is it my shoes? I can take them off."

"Don't be silly. It's just that I have appointments all evening." She turned and pointed across the oval, at a purple door. "If you knock three times on that door, you'll be more than pleased with the counselor who comes out."

"Is it a man or a woman?" Simon asked.

"A woman."

"Is she beautiful like you?"

"Better. She's available."

Simon poked Baldwin.

"Wait for me."

They watched in silence as Simon walked to the purple door, knocked on it, and when it opened, disappeared inside.

"I hope I didn't hurt his feelings," Hetta said, turning to Baldwin. "He seems rather fragile."

"Don't worry. He's actually rather hard."

"I see." Hetta smiled. "But I didn't lie: I do have someone to touch."

"That's okay. You don't have to stay with me. I can wait outside."

Hetta drew close to Baldwin.

"You don't understand. It's you. I want to touch *you*."

Baldwin pulled away.

"I'm sorry, I can't."

"Why?"

Baldwin blushed. He looked back down at the ground.

"I'm in a romantic union. And…"

"You think you're betraying your lover by being touched by someone else," Hetta said, taking over his words. "Don't think that way. I touch many men and women who are in romantic unions. Some come to me in love with their lover and leave the same way. Some come to me hating their lover and leave the same way. And some just come to me for love."

Hetta moved closer. She put her hand under his chin and forced him to look directly into her eyes.

"We can just talk if you like," she said, her voice low and soothing. "I can listen as well as I can touch."

"I don't know."

"I mean it. I don't know what your situation is with your wife – if it is good or bad or indifferent. But you don't look happy."

Baldwin's throat constricted. He reached up and wiped his eyes, felt moisture.

"We're having problems."

"I'm sorry."

"It's not your fault."

"I'm still sorry."

Her touch began to relax him, the skin around his chin warming against her fingers.

"You're kind."

"No. I'm empathic. I'm in a bad union too. But I decided not to let the relationship define me. What I want is what I want. What I do is what I do. What I am is what I am. My husband is no more a part of me than any other part of me. Once I accepted this I was freed. Once

I let go of hope I found hope. You can do the same."

"It can't be that easy."

She released his chin and took hold of his hand.

"Come," she breathed. "Let me show you."

9 HOT BED

The room was small, square and without windows. Four fat candles burned quietly in each corner. A cement slab, as long as Baldwin was tall and rising up to his waist, took up most of the space. The air felt warm, but not hot.

"Can I leave my clothes on?"

"The stone is damp," Hetta said. "They'll get wet."

Baldwin fidgeted nervously.

"I'll turn around while you undress, if that helps," she volunteered.

"Thank you."

Baldwin waited for Hetta to turn her back before removing his clothes, the scarf last, and placing them in a wicker basket below the slab.

"Are you ready?"

"Almost."

Baldwin climbed up on the stone and lay face down. He rested his head on his folded arms and tried to calm himself.

"Okay."

"I'm going to put out a few candles to dim the light."

Baldwin listened to her footsteps, and then smelled the sweet yet acrid scent of smoke mixed with wax.

The footsteps drew close.

"Are you comfortable?"

"Yes. Thank you."

"Let your arms hang over the sides."

Baldwin did as he was told.

"I'm going to touch you now. Is that okay?"

"Yes."

He felt a single finger trace a smooth line from his neck to his shoulder, stopping on the damaged collarbone.

"What happened here?"

"I broke it."

"When?"

"About two years ago."

She probed deeper into the flesh, pushed hard onto the bone.

"Does that hurt?"

"A little."

She released the pressure.

"How did it happen?"

"A deer connected with me."

"*Connected?*"

"It ran me over."

"Oh."

"But it could have been worse."

"How so?"

"I could have died."

She again traced the wounded area.

"This will never heal. The bone is split too far apart."

"It was a big deer."

"I imagine so. But it did you a favor. You'll live long because of the break. Consistent pain tricks your body into thinking it's under attack, and so it fights each day to repel it. It makes you strong…and hard."

She paused.

"Baldwin."

"Yes."

"Turn over."

Baldwin did not move.

"Please."

"I'd rather not."

"Why?"

Baldwin hesitated. He pressed his forehead harder to the rock.

"I'm scared."

"Of me?"

"Of everything. It's bad what I'm thinking."

"What are you thinking?"

"That I like you."

"That's not bad. I like you too."

"But we're both in unions."

"Bad ones."

Baldwin exhaled. He felt lightheaded with excitement and fear.

"If I turn around, will you promise not to touch my—"

"Heart?" Hetta laughed. "I'm just teasing. I promise my hands won't touch you there …wherever that is."

Baldwin turned over. Hetta's hands glided over his torso, around and under his waist and buttocks. The pleasure of her touch was so intense he winced as if in pain.

"I like you're body," she said, continuing to explore it. "Your skin is in harmony with your bones, even the broken ones."

"Thank you."

"I'm going to come on the stone. Is that okay?"

"Okay."

Baldwin inhaled as she pulled herself up onto the slab. She spread herself atop his body so that her nipples pressed tight against his own.

"You promised not to touch me there."

"I promised not to touch you with my hands," she breathed.

"We have to stop."

"I can't."

"You have to."

"No, you have to." Hetta pressed her pelvis against his erect penis. "Do you remember what the woman asked me to do in the dream? Her exact words."

"Yes."

"Say it."

"Free him."

"Say it again."

"Free him."

"Again."

This time Baldwin shouted it out.

"It's time." Hetta said, gasping as he finally let go and entered her. "Now is the time."

10 PIECE MEAL

*H*etta walked him to the door. They held hands as they parted, looking at each other with insecure excitement, like new lovers unsure how to handle the responsibility of their growing bond. Baldwin finally let go of her hand and drifted across the warm wash, content to float with the feeling. With the sun having set, the heat had dropped, and not a lick of wind could be felt. It was so pleasant, so devoid of irritating stimuli, it made him doubt his very existence. Then he remembered he had come with Simon.

He looked about but did not see his neighbor, either standing alone or in one of the groups. The purple door was still closed and he walked toward it. When he got close enough he heard grunting and moaning noises inside. He decided it best to wait somewhere else.

It was quicker moving through the pipe without Simon, and he popped out relatively unscathed by spider web or strain.

"Grateful to see you again."

"Likewise."

The counting counselor was sitting on a stump, the chit bucket at his feet. He shot Baldwin a gummy smile.

"Enjoy yourself?"

"I did, thank you."

Baldwin rubbed at his collarbone.

"The person I came in with. You didn't notice if he came out yet?"

"The fat one?"

"I suppose."

"I didn't see him," the counting counselor said. "He's either still inside or he went over the wall. Some do."

"I'll wait for him here then, if that's okay with you?"

"Help yourself."

They were silent, giving Baldwin time to replay in his mind what had just happened with Hetta.

"I'm Nathan, by the way," the counting counselor said, interrupting his thoughts. "What's your name?"

"Baldwin."

"I once knew someone named Baldwin. But I'm pretty sure he passed."

"I'm sorry."

"Don't be. I didn't like him."

He smacked his lips together.

"Say, Baldwin, you might not have a vial of impure on you?"

"Sorry, I don't."

"That's a shame. I'm past the age of counting, but it wasn't so long ago when there was so much impure around you almost drowned in the stuff. You could drink a bucket a day and still have three buckets left. Now you have to empty out your entire chit supply just to get a thimbleful."

He rubbed a freckled hand wearily over his freckled scalp.

"How about you, Baldwin? You like impure?"

"Once. But I lost my taste for it."

"I wish I had. I can't get enough. Takes all of my chits and then some to keep up with my thirst."

Baldwin felt a sudden wave of fatigue. There was a tree stump next to him and he sat down and stretched out his legs.

"It's not fair the way the Circle doles out its doses," he continued. "It's like they want you to feel better, but not so much that you don't want to feel even better."

"Excuse me?"

"I was talking about impure. Didn't you hear me?"

"I'm sorry," Baldwin said. "I'm just tired. I don't mean to be rude, but I might close my eyes a moment to rest."

"Do as you like. I was only talking to talk anyway."

Baldwin did as he said, but still he saw, at least in his mind's eye, a hazy swirl of orange and red color, a moving prism that only invaded when he desperately wished for the blackness of sleep. There was also the memory it brought up: the pyres that ravaged the Circle during his childhood, enormous bonfires ignited by waste counselors who were encouraged to turn combustible refuse into nutrient-rich ash. That wasn't such an awful time, he thought, drawn in deeper to the colors. Or maybe it *was* an awful time, and the many years that had passed since that time made the time seem not as awful as it really was. He thought it interesting to think how one can heal without doing anything but getting older. It was also interesting how just sitting on a tree stump with eyes closed and looking at color might be a trigger for so many remembrances and thoughts and ideas and…

The nightmare enveloped Baldwin before full sleep did. He was conscious of his head bobbing without tether and his chin knocking against his chest and his lips parting just enough to let a long line of cool drool fall onto his right foot and pool between his toes. But still he could not stop his mind from slipping into the suffocating blackness of the dream where he awaited, powerless, as the deer came at him at full speed, emerging like the moon out of darkness, galloping at him with clattering fury, its open mouth overflowing with chits. Baldwin did not flinch, knowing, even in this unconscious state, that it would never hit him, that he would snap wide awake right before impact. But it did connect, hard, toppling him into a continuous backward somersault that he could not escape from.

"I got you."

It was Nathan, the counting counselor. His face was inches from Baldwin's.

"You were rolling toward the drop-off," he said, pointing to a steep downward incline.

"I must have been sleeping."

"Try shouting."

"It was a nightmare."

"Well, you're awake now."

Baldwin stood and dusted off his pants and shirt. He walked with care to the edge of the incline. The slope was steep, flattening out to a clearing of low brush and scrub oak, anemic-looking trees with speckled leaves and dusty bark. A hundred paces in was a square pit ringed by cement. Inside the pit he saw flashes of movement.

"Deer," Nathan said, as if intoning Baldwin's thoughts. "Poor things fall in at night and can't get out. Every week a few nutritional counselors come and harvest the dead ones."

Nathan spat and dug the saliva into the dirt with the ball of his foot. He wasn't wearing shoes, but brown socks encased in clear plastic bags. A rubber band around each ankle secured the bags. He looked to Baldwin more like a scrub oak than a man.

"Actually," Nathan continued. "They just burn them all – dead or alive. I've watched them do it from up here: they throw in sticks and paper, make a big fire, then scoop out the pieces that are left with a pitchfork."

"That's horrible."

"Sure it is. But people like meat in their bags."

Nathan turned his head toward the pipe.

"Your friend's coming."

He was right. Simon stumbled out and immediately doubled over, his belly hanging below his knees, his mouth wide and sucking air greedily.

Baldwin left Nathan and walked over.

"Are you alright?"

Simon straightened. The bra hung around his neck. His thong was coated in white webbing. His shoes were missing.

"I'm sorry to keep you waiting," Simon said, panting. "It's just that my counselor was amazing. After she rubbed me with her hands, she walked all over me. The bottoms of her feet are softer than moss. I never thought toes could move like that. It was like ten people working on me at one time. I think she liked me, too. I know what I said earlier, but I really think she liked me. I mean, I felt something between us. She even told me I had "needy" skin. That's a compliment, right?"

"I imagine so."

Simon fixed his bra. His breathing had slowed to almost normal. He eyed Baldwin and then smiled.

"I was right – you got touched."

Baldwin decided to lie, not because he did not want to give Simon the satisfaction of being right, but to keep private what happened with Hetta.

"No."

"Then where's your scarf?"

Baldwin looked down, surprised. He realized he must have left the scarf in the hamper.

"I was hot so I took it off. I must have left it inside on the railing."

"So go back and get it."

"I'm sure it's safe. I'll get it another time."

"You're too trusting of people."

Nathan came over. The bags on his feet gave off a crinkling sound as he walked.

"What about you?" he asked Simon without introduction. "You wouldn't have any impure to share?"

"No."

"You mean you don't have any on you, or you don't want to share?"

"Both."

Simon pushed past Nathan.

"Let's go," he said to Baldwin. "It's certainly dark now."

Simon was not lying. The moon had settled in behind a cloudbank, crowding out any available light and making it difficult for Baldwin to see Nathan's face as he passed. But he did find his hand, slipping the counting counselor the last chit in his pocket, before falling into place behind his neighbor.

11 TIGHT ROPE

*B*aldwin smelled Hetta on his skin and suffered a new wave of excitement and guilt. This mix of emotions began to bother him after awhile (plus, a reborn erection began to chafe his left inner thigh as he walked), and so he made a concerted effort to think about something else.

His thoughts settled on Manu. He hoped his utility partner was feeling better, had not suffered any more seizures, was resting, and, more importantly, was not doing something with the conflict counselor he shouldn't be doing. Baldwin, after what had just happened with Hetta, was not in a position to judge Manu for falling so quickly in love, or even acting on it in a sexual way, but there was something about Ramson, the conflict counselor, that alarmed him and made him fear for his friend's safety more than his heart.

Baldwin had hoped to continue to focus on Manu, perhaps review some of his other romantic relationships and the result, when his mind, as if tiring of the subject and taking control, pulled him toward his mother, and then to her favorite phrase, which she borrowed from *The Book of Ash*, and which now rang in his head like the sunrise gong upon waking: 'The past only exists if you believe in the future.' When he got older, and thought to ask her why she so valued the words, she told him that it gave her comfort to think that letting go of hope for a better tomorrow could erase the sadness of a bad yesterday. It had made him sad then to think her so unhappy, and it still did, perhaps even more, now that she was without breath. All of it he blamed on Leonard.

"I need a break."

Simon stopped and blew out his cheeks. His white legs emitted a phosphorous glow in the darkness. His skin shined with sweat. They had walked a considerable number of paces without speaking since leaving the warm wash.

"The touch counselor took more out of me than I realized," he said with a labored breath. "She grabbed me down deep and pulled everything out."

Baldwin winced at the image. He peered ahead.

"Are we close?"

"A few hundred paces should get us to a community garden," Simon answered. "And after that is the rust field."

"Is it a big one?"

"The garden or the rust field?"

"Both."

"They didn't seem big last night. But I was alone and walking fast. Talking is slowing us down."

They continued on in silence, walking in rhythm, their footfalls muting each other. Baldwin began to struggle again with thoughts of his mother when they reached the garden.

"I was almost right," Simon said. "Ninety-eight paces." He sniffed loudly. "Smell that soil. This dirt's seen a shovel today for sure."

"I don't smell anything."

"Then something's wrong with your nose. I usually have clogged nasal passages. But the touch counselor must have cleared them. My senses are wide open."

The scent finally came to Baldwin. It was harsh and chalky and sickly sweet. It was the smell of his youth, when the Circle had done most of its soil reclamation work.

"We should go around," he said to Simon. "Otherwise we'll leave holes in the soil and they'll have to bring in leveling counselors to fix them."

"Don't be silly," Simon said, venturing into the garden. "This is the fastest way."

Baldwin shook his head. He never liked creating a need for utility when it was not needed. He took a step backward, made sure he was on hard ground, and began to navigate around the garden's edges.

"Hurry up," Simon shouted over to him. He was already through the garden and looked impatient. "Just cut through."

Baldwin ignored him and kept to the longer route. He had just sidestepped a patch of briers when he heard a jostling noise to his left. He stopped, listened. The noise came again, more distinctive this time, like sticks snapping. He clenched his fists, the muscles throughout his body twitching in anticipation. His mind locked into a defensive stance, providing him with a flash list of evasive maneuvers to thwart any attack. When it didn't come, he quickened his pace to catch up to Simon.

"I told you to follow me," he said to Baldwin. "We lost a lot of time."

"I hope we're close."

Simon pointed to the ground.

"Is that close enough."

Baldwin looked down at a hole as wide and round as Simon.

"This is where you fell through?"

"Like a stone."

"How did you get out?"

"I just pulled myself out."

Baldwin eyed Simon's ample stomach and skinny arms.

"I don't know about this."

"Don't worry," Simon said. "I told you I have a rope."

He walked a few steps to his left, bent over, and began digging in the orange dust. When he stood, an edibles bag was in his hands. He reached in and pulled out a stretch of thick yellow cord.

"I came this morning and buried it," Simon said. "I also made a torch."

He pulled a forked branch from the bag. Stretched across its diametrically pointed ends was a red thong with emerald sequins.

Simon saw Baldwin looking at the underwear.

"I figure I'll get a lot more down there," he said. "And besides, I only offered it to you because I don't really like it."

"Okay."

"Anyway," Simon continued. "I soaked it in impure so it will burn bright."

Simon pulled a matchbook from the bag and lit the shorts. Baldwin felt an immediate heat on his face. The smoke made his eyes water.

"I'll hold the rope," Simon said. "You go down and set up the torch. Then throw everything to me and I'll pull you back up."

"I thought I was to hold the rope and you go down?"

"Is that what I said? I must have misspoken again."

"I thought you only did that with 'f' words."

"That's true," Simon said. "But also in the morning. I think it's because my body is hungry after the long night. I have a needy system when it comes to nourishment."

Baldwin peered into the hole.

"I'd still prefer to hold the rope."

"And I'd prefer to be skinny. But I'm not. And let's face it: you're not strong. It makes no sense to go against our bodies. The logical thing is for me to hold the rope."

Baldwin checked out the hole again. He could not see the bottom.

"Are you sure it's shallow?"

"Would I be here if it wasn't?"

Baldwin blew air out his nose. Ordinarily, he might have stood his ground and convinced Simon to let him hold the rope, or even give up on the project and go home. But he felt empowered by his time with Hetta and more daring.

"Just make sure to hold me tight."

Simon tied one end of the rope into a wide loop and passed it to Baldwin.

"Put your head through and then cinch it under your arms.

Baldwin did as was instructed.

"Now what?"

Simon handed him the torch.

"You go down."

"Aren't you going to grab the rope?"

"Right," Simon said, picking up the other end and twisting it around his wrists several times. "I get forgetful when I'm excited."

"Well, make sure to keep your head. And make sure to keep the rope taught until I get to the bottom."

"Of course," Simon said, bracing his knees for support. "I've done this before."

Baldwin thought of Manu's favorite number.

"I'll go on four," he said. "One, two, three...four."

For a moment, he was suspended in the air, his feet dangling, floating as if weightless. And then he was falling, gravity regaining control, pushing him down into the darkness. He hoped that he was dreaming again, that he would wake before impact, perhaps in his own bed, with Nadine nestled beside, or with Hetta on the stone slab. But it was not a dream. Not a nightmare. He was awake and alone. Simon had lied. It was a deep hole. And as is always the case when one finally accepts the reality of an unpleasant situation, the truth hurt.

He landed with a thud.

ENCOURAGEMENT 55—TURN AGAINST LOVE

When we thirst for love it dries up. When we search for love it disappears. When we fight for love we beat it into submission. But when we leave love alone, turn our back to its pull and embrace the emptiness of our lives, it will greet us with a kiss and never leave our side.

Reaction Step: Take time to select in your mind the person you are most in love with. It might be a spouse, a romantic interest, even a stranger. Then formulate a strategy to make this person hate you.

12 HANG OVER

*B*aldwin woke with the clang of the sunrise gong. He stared up at the ceiling, not wanting to move. For a moment he felt safe, sheltered, separated from life in the Circle.

But then he heard the familiar voice of a stranger.

"I'm grateful to see you."

Baldwin looked fast to Nadine's side of the bed. It was empty.

"Over here."

Baldwin's eyes moved faster than his neck could turn. Ramson was sitting cross-legged on the floor, his back against the wall facing the bed. He was holding Baldwin's copy of *The Book of Ash*.

"What are you doing here?"

"Just thought I'd stop by to see you," Ramson said, flipping absently through the pages. "Is that wrong?"

Baldwin tried to calm himself. It was not uncommon to be surprised in one's home by an unexpected visitor. The Circle did not allow for locks on living unit doors, and people were encouraged to make connections with residents they did not know. Once, Baldwin and Nadine had come home from an evening walk to find a young couple making love on their conversation room floor. Although the man and woman invited them to join, they declined and waited patiently in the kitchen until they finished and left.

"I guess you startled me."

"That wasn't my intention. But I won't apologize. It's good to wake with a jolt – gives you a leg up so to speak for the rest of the day."

"Anyway" – Ramson held the book up – "what do you think of this Ash character? Do you really believe in all these encouragements?"

Baldwin hesitated. He was still groggy from sleep as well as the chaos of the night before. But he knew it was best to be cautious when discussing *The Book of Ash* with anyone in the Circle, but particularly so with a conflict counselor, a utility entrusted with making sure the text's encouragements were followed.

"I follow the encouragements to the best of my conscious ability," he said, giving a response he had often used to the question.

"I didn't ask if you follow them," Ramson returned. "I asked if you believe in them."

"Is there a difference?"

"I suppose not. As long as you know the difference."

Ramson tossed the book up onto the foot of the bed and stood. He was still wearing his black boots, and was again shirtless, but he now sported white leggings a shade lighter than his learning stick. The purple makeup around his eyes and on his lips was also slightly different, less intense that it might be described as pink. To Baldwin, he looked bored and dangerous.

"But I found there are two types of people in the Circle," he continued, stretching his long arms overhead so that his fingertips brushed the ceiling. "There are those who will follow an encouragement even if they don't believe in it, and those who will believe an encouragement and still not follow it. I'm wondering which one of those you are?"

"Like I said, I follow the encouragements—"

"To the best of your conscious ability." Ramson dropped his arms, clasped his hands together and cracked the knuckles. "I heard you the first time, but I was hoping I might convince you to tell the truth."

"I am telling the truth."

"Sure you are. I'm sorry. I get so used to hearing lies in my utility, that when someone tells the truth I immediately think they're lying. Maybe it's conditioning or even that I'm growing lazy. The truth is deceitful people are always easier to control than honest ones, at least when it comes to ending conflict. It's gotten to a point now in my life that I want everyone to be liars." He paused. "What about you, Baldwin? What do you want?"

At the moment Baldwin wanted to know if Nadine was home when Ramson sneaked in, and he also wanted the conflict counselor to leave, but he dared not ask about the first, or encourage the second.

"What everyone in the Circle wants," he finally answered, "a reason to wake up in the morning and to go to sleep at night."

Ramson laughed through his nose.

"I see you have been conditioned as well. Anyway, like I said, I just stopped by. But since we're getting on so well why don't we have a real talk and get to know each other better. Doesn't that sound nice?"

Baldwin also knew better than to say no to a conflict counselor, especially when they were being nice.

"I'd like to wash up first."

"Go ahead. I'm in no rush."

"Perhaps you can wait in the kitchen while I get ready."

"Sure. Manu told me you're shy. I hope that's not another way of saying you have things to hide."

"I just like privacy."

"Who doesn't?"

Baldwin waited until Ramson left the room before easing out of bed. His body was sore and his face was dirty. He was glad Ramson was not there to see that he had slept in his clothes. As he washed up in the connecting bathroom, he teased out of his memory what had happened after the fall.

He must have been knocked out for some time, because when he regained consciousness the torch had gone out and the thong, charred as it was, felt cold to his touch. The moon must have changed position, as its light shot through the opening above, providing enough illumination for him to see inside the timehole. Simon, it appeared, had also lied about the contents. The room was completely bare, save for a wooden table, a wooden chair, and a wooden footstool, laid out in a row of descending height. It gave him an idea and he dragged the table under the opening, put upon that the chair, and then topped the structure with the footstool. It took him several tries, but he managed to climb up the makeshift ladder without toppling over, and on the tips of his toes gained enough height and leverage to pull out of the hole. He staggered home, nearly blind with shock and exhaustion, vaguely remembering an open door, collapsing into bed…and waking up to Ramson.

Who was now sitting at the kitchen table, peering into the evening's edibles bag. Baldwin did not recall taking it in when he came home. Of course, he did not recall much of anything once he left the timehole.

"I see you still have a full bag," Ramson said. He took a final peak into the bag and then let it go. "I guess you weren't hungry last night."

"Not really."

"That's a shame. I see you got peaches. My favorite."

"Have one if you like."

"No thanks," Ramson said. "I only eat what I get, not what I'm given."

Baldwin sat down gingerly.

"Are you okay? You move like you're past the age of counting."

"I must have slept wrong."

Ramson studied him a moment.

"Tell me the truth, Baldwin."

"It's the truth."

"I'm not talking about sleep. I'm talking about you. Specifically, how you feel about me. I get the sense you don't welcome my visit this morning. I also suspect that you don't like me."

Baldwin was wary of the question. Conflict counselors had a reputation for encouraging people to admit truths they wished were false.

"You seem fine."

"Fine?"

Baldwin rethought his words.

"I don't know you well enough to give you a better compliment."

"I feel the same about you. So let's get to know each other."

Ramson tapped his right index finger on the table.

"I'll start. Tell me about your father."

"I don't have a father. Not one I know, at least."

"I think you know who I'm talking about."

"If you mean Leonard Living, he's my stepfather. There is no blood between us."

Ramson smiled.

"Manu did say you hated him."

"He shouldn't have said that. You see, I don't hate anyone."

"Then you must not love anyone either."

"Why do you say that?" Baldwin asked defensively.

"Because you said you don't hate anyone."

"I don't."

"Then you can't love anyone. Love and hate only exist as parallels. You can't have one without the other."

Ramson licked at his lips, causing the purple makeup to glisten.

"I'm not trying to make you feel anything you don't want to," he continued, "but let's pretend for a moment you do hate your father—"

"Stepfather."

Ramson frowned.

"If I call him Leonard, will you stop interrupting me?"

"Yes. I'm sorry."

Ramson took the apology with a nod.

"As I started to say, let's pretend you hate...Leonard. What if I know a way to make that hate go away? I imagine it's awful to carry around such an ugly and destructive emotion. Don't you want to let it go?"

Baldwin did not like the way he was being drawn into Ramson's suggestion. He understood, deep down, that he did harbor an acute dislike of Leonard, but to admit it crossed into hate was to go against his training, his mother's admonishments, his identity as a person that does not hate, who is always nice, helpful to a fault. He was afraid to accept that a "hateful" Baldwin was inside him. Perhaps he knew, if unleashed, this other person would overpower the one currently in control.

"What do you say, Baldwin?" Ramson continued. "Are you ready to let go?"

Baldwin shook his head, more to convince himself than Ramson.

"Believe me, I don't hate Leonard. And even if I did, which I don't, I hardly see him anymore since my mother passed. So I have no reason anymore to feel that way about him, which I never did."

Baldwin tried to swallow to slow himself down, but his mouth was very dry and he could not work up enough saliva to complete the action. Ramson, watching him closely, reached into the bag and pulled out a peach. He rolled it across the table, its momentum carrying it to a perfect stop at Baldwin's forearm.

"That'll help," he said. "It's juicy."

"Thanks," Baldwin said, but he did not pick up the fruit.

Ramson resumed his finger tapping.

"Manu says you lost your mother recently," he said.

"Yes. She passed ten seasons ago minus one."

"My mother left the Circle not long before that." Baldwin suspected by Ramson's faraway look that he was remembering the woman. "I guess we share the same sadness."

"I guess."

"It's like breaking a bone, right?" Ramson said.

"What is?"

"Losing a mother. The pain is immediate and intense, but then it goes numb, the bone eventually heals, and you can put weight back on it. It's different with fathers; the loss doesn't start hurting until much later, and it never goes away."

Baldwin eyed the peach. It was pink with green tints. A single green leaf stuck out of the stem. It looked lonely.

"I don't have to worry about that," he said. "A stranger inseminated my mother. Leonard came later."

Ramson grunted with displeasure.

"I can't believe the Circle used to encourage anonymous penetration. Now there are so many men about that even the most desperate women can find a willing conception partner."

"My mother wasn't desperate. She was beautiful."

"If you say so."

Baldwin began to feel claustrophobic in the small kitchen.

"Are we done getting to know each other?" he asked. "I do have other things to do today."

"Sure. We're almost done. Just as soon as you admit you hate Leonard?"

"I can't admit something I don't feel."

"But you do."

"I don't."

Ramson slapped his right hand hard to the table.

"Just admit it."

"No."

Ramson slapped the table again, this time with both hands.

"Admit you hate him. Admit you wish he was no longer breathing."

"No. I don't hate anyone."

"Then I'm right: you don't love anyone. No wonder your wife isn't here. Manu told me all about it. How she bullies you. How she's probably cheating on you. You must like it. I'm sure Leonard bullied you growing up, and your wife took over where he left off. Maybe she's just like your mother. Did she bully you too? Or did she just sleep around?"

"Be quiet."

Ramson leaned forward.

"Make me."

"I want you to leave."

"I will," Ramson said. "When you admit it."

"I won't."

Ramson stared at Baldwin, his gaze no longer holding rage but sympathy.

"The saddest thing about hate is when it's wasted," he said. "But those with the courage to own it, to tap into it, reach heights of happiness they've never dreamed. And by doing so, they lift all those around them to the same heights. I came here hoping to convince you to use your hate, not just for your own good, but for mine as well."

"And how would I do that?"

"By killing Leonard."

"You're not serious."

"I'm always serious. It all makes sense: I save Manu's life, he tells me about yours. I realize we share the same pain and both have something to gain from Leonard's death. And with the Day of No Consequence nearing, our dreams, our wants and desires, can be attained. See how your hate is connected to our fate? Your past is our future."

"I don't understand."

"It's simple: I want to be the Mentor of Self Esteem, you want to be free of hate. The only thing blocking the attainment of these goals is Leonard."

"So kill him yourself."

Ramson shook his head.

"It has to be you. Ambition isn't encouraged in the Circle. The people would never accept a leader who goes to such lengths to lead. I have no other reason to murder Leonard than my own advancement. They would know why I did it and never give me what I want. But your motivation to end Leonard's life is personal, even common. Sons have always killed their fathers on the Day of No Consequence. It happens so much it's almost boring."

"This is absurd."

"You're absurd," Ramson snapped. "Why wallow in hate and be miserable when there's a chance to be free and happy."

Baldwin mustered his courage.

"I'm free and happy enough. And I'd never kill anyone for any reason. I won't ask again: I want you to leave. It's the only thing in the Circle I want or desire."

"Then I feel sorry for you."

Ramson stood and moved past the table in slow sections. When he reached Baldwin he stopped, his right hand gliding over the learning stick before falling to the table and picking up the peach.

"I thought you only eat what you get," Baldwin said. "I see you lie too."

"I never said I didn't."

Ramson smiled as he placed the fruit under the front waistband of his leggings. "But you see," he said, leaving the room, "this is for Manu."

13 BABY SIT

*R*amson left and Baldwin ate the three peaches left in the bag. It was not a day of utility and he was not eager to leave the unit, let alone the table, still quite shaken by the fall into the timehole and the morning's confrontation with Ramson. But he needed to talk to Simon, needed to find out exactly what had happened. Had Simon lost hold of the rope? He was sure it hadn't slipped off him as he was being lowered, but when he came to later it was no longer looped under his arms. Perhaps Simon had tried to pull him up and the knot had come undone? But where was Simon? When he finally extricated himself from the hole his neighbor, and the rope, was gone.

Baldwin went to the bathroom to rinse peach juice from his hands and face. His image in the mirror above the sink made him pause. He looked older, not so much tired as drawn, his skin, usually somewhat oily and shiny, dry and dull. He also noticed a single gray hair amidst his black bangs. It looked lonely and outnumbered and he pulled it out with a yank.

At the door, he stopped himself and peered through the peephole. He didn't see anyone and so opened it.

"Hello, Baldwin."

He jumped back, but then saw it was Hetta. She was standing just left of the doorframe. A white sheet covered her body. Her head and arms poked through jagged holes in the material. The bottom of the makeshift dress stretched to the floor, covering her feet.

"Hetta."

She began to cry.

"What's wrong?"

"Everything."

Hetta stepped toward Baldwin and clasped his left forearm with both hands.

"I need your help."

"Of course. What is it?"

She pulled tight to him.

"Right now, can I encourage you to hold me?"

Baldwin followed the encouragement. He wanted to follow it, even desired to follow it. He was certainly content holding her, oddly happy as her tears soaked through his shirt and touched his skin.

"Thank you," she said, looking up at him. "I already feel better."

"I'm glad. But what's the problem?"

She pulled away gently and lifted her hair to reveal her right ear. It was bright red, the lobe swollen.

"He hit me last night."

"Who?"

"My husband. That's what he does after he drinks impure. And all he does is drink impure."

"I'm sorry."

"Don't be. Remember what I told you, that he's only a part of me. Well, this makes him an even smaller part. Every day he becomes a little less. Soon, there won't be any part of him left."

She steadied her gaze on Baldwin. Her blue eyes were moist.

"The problem is I have a meeting this morning with a conception counselor. I can't bring him. He's not fit to be a husband, let alone a father. They'll turn me down and I'll have to wait another year before putting in a new application. I know my body. I can't wait any longer. I need approval to conceive now or it will never happen."

"You're young. I'm sure you have time."

"No. My mind and body are in agreement on this. I think the orgasm confirmed everything. Now is the time."

Baldwin hesitated.

"I'm not sure how I can help."

This time Hetta paused.

"I know this sounds strange. But I need you to be my husband."

"I don't understand."

"This morning, at the meeting. If you pretend to be him, I know your goodness will shine through, and I'll be approved to conceive. Then I can have a baby."

"But what if we get caught?"

"We won't. I've never seen this counselor before."

"Maybe I have."

"Have you and your wife ever gone to a conception counselor?"

"No."

"Then there's no worry."

"But if you get approval, then what?"

Hetta smiled happily.

"Then we can have a baby."

"We?"

"Don't worry. I'm just trying to get into character so we can be convincing as a couple in the meeting. But it wouldn't be such a horrible chore to make a baby with me, would it?" She rested her hand on her stomach and smiled. "Maybe we already have?"

Baldwin exhaled. The fall into the timehole and that morning's encounter with Ramson had pushed back in his mind what had happened with Hetta at the warm wash.

"But what if they ask questions about us? What if they ask how we met? How we fell in love?"

"We tell the truth – a miracle brought us together."

Hetta placed her hands around Baldwin's neck and drew him close.

"Please pretend to be my husband."

Baldwin knew he could not resist the role. But he wondered if he still knew how to play it.

"Please say you'll do it?"

"I'll do it," he said. "But you never told me your husband's name?"

"Don't laugh."

"I won't."

"Ernest."

"I remember. You told me your second name when you put in for your miracle. But what's his first name."

"That's it. Ernest. His name is Ernest Earnest."

Baldwin didn't laugh. Perhaps because she was kissing him.

14 NOTE WORTHY

*B*aldwin had never before seen the conception counselor. She was a tall woman with a shaved head of red bristles and deep laugh lines that ringed her large mouth. She motioned for them to sit down in chairs placed neatly in front of her rather formidable desk. When they did, she folded her hands and smiled without showing her teeth.

"Let's start with gratitude," the conception counselor said matter-of-factly. "I'm grateful to see you both, and I'm sure you feel the same. Agreed?"

Hetta and Baldwin nodded their heads.

"Good. Now your names, first and second, in that order please." She motioned to Hetta. "Let's start with the female."

"Hetta Earnest."

"And the man?"

Baldwin cleared his throat.

"Ernest Earnest."

The conception counselor blinked.

"Ernest Earnest?"

"Some people call him Ee-Ee," Hetta volunteered.

"I hope not too many," the conception counselor snapped back, her long face reddening. "We have double syllable names in the Circle for a purpose: it helps with memory, it helps with order, and most important, it helps with discipline."

"I'm sorry," Hetta said.

Baldwin raised his hand.

"Yes," the conception counselor said.

"I'm sorry too. I mean, about the name."

"Noted. But no more raising your hand to speak. This isn't a classroom, I'm not a teacher, and you're not children. Agreed?"

They nodded again.

"Now that we got that straightened out, let's get to the real reason you're both here. Tell me, the female first, why *don't* you want a baby?"

"But I do want one," Hetta said.

"Perhaps so, but with every desire is an opposite desire. I want to know about the opposite."

Hetta bit at her lip. After a moment she said:

"Baby's cry. I hate crying."

"And the man?"

"I don't like crying either," Baldwin said.

The conception counselor looked concerned.

"So you think alike. That worries me. I'm not someone who thinks opposites always attract, but they certainly make for a better time. I hate to think of two people in love agreeing on everything."

Baldwin began to raise his right hand, then remembered the conception counselor's scolding and shoved it under his buttocks.

"If it's not too late," he said, "I'd like to add that while Hetta *hates* crying, I only dislike it. There's a big difference."

"Noted." The conception counselor kept her eyes on Baldwin. "Let me ask you, when you're penetrating the female, do you prefer the bottom or the top? That is, would you rather look down on her or up to her when making love?"

Baldwin shifted nervously in the chair.

"I'm not sure. I suppose both views have their attributes."

"But you must have a preference? That's one thing about sex – everyone has a preference. People might say they are egalitarian when it comes to pleasing their partners, that it doesn't matter when or how they do it, but trust me, everyone, at their core, knows just how they like it. If you don't know that's a problem."

"He prefers the bottom," Hetta spoke up. "I like the top."

"Noted. And very good. Opposite attractions working toward a communal pleasure. That's very good."

The conception counselor unfolded her hands.

"I'll get right to the point. I imagine you came in here thinking I was going to ask you about your relationship and your views on parenting, but my experience is the more I learn the less I know. Let me give you an example. Let's say the man" – she pointed her middle finger at Baldwin – "tells me he can only get an erection if he sees the female" – she turned the digit to Hetta – "wearing his underwear. I might deduce from the statement that the man has latent sexual feelings for men, and the female wearing his briefs provides him with the fantasy that he is actually having sex with a man. Or perhaps his mother wore men's underwear when she was nursing him and he's just recreating a pseudo-sexual suckling relationship with her. Maybe he's just turned on because something that is usually close to his genitalia in now close to the female's genitalia. You see how many ways I could go with the slightest bit of information. That's why I try to keep my mind as narrow as possible when I talk with a couple. In fact, it's really better if I don't think at all. What I'm trying to say is that I actually don't have a clue what makes a good parent or a bad parent. So rather than make a decision based on chance, I let chance make the decision."

The conception counselor opened a drawer and pulled out a crude looking knife, its handle white, the metal blade rusty with deep serrated edges. She pointed the tip between them.

"What I'd like to do is slice one of your palms. Then the two of you hold hands while I count to twenty. If the bleeding has stopped when you unclasp your hands, I approve your claim for conception. If not, I reject it."

"There's no other way?" Hetta asked.

"Not in this office. So who wants to get cut?"

"I'll do it. Take my blood."

Baldwin reached over and pulled back Hetta's hand.

"No," he said. "Take mine."

He extended his right hand, palm up. It was shaking.

"Maybe you should close your eyes," the conception counselor suggested.

"I'm okay."

"Alright, on four. One…two…three…four."

The blade dug into his palm. The pain was sharp but bearable. He saw a line of blood press up from the skin.

"I encourage the man to hold hands with the female."

Hetta and Baldwin brought their hands together. The conception counselor began counting. Hetta closed her eyes.

"I'm sending your blood a positive message," she whispered.

At twenty the conception counselor encouraged them to let go of each other. Baldwin looked down at his palm.

"Now you can raise your hand," she said to him.

Baldwin did as he was told. The blood had stopped.

"Congratulations," the conception counselor said. "On behalf of the Circle, I encourage you to conceive. Starting next month, your monthly allotment will include an extra chit, which you will receive for a period of nine seasons. I'm encouraged to tell you that this extra chit must be used to procure items that will heighten your sexual activity or, in the case that the female becomes pregnant before the nine seasons mark, to decrease your sexual activity. Do you understand?"

"We do," Hetta said.

"And some practical advice for the man," the conception counselor continued. "I know you prefer the bottom during sex, but for conception sake, it's always better to move downhill. Think you could do that for a while and still enjoy yourself?"

Baldwin nodded. Happy, at last, to be telling the truth.

15 DATE LINE

*B*aldwin and Hetta held hands as they left the conception counselor's office. For a brief moment he forgot that Hetta was not his wife, that he was only impersonating her husband, and that his real wife, Nadine, was somewhere in the Circle. It was a nice moment, a clear moment, but then it passed, and he pulled his hand away with reluctance when another couple approached the office.

"Can I see you later?" Hetta asked, blinking as the sun shone hard upon her face. "I have to go to the warm wash for the afternoon, but if you come before sunset we can take a walk. There's a blueberry bush not far that's ripe. We can pick some for dinner. Wouldn't that be nice?"

Baldwin smiled at the thought. He and his mother used to go blueberry picking often when he was small, filling a large wooden bowl with the fruit and then mixing in chopped honeysuckles. It was the sweetest, gentlest combination of flavors he had ever experienced.

"So is it a date?"

Baldwin hesitated.

"I have to go to my life counseling session. And then I should really go home."

"Oh."

"It's just that I haven't seen my wife in days. I need to talk to her."

"You don't have to explain wanting to be with your wife."

"It's not that. I think I should tell her about us."

"Why would you do that?"

"It's only right. I'm not a deceptive person."

"So don't be. You have a right to live your life, not explain it."

Hetta bit at her lower lip.

"I'm sorry," she said. "I crossed the line. I guess I'm not use to dealing with honest people."

"I'm not always honest."

"But at least you want to be." She paused. "What will you tell her?"

"I'm not exactly sure. I might just say I met someone I like. She probably won't even care. She might even be relieved. I don't think she loves me anymore."

Hetta patted Baldwin's arm.

"I think for now you don't need to share us with anyone. You don't have to rush things. I'm not going anywhere."

"Except to utility."

Hetta laughed.

"Which is why I deserve a reward; for performing my utility when everyone else isn't. So forget about the truth for now and meet me before sunset. Okay?"

"I'll try."

"Try hard."

Baldwin watched her walk away, the white sheet clinging to her marvelous frame, the bottom dusting a path around her feet. He had no doubt he would end up at the warm wash before sunset. He turned and headed to his weekly life counseling session with Harold. There was a lot to talk about. He just didn't know if he should.

16 BLOOD SUCKER

*T*he building where Harold lived was short and squat and made of brick. It consisted of three floors and a basement. Harold lived in the basement. The unit was windowless and dank, but blessedly cool. So much so that Baldwin sometimes welcomed the end of sessions to get back outside and warm up. It always made him feel grateful for the sun, as opposed to the many times when he cursed its unrelenting heat.

Baldwin entered the building from behind, stepping down a narrow cement stairwell to a light blue metal door dimpled with dents. Baldwin aimed his knuckles into the largest dent and knocked twice. He heard movement inside, and then a loud belch. The door opened to the inside with a pained whine.

"Come in."

Harold was clad in a red velvet robe, cinched at the waist by a lavender belt. He motioned with his hand for Baldwin to enter, swallowing and belching again as he led them into the unit's conversation room. They settled into matching orange felt chairs, facing each other about five feet apart. Harold's chair had a footstool. He propped his bare feet up on it and wiggled his toes at Baldwin.

"We're grateful to see each other, right?"

"I think so."

"Good. What's up?"

Baldwin scratched at his forehead. He did not know how or where to start. So he delayed.

"Not much. How are you?"

Harold used his right index finger to pick at his front teeth.

"No complaints," he said, pulling out the finger and staring at the print. "I ate some good spinach this morning. At least it tasted like spinach. It might have been collards. In that case, it was bad collards."

Harold took another pass at his teeth and then rested his hands in his lap. He nudged his chin at Baldwin.

"What's wrong with your hand?"

Baldwin had forgotten about his palm. He looked down. It was bleeding again.

"I must have cut myself."

"With what, a hatchet?"

Harold rose from the chair and left the room. Baldwin heard him rummaging around in the kitchen. He returned holding a glass jar filled with what looked like grape jelly. He unscrewed the lid and held the jar under Baldwin's nose.

"I made it myself – crushed grapes, a thimble of impure, and enough cane sugar to put holes in your teeth. Take a scoop and spread it over the wound."

Baldwin did as he was told.

Harold sat back down with a groan. He returned the lid to the jar and set it on the floor.

"You can leave that on all day, by the way. With air it will harden just like a scab. Then you can break it off and eat it."

Baldwin made a face.

"I'll pass."

"Don't be swishy," Harold scoffed. "The best things to eat look disgusting."

He raised and lowered his eyebrows.

"Now tell me what really happened to your hand."

Baldwin hesitated.

"It's complicated."

"And I'm simple. We can work it out."

Baldwin eyed the jelly coagulating in his palm.

"I met a woman."

"And she stabbed you?"

"No. It wasn't like that. Right before I came here, a conception counselor cut me to decide if we can have a baby or not."

"Strange decision making process. But to each his own. I don't remember you telling me you and Nadine were seeking to conceive."

"We're not."

Harold narrowed his eyes. He scratched the bridge of his nose.

"Let's go back. What's the woman's name, the one you met?"

"Hetta."

"I like her already. Is she pretty?"

"Very."

"And what is her utility?"

"She's a touch counselor at a warm wash."

"Is that where you met?"

Baldwin shook his head. He closed his hand into a fist, causing the jelly to worm through his fingers.

"She came to my office yesterday morning about a miracle."

"And then she invited you to the warm wash," Harold said knowingly.

"No, that was by chance. My neighbor invited me after utility. I didn't know she worked there. It just happened she was on duty and free."

"So she touched you?"

"Yes."

Harold waited for Baldwin to continue.

"Maybe we did more."

"Maybe?"

Baldwin was not a good liar, but he was worse at withholding information, mostly because he assumed people could see through him and would think him deceitful if he didn't tell them whatever they asked or what he was feeling. The whole thing was even more complicated with Harold. As his life counselor, it was Baldwin's reverse utility to tell him everything and anything in sessions. But there were times he did not want to share, did not want to explore, did not want to analyze or strategize his actions, and so he would hold back. The problem, though, was that it never felt as good as when he let it all out. He weighed all this in his mind, balancing an urge to shut up, to keep what had happened between he and Hetta private, versus speaking it out with Harold, widening the circle, so to speak, of people involved in their affair; even legitimizing it.

"I touched her back."

Harold nodded.

"How did that feel?"

"Good. She's got nice skin."

"Anything else about her you like?" Harold asked.

"She's missing an ear."

"Which one?"

"Her left."

"She can hear out of the other one?"

"Yes."

"Then I suppose not having the other ear isn't much of a deficit. I once dated a woman whose nostrils wouldn't open. It gave her nose a rather sleek look. But the problem was she had to breathe out of her mouth. It made for clumsy kissing – stop and go, you know, so she could come up for air. It made it impossible to get into a rhythm."

"So you broke up with her?"

"I wish. She left me before I had the chance to even consider it. Took up with a man she met at a confidence rally. You're probably too young to know about them, but the Circle used to encourage single people to gather on full moons, inside rust fields, and speak to each other in compliments. Nothing else. That kind of phony talk always bored me. And I never liked to get rust on my shoes, so I never went. But one night she did and met this fellow. Maybe he had nice things to say about her nostrils."

Harold paused, shook his head and smiled.

"That wasn't such a bad thing to remember. It always does a person good to recall instances from their life that seemed so important at the time, and really they are just about the most unimportant thing that could ever have happened. You'll find that the more you age, whatever bothers you most at the moment, won't be worth a trifle later."

"I hope you're right."

"Of course I am. Don't underestimate the power of the human mind to progress as it decays. The older you get, the less you remember. It's the perfect coping mechanism to prepare for death."

"You're cheerful today."

"That's because I met a woman too."

"Congratulations."

Harold raised a hand.

"Please. She's nothing special, but she likes me and can cook, and that's enough for now."

They were silent a moment?

"What was her miracle?"

"Excuse me?"

Harold cleared his throat.

"The woman you met. Hetta. You said she came to you about a miracle."

Baldwin flushed.

"Normal stuff."

"I wouldn't think miracles were ever normal."

"They are when you hear enough of them."

Harold rubbed at his chin.

"You seem drained. Is it emotional or from loss of blood?"

Baldwin smiled. Harold's sarcasm always provided him with the option to go deeper into a conversation, or to escape it.

"Just tired. It was a long week."

Harold continued to rub his chin.

"It's not over yet. Any fun plans for the Day of No Consequence?"

Baldwin thought of what Leonard told him: the threat on his life. That worry had been buried under the intrigue of meeting and falling in love with Hetta.

"Maybe I'll hide this year," he said.

"Any particular reason?"

"Just to be safe. Sometimes people get mad when their miracles get rejected. You never know who wants revenge."

"Well, at least you have some excitement in your life. I'm sad to say I can't think of one person who has any intention of doing me harm this year. Makes me think I'm rather boring."

Harold released his hand and slapped his knee.

"Should I encourage you to leave now?"

"I think so."

Harold rose from the chair. He waited for Baldwin to stand, and then walked him back to the door.

"I'm just curious," he said. "Was Hetta's miracle a miracle?"

"What do you mean?"

"Did you approve it?"

"I did."

Harold paused.

"She must have been grateful."

"I suppose so."

He patted Baldwin's shoulder.

"It's nice to make people happy. But remember, sometimes it's nice to make people sad, too."

Baldwin waited in the stairwell a moment after Harold closed the door. The chill gained from the unit left his body with the heat. It was very sunny. He opened his hand. The jelly scab had already hardened. He pushed his palm to his mouth and bit it off. Harold hadn't lied. It tasted good.

17 WASTE LAND

Leonard strolled up to him not far from Harold's unit. His stepfather was wearing his "browns" and holding *The Book of Ash*. In his left hand was a lemon wedge, which he held out to Baldwin.

"How grateful I am to see you again."

"Likewise."

"Want a lick?"

"No thank you."

"Are you sure?"

"Yes."

"Well, I'm done with it."

Leonard tossed the lemon aside. He wiped his hand on his shorts and pointed behind him.

"I just came from reading some encouragements over a patch of reclaimed soil, not five hundred paces away. Nasty smelling dirt, but it has a nice airy look to it. Of course, the Mentor of Cultivation chose the wrong seed for such light fare. Only plants with deep roots can thrive in loose structure, but he's going to sow lettuce anyway. I swear that man loses his head when it comes to greens. Trust me, the first hard rain and every sprout will wash away. But what do I know – I'm just responsible for people feeling good about themselves, even if they don't have anything to eat."

"I'm sure it will grow well if given the chance."

"Let's hope so."

Leonard peered over Baldwin's shoulder.

"Isn't that the building your life counselor lives? Herbert, isn't it?"

"Harold."

"Yes, Harold. Now I remember him. He has a humorous bent, does he not?"

"I suppose."

"I hope he's at least serious about fixing your problems. If not, I can get you someone new to talk with. Maybe even a woman. There's something to be said about working through problems with the gender that gives you the most problems."

"I don't want anyone else. I'm happy with Harold."

Leonard's lips spread into a tight smile.

"Then I won't give it another thought. I'm actually pleased to hear you praise his work. You can't imagine how many people come to me with complaints about their life counselors. Most times the fault lies in the person doing the complaining."

Leonard raised the book, but this time it shielded his eyes, not Baldwin's, from the bright sun. He said:

"Encouragement 10, paragraph five, line six: 'To want more from a relationship is to expect less from yourself.' Perhaps that's why I'm always grateful to the people closest to my life...I don't expect much from them."

Baldwin watched as Leonard kissed the book and lowered it.

"It's fortunate I ran into you," he continued. "There's more to what I told you yesterday, about the person who wants you dead. I'm afraid it's not pleasant, perhaps even shocking."

Baldwin's stomach clutched.

"It's Nadine," Leonard said.

"Nadine?"

He nodded.

"She's the one who wants to kill you."

"You're kidding."

"I wish it so. The fact of the matter is I'm somehow connected to this desire. What I'm saying is she's in love with me. Perhaps *infatuated* is a better description."

Leonard raised the book again.

"Encouragement 15, paragraph 7, line three: 'Lust is nothing but imagination meeting desperation.' I'm afraid your Nadine is filled with both."

"You two are having an affair?"

This time Leonard gave the book an angry peck and then shook it at Baldwin.

"You're not listening. I would no more penetrate Nadine than you. The only guilt on my part is not telling you sooner about her obsession. The truth is I've felt her eyes on me since the time you met her, but even more so after your accident with the deer. I'm sure she was moved by my nurturing nature to you during that period. Remember how I came over each night while you were stuck in bed and read over the encouragements. Women are never more vulnerable to love than when they see it being provided by another. I think that's when she could no longer control her desires. As you know, I'm an astute perceiver of human intention through nonverbal cues. It was clear by her protracted nipples, the angle of her hips, the purse of her lips, even the dab of saliva atop them, that the sight of me caused within her an acute erotic tension. I won't lie and say it wasn't flattering to have such a young and attractive woman addled with arousal on my account. And I suppose I might have let her continue on this path of sexual admiration if not for her recent desire to kill you. I imagine she thinks with you dead we can form a union. I told her this was lunacy and encouraged her not to harm you in any way. Basically, I gave her a good scolding."

The delicate wrinkles under Leonard's eyes twitched. There was an almost imperceptible aging that had occurred in the short time of their conversation. His face looked almost hollow, as if his eyes and mouth had been pulled inward.

"It's the real reason I was going to your unit yesterday," he continued. "I was worried my words to her were too harsh. I wanted to make sure she was okay and accepted the reality of the situation."

Baldwin's thoughts swirled.

"I wish you told me this yesterday."

Leonard bowed his head.

"Your mother agrees with you," he said softly. "She came to me last night in a dream – gave me a scolding as well for not telling you all about Nadine."

"Don't talk about my mother."

"You mean my wife."

"She was my mother first."

Leonard's derisive laugh lingered in the warm air.

"And so we fall to the same conclusion," he said, shaking his head. "You think I stole your mother from you, and you hate me forever for it. Or despise me, or dislike, or whatever word you want to use to shade your animosity. But the truth is your mother *chose* me. You, she merely had."

Baldwin felt the urge to strike, to kick Leonard, to pummel him with punches, bite at his flesh, and gouge out his eyes. Instead, he looked down at his palm. It was bleeding again. He squeezed the hand into a fist to stop the flow, looked hard at his stepfather.

"I loved her more than you. I'll always love her more than you."

Leonard's eyes glinted with compassion.

"I wish you wouldn't waste your time trying to feel something you've already felt. It's the same as putting good seed into bad soil: nothing good will come from it. The best thing for your mind is to put your mother out of it."

"You're wrong."

"Then so is Ash."

For the third time, Leonard raised the book.

"Encouragement 80 – 'Find What You Have, Lose What You Lost.'"

He kissed the cover, but also his hand, before lowering both.

"All I'm saying is you should concentrate on the present," he said. "And not on Nadine."

"After what you told me, I don't care about her anymore. She can do whatever she wants with whoever she wants."

"You sound more confident than yesterday."

"Yesterday I didn't know it was Nadine."

"You're not scared of her?"

Baldwin smiled. Anger made him brave, or at least less fearful.

"Why should I be?" he said. "Encouragement 12 – 'Never Feed the Hand that Bites You.' Meaning, Nadine's your problem now, not mine."

And with that Baldwin turned and walked away, realizing he had done something he had never done before with his stepfather: he had gotten the last word.

18 WILD LIFE

*B*lood. Baldwin stopped walking. He unleashed his fist. The palm was smeared red, a pretty, heart-shaped stain, a reminder there was still someone to love in the Circle, someone who did not want him dead. It was hard for him to believe. Despite their troubles, he did not think Nadine so desperate to escape their union that she would kill him to achieve it. And while he could imagine her being reckless enough to have a dalliance with Leonard, he could not imagine her falling in love with his stepfather to the point of irrationality. If anything, Nadine became more clear-headed, more responsible, more grounded and resolute when in the throes of passion – at least that was how she was leading up to their union.

He started up again in the direction of the warm wash. It was early – Hetta had asked him to come right before sunset – but he could think of nowhere else to go, certainly not home. Each step brought him deeper into thought, analyzing the validity of Leonard's words, of Nadine's capacity for infidelity, to do him mortal harm. His doubts in her defense were based more on compassion than confidence, a feeling honed during their union, when he downplayed her brusque slights, manic fits, and melancholic moods as the rightful anger of an abandoned child. Neglected, ignored, and often forced to stay with neighbors while her parents drank impure and explored love relationships outside their union, Nadine grew hard, petulant and unpredictable, the type of girl who punched boys in the teeth if they made a pass at her, and then invited their hands down her pants while they bled. There was a cloak of dangerous contradiction about her, a hood either hedonistic or heartfelt, which she raised and lifted without logic or worry of consequence. When they met, this capriciousness spoke to Baldwin's rebellious desires, feelings fermented in the lidded cauldron of Leonard's trailer. But he soon realized he could never match her torment, her temper, her zeal for unreality. Despite his hope that he had found in Nadine a kindred spirit, really, all he had found was a wild one.

There was no one outside the warm wash when he approached. The sun was falling, but not enough to cool the air, and his skin, from the hard walk and hard thinking, was coated in a fine sweat. He hesitated to head inside, not wanting to disturb Hetta if she was with a client, but he was hungry to see her, desperate to distract himself from the thought of Nadine and Leonard, to hold someone who wanted to hold him back. His desire for her built as he rushed through the pipe and stumbled out into the wash. This time there was no one standing about. All the doors were closed, except the one to the room Hetta had taken him the day before. He headed toward it, excitement crawling over him, his penis stiffening.

He opened the door.

"Hetta."

The room was again lit by candles. His mother's scarf, which he had forgotten the last time, was laid neatly on the slab. He took in a deep breath, took in Hetta's scent, grit his teeth as desire burned through him. She was near, perhaps waiting behind another door, merely testing to see what he would do once inside – to see if he would welcome this invitation into her heart. He needed no more encouragement. He removed his clothes, picked up the scarf and looped it around his neck, and climbed onto the slab. He closed his eyes, content to wait. Hetta would come soon. He was almost certain of it.

19 LIGHT HEADED

*B*aldwin woke with a start. The candles had burned out and the room was black. He hurried off the slab and groped with his hands on the floor until he found his clothes. He slipped them on in quick motion and stepped outside. The moon was high and bright. He called out Hetta's name and opened all the doors inside the wash, but found no one.

He moved toward the pipe, buttoning his shirt as he walked, puzzling on Hetta's whereabouts. At the top button he stopped, realized something was missing – his scarf. He was certain he had put it on before lying down, but it was now gone. There was the possibility he had removed it while asleep, his hands obeying nocturnal commands, but there was also the possibility that someone else's hands had done the deed, and not Hetta's, as she surely would have woke him or at least stayed with him until he roused. He gave the mystery a few more seconds of thought, didn't like his conclusions, and dove into the pipe, moving forward as fast as he could in the confined space.

Despite skimming the walls several times, he made it through relatively unscathed, save for some webbing, which clung to his nose and both ears. He cleared away the strands, straightened and stretched, and took in a long breath. A firefly lit up next to him, and then another, and another, but they were not acting at all like the instinct, their brightness not ending when they hit the ground. He realized it was embers, red-hot ash, a descending halo of sparks aimed right for his head. He backpedaled to avoid getting burned, swatting at the embers as if they were marauding gnats. Another shower of sparks pushed him further back, to the edge of the ravine, where he had almost tumbled the evening before. This time there was no one to stop his fall. With a final backward step he plummeted, somersaulting a few times before evening out and sliding on his backside to the bottom. He finally came to a stop when he hit the pit's cement wall.

Baldwin lay a moment, stunned, but not hurt. He saw now where the sparks had come from: the pit was ablaze. He stood and raised himself on his toes to see inside. A ferocious wave of heat enveloped his face. The smell of burning meat was overwhelming.

"Turn around."

Baldwin obeyed. It was Nathan, the counting counselor from the warm wash. His gray eyes refracted the jumping flames. His sunken face was smeared with ash. He was holding an empty edibles bag and a pitchfork. The latter he pointed at Baldwin's stomach.

"You a nutrition counselor?"

"No."

"Then what are you doing here?"

"I fell."

Nathan waited for a stream of black smoke to pass. When it did, his eyes flickered with recognition. He lowered the pitchfork.

"I remember you. You gave me a chit yesterday. What's your name again?"

"Baldwin."

"That's right. So I see you want some meat after all. I don't blame you, seeing as I'm here for the same."

"That's not it. I really did fall. I was looking at the fire from up the hill and lost my footing."

The old man looked up the incline.

"What were you doing up there? The warm wash isn't open."

Baldwin thought it best not to mention Hetta and their date.

"That's what I found out. I guess I got my days of utility mixed up."

The white of Nathan's eyes gleamed because of the black soot surrounding them. He looked to Baldwin like a rabid raccoon – feral and fragile.

Nathan spat and wiped his mouth, smearing the ash on his lips.

"Well, you're here now," he said. "Might as well take advantage of the opportunity and grab some meat. There's plenty inside the pit for both of us."

"I'll pass."

Nathan spat again.

"The truth is I could use your help. There's a ladder on the other side of the wall, with a board attached to it that juts out over the pit. It's high enough that I won't get burned if I crawl out, but I need to lean over pretty far to get my fork into a deer. I already tried a few times and nearly fell in. If you hold me steady, I can get the leverage I need to rip out some good pieces. I'll give you half of what I pull up if you help."

Baldwin eyed the flames, the black smoke crawling over the wall.

"I'm sorry, but I think I'll just head back."

"Maybe I can tempt you with something else," Nathan said, the corners of his mouth curling slyly. "Seems you like the warm wash, so how about I turn my chit bowl away the next few times you come. I can even arrange for one of the touch counselors to visit your living unit. Nothing beats a rub at home."

"You can do that – arrange home visits?"

"Sure. I usually get a chit from the counselor and a chit from the client. But I'll waive my fee if you help me out. You can even tell me what kind of counselor you prefer and I'll make it happen – blonde, brunette...bald."

Baldwin paused.

"How about Hetta?"

Nathan shook his head, causing flakes of ash to fall from his cheeks and chin.

"So you like her I see. Don't blame you a bit. She's a looker and nice too. But I'm afraid I can't help. She's the one touch counselor we have that's untouchable."

"What do you mean?"

"I mean, she's not mine to sell. She's run by someone much more connected than me, someone who sets her up with mentors. At least that's what I hear."

Baldwin felt a mix of jealousy and fear.

"Who is this person, the one who sets her up?"

Nathan studied him a moment.

"Boy you got it bad for Hetta, don't you?"

"I'm just curious," Baldwin said, trying to feign indifference.

"Curiosity comes at a cost."

"Remember, I already gave you a chit."

"And I already spent it."

"What do you want then?"

"Meat."

They went around the pit and found the ladder. Baldwin was surprised by Nathan's agility as he climbed up the metal steps and then crawled out along the board, which bent and bounced with his movements.

"Now grab me tight and hang on," Nathan said when he reached the end.

Baldwin did as he was told, gripping the old man's ankles and lowering his head to shield his eyes from the falling ash. He did not want to look down, did not want to see what was happening to the deer.

"Almost got one," he heard Nathan grunt out. "It's a big piece. Just a little more…"

His scream was high-pitched and girlish. Baldwin looked up. At the end of Nathan's pitchfork sat Simon's head. The skin of his neighbor's face was smoldering and swollen, his forehead encircled by the blue velvet thong. Apparently, unlike the red variety, this one was fire resistant. Baldwin thought as much before throwing up.

20 BACK WATER

*T*heir relationship started in a conversation club called The Silo, a narrow, circular structure with cinder block walls and a white conical dome. Baldwin was newly on his own, just beginning to enjoy the possibilities of life without the smothering tether of family, when he noticed Nadine enter the club, her blond bob perched atop her thin head like a wary sentry. He lost sight of her in the crowd, and it was not until much later, as he was angling toward the door to leave, that she appeared at his side, almost as if she had risen up from the floor. She looked at him, took a hit from the vial of impure water in her hand, and without a blink said he reminded her of a "tree with no leaves." Baldwin might have been offended by the comparison, except she rose up on her toes after saying it and kissed him. They spent the next hour talking, and then he walked her home. This time he made a move to kiss her, but she pulled away.

They began dating, spending most evenings sitting on cement slabs hidden by trees or brush, talking, kissing and groping each other to the point of frustration. One night, Nadine halted a particularly impassioned pelvic thrust of his to explain the difficulties of her childhood. "That's why we can't get closer than this," she said, when finished, her brown eyes exhausted from the torrent of tears that accompanied her story. "I don't think I can love anyone in a normal way." It was a final blow to his short-lived freedom. Her words had roused in him a monumental compassion, an emotion far more powerful than lust, and removing his hand from inside her pants, he vowed he would never leave her.

Yet even as their relationship followed a traditional arc toward marriage, Nadine continually warned Baldwin that entering into a romantic union with her was a great risk. But whenever she tried to convince him of her inability to connect in a healthy way, he would work just as hard to convince her that she could. And so he pushed and pushed and pushed, shrugged away her denials of stability, turned his head from her promises of future rage, and coaxed and cajoled and complimented her until, at last, she conceded that she might make him a suitable wife, perhaps even a good one.

It had all started at The Silo, and now, with their union seemingly irreparable, the main problem being (if you believed Leonard) that she wanted him dead, he was staring at it again.

"I'm going in."

He and Nathan had made a concerted scramble off the board, down the ladder, and away from the pit after spearing Simon's head, the two of them running through a sparse wooded area in the opposite direction of the warm wash. Baldwin was surprised by the old man's speed and stamina during the long scamper, but when they finally slowed he collapsed, falling to the ground face first, as flat and still as a trampled leaf. Baldwin feared Nathan had lost his breathing, but when he rolled the old man over his eyes were alert and his nostrils flaring.

"I didn't like that face a bit," he said, raising fast to his elbows and shaking his head. "It was like he was grinning right at me."

"It was my neighbor, Simon," Baldwin said. "The one you met yesterday."

Nathan struggled to his feet.

"Are you sure?"

"Pretty sure. I recognize his thong."

"That was peculiar."

"I guess we should get a conflict counselor."

Nathan recoiled as if punched.

"You do what you want," he said, "but leave me out of it. Forget for a moment that we were taking meat we were not encouraged to take, which is bad enough to get us sent to a gratitude farm, but telling a conflict counselor we pulled a man's burning head out of a fire with a pitchfork adds a whole other layer of bad to the thing. For sure they'll dig into your friend's life, try to find out what happened to him, how he ended up in the pit. Who knows – maybe it's innocent and he fell in doing what we were trying to do? But maybe someone *encouraged* him to take a dive? If that's the case, that same someone might not appreciate us pulling something out of the ashes that was supposed to be ashes."

"So what are you saying?"

"I'm saying we don't say anything. I say we let the fire complete its utility. I imagine by now he's burned to a crisp. Just one more piece of charred meat."

Baldwin shuddered at the image of Simon's face, the melting skin, the twisted thong atop his smoking head. He eyed The Silo. It offered a quick solution to his disturbing thoughts.

"I'm going in," he said again, to Nathan. "To have some impure. Do you want to come with me?"

"For sure."

Nathan fell directly behind Baldwin as they approached the entrance. A man of massive proportions leaned against the outside wall. His shoulders spread out behind him like two mature pumpkins. His chiseled cheeks stretched and contracted as he chewed on a wedge of sapling. His wide head, defined by a mop of sandy colored hair, slanted toward his broad chest

"I'm grateful to meet you both," he slipped out in a low tone without looking up.

"Likewise."

"One chit each," the big man said flatly, still not looking up. "That includes all the conversation you want and two vials of impure."

Nathan nudged Baldwin.

"Can you spot me? I didn't plan on going out, you know."

Baldwin reached into his pocket. He had taken four red chits out from Nadine's reserve pouch before leaving for the conception counselor's office with Hetta. He pulled out two and handed them over.

"For both of us."

The big man straightened up. He also opened his eyes. They were blue, but not a pretty shade. More like a bruise. He shook the chits like dice as he spoke.

"Just remember, no talking when someone else in your party is talking. One-at-a-time at all times. Got it?"

"We understand," Baldwin said.

"Make sure you do. Also, the encouraged topic tonight is false empathy."

"False empathy? What does that mean?"

"Beats me," the big man said, returning to his slouching position. "I don't pick the topics, and I don't listen to them either."

The club was well lit, the walls lined with thick candles, in black metal holders hammered into the cement. The room was crowded. Each of the stools lining the perimeter was occupied, and the four round tables in the center were also full. Nathan tugged at Baldwin's sleeve. He pointed across the room, where a pale-skinned young man stood holding a ladle over a large metal pot.

"There's the impure," he said. "I'll get the first round."

He was gone only a moment. When he returned his lips trembled with excitement.

"Look how filthy this is," he said, passing a vial to Baldwin and holding up his own. "I haven't seen stagnation like this in a while. The pourer says it's not part of the Circle's stock. He says it comes from a sump hole they dug out themselves."

Baldwin raised the drink and sniffed it. It smelled as if someone had mixed lemon and sulfur inside a dirty slipper. The color was curious as well – a silty mix of blue, gray and green that barely moved when he gave the vial a swirl.

"Of course, the kid could be lying to justify the chit," Nathan continued, bringing the vial to lips. "Plenty of pure water gets passed off as dirty nowadays."

He downed the shot without swallowing. When he looked at Baldwin, his eyes were shining.

"Your turn."

Baldwin hesitated. He had not finished an entire vial of impure in one sitting in years, mostly because Nadine did not like the confidence it gave him, which she felt leaned more toward bravado, something she found disruptive to her digestion.

"It doesn't taste too bad if you shoot it right down," Nathan cajoled.

"Okay."

Baldwin brought the vial back to his lips and sucked it in with a gulp. It took him three swallows to get the viscous liquid down, and then all his will not to spit it back out. But the urge to vomit was overwhelmed by a sudden burn in the pit of his stomach. He closed his eyes and waited for the pain to subside.

"Good, huh?"

Baldwin opened his eyes. The room seemed brighter. He couldn't feel his toes.

"My stomach is on fire."

"It will pass," Nathan said. "Give it time to get into your veins."

Baldwin exhaled. The pain began to subside. Feeling came back to his extremities. A piercing pang of happiness gripped him. His eyes welled with tears. He had the urge to wet his pants.

"Feeling better?" Nathan asked.

"Much."

"Me too." Nathan rubbed his hands together as if cold. "Being around young people does me good. I'm not in a union and I don't live with anybody. I don't even have a life counselor since he stopped breathing. I guess the Circle thinks I'll mimic the behavior soon, so they're not assigning me another. But let me tell you, the closer you come to the end of your life the more you want to talk about it. I actually envy old people who can't think for themselves, who can barely remember their names. That's the best way to go out, unaware, not knowing who you are or what you're doing. But if your mind is clear like mine, you live each day painfully aware that each breath you take in means one less you'll push out."

He licked the inside of his vial.

"Impure helps of course," he continued. "Tricks you into thinking you're never going to die, while at the same time hurrying along the process."

Baldwin's happiness began to deflate. He had a hard time connecting the feeling to words, but finally came upon an idea.

"Life isn't all about death," he said. "In fact, my fake wife and I were approved to conceive yesterday."

"Fake?"

"Did I say that? I misspoke. I have that problem with 'f' words."

"Who doesn't?"

Nathan clapped him happily on the shoulder.

"Well, congratulations. Do you want a boy or a girl?"

"I'm not sure. Probably a girl."

"How come?"

"They seem nicer."

Nathan licked the vial some more.

"I'm not exactly sure if it works," he said, "but when I was an insemination counselor, they encouraged us to penetrate from behind if the woman wanted a girl, and from the bottom for a boy. I don't think it matters from the top."

"You were an insemination counselor?"

"My first utility. Can you imagine – paid to penetrate. I loved that job. And I was good at it. My style was to come late to the appointment, so that the woman thought the whole thing was off. I'd sneak into the unit and curl up with them while they were sleeping, like I was a husband coming home after a long night. I'd kiss them in the ear, snuggle, rub their backs, and then when they woke up I'd get down to business."

"Problem is that it's a young man's job," he continued. "Not so much the physical aspect, but the mental one. You get older and you start wanting more from the women you're penetrating. You want to know more about them, want them to know more about you than just your penis. At least that's what happened to me. I couldn't stop visiting the women I inseminated, showing up at their units to share their edible bags, some impure, and to talk. A few complained and here I am holding a chit bucket."

Baldwin belched. The impure was chipping away at his natural inhibitions. He no longer understood the concept of shame or caution. If anything, it felt injurious to his mind and spirit to hold anything back.

"Maybe you're my father."

"What?"

"My mother used an insemination counselor to have me. She never saw his face. She said he came in the darkness and left a flower on her pillow to find in the morning."

"Then it's not me," Nathan said. "I never left anything behind except what was inside of me first."

"You sound relieved I'm not your son," Baldwin said, feeling somewhat disappointed.

"No offense, because you seem a good sort, but I am." Nathan stared at the empty vial. "Even though it was my utility, I feel guilty sometimes, like I did something wrong by giving a child life and then not being in it. I imagine they hate me even though they don't know me, or *because* they don't know me...I mean, how do you feel?"

"About what?"

"About the man who inseminated your mother? Do you hate him?"

"I don't hate anyone."

"But do you ever think about him?"

"Maybe when I was young, before my mother got married. Then I figured it didn't matter anymore. Even if I found out who my real father was, Leonard would never allow me to pursue a relationship – he'd probably even kill him."

"Leonard?"

"My stepfather. Leonard Living."

Nathan blinked with surprise.

"Leonard Living is your stepfather?"

Baldwin nodded.

"Well, I'm certainly in good company tonight." He grabbed Baldwin's empty vial. "I'll get us refills."

As Baldwin waited for Nathan to return, he realized, almost with a start, that he had forgotten about Simon. The incident in the pit now seemed to have happened long ago, a distant memory stored neatly in his mind, not as an open question, but a closed thought, a number rounded to its final degree. He tried to draw up concern that Simon's demise was related to what happened between them at the timehole, but the impure would not allow his brain to make such complex connections. It was as if his thoughts were pebbles sliding down a hill, but as Nathan approached, one pebble, one thought, came to a stop.

"You never told me his name," he said, taking the vial from Nathan. "The person who arranges appointments for Hetta."

"Do I really have to?"

"We made a deal."

"But we didn't really get any meat."

"That's not my fault."

Nathan frowned.

"You have to promise never to tell anyone I told you – especially him."

"I promise."

"Even if he threatens you?"

"Even if he threatens me."

Nathan took a small sip from the vial, licked at his lips, and then finished the rest off in a gulp. The veins in his thin neck bulged out as he talked.

"His name is Franklin Ramson. He's a conflict counselor. He's the one you to go to if you want Hetta. From what I hear, she'll do anything he wants her to do to anyone he wants her to do. So it's good to get on his good side."

Baldwin finished his drink fast. This time, his stomach did not burn. In fact, he felt nothing, no sensation whatsoever, from the neck down. And then he was floating, rising above the crowd until he reached the top of the conical tower. There he hovered happily, peacefully, contentedly, traveling back many years in an instant, seeing the door of the club opening and a youthful Nadine walking in, her eyes darting with mischief, her blond bob pointing at him, beckoning him to come down and join her.

21 DUMB WAITER

*N*athan yanked at Baldwin's sleeve.

"Let's sit down."

Baldwin shook his head. He was no longer floating. His two feet were back on the ground. He blinked and looked around the room. Nadine had disappeared, but he did see two empty chairs at a table within ten paces of where they stood.

"Hurry," Nathan said. "Before someone takes them."

Baldwin followed the old man. An attractive woman of about thirty stood to greet them. She was heavy at the waist and petite around the shoulders. She had a wonderfully long neck with defined wrinkle lines at the base. Her hair was dark brown and long. She was wearing a red tube top and no bra. She had large breasts that jiggled when she talked.

"We're grateful you decided to join our conversation," she said, her voice husky. "I'm Christine." She pointed a long finger across the table. "This is Ee-Ee."

"Ernest," the man returned flatly.

Christine ignored the correction and nodded at the chairs.

"Please sit."

Baldwin took the chair next to Christine. Nathan sat to his right. Ernest, or Ee-Ee, paid them no attention.

"So what brings you two here tonight?" Christine asked pleasantly.

"Trauma," Nathan blurted out. "I saw something I want to forget."

"That sounds interesting. Care to share?"

"Not really. Like I said, I'm trying to forget."

"I see."

Baldwin took in a long breath. The impure was playing tricks on him, weaving him in and out of lucidity.

"And what about you?" Christine asked him.

"Excuse me?"

"Are you trying to forget something as well?"

Baldwin had forgotten completely about Simon.

"No. I'm celebrating."

"That's fun. Care to share?"

"About what?"

Christine smiled sweetly.

"What are you here to celebrate, dear?"

"Oh," Baldwin said. "I'm happy I can conceive. I'm encouraged to have a baby."

Ernest finally looked up. He had large brown eyes spread too far apart, making his plump nose look like a lonely potato. The rest of his face was flat and lifeless.

"Congratulations," he said. "You'll make a great mother."

Christine widened her nostrils and exhaled.

"Don't mind him," she said. "He thinks he's funny."

She smiled again.

"I forgot to ask your names."

"I'm Baldwin, this is Nathan."

"Well, nice to meet you Baldwin and Nathan," she continued. "I'll catch you up on what we're discussing. I was telling *Ernest* that it's easier to detect false empathy in men, simply because women are incapable of false empathy and men are incapable of real empathy."

Ernest grunted with a mix of amusement and derision.

"And I was telling Christine that not only do I understand where she is coming from, I encourage her to go back there as soon as she can."

"Which led me to question if a bad joke is another form of false empathy?"

"And my answer was yes, but only if the person who tells the bad joke is incredibly good looking…or has a big penis."

Nathan shot out a laugh that turned into a coughing fit. When he was done his face was bright red. He cleared his throat and looked desperately at Baldwin.

"My throat's dry. Can you spot me another vial?"

"You already had two."

"Three is my lucky number."

"I only have two chits left."

"Please."

Baldwin reluctantly reached into his pocket and handed him another chit.

"Thanks."

"Wait a moment."

Ernest flipped a red chit across the table.

"Bring back a vial for me and this deluded young lady as well."

Nathan scooped up Ernest's chit and hurried across the room.

"So where were we?" Ernest said, his eyes hinting at mischief. He turned them on Christine. "I remember, you were saying I have a big penis."

"You mean, you were saying."

"Well, someone was."

Christine raised her chin, flared her nostrils again, waited a moment, and let out a dramatic exhale.

"The only reason I tolerate Ernest is because he's so stupid," she said playfully to Baldwin. "It's good for my self-esteem to be around someone I can always beat in an argument."

Ernest winked at Baldwin.

"Remember that. If you want a woman to like you, let her think she's smarter than you. But if you want to hate her, let her prove it."

"Aren't you clever," Christine said returning her attention to Ernest. "Thank you."

"You're welcome."

Baldwin was dizzied by their back and forth. He grabbed the seat of his chair to steady himself.

"I'm back."

Nathan placed two vials on the table and sat down.

"Where's the other two?" Baldwin asked.

"I drank them."

"Both?"

"I think so."

Baldwin stood and handed Christine a vial, and then gave Ernest his. When he sat down again he was surprised to see Nathan's head on the table, or at least the point of his chin. The old man had closed his eyes and was snoring lightly through his nose.

Ernest took a hit from his vial, nodded at Nathan.

"Now that's false empathy."

Christine clicked her tongue.

"I don't know how you can be so mean."

"Practice."

Christine shook her head. She turned to Baldwin, patted his arm.

"Tell me, what do you do? I mean, what's your utility?"

"I'm a miracle counselor."

Christine clapped her hands.

"That's fun. Tell me some of the miracles you heard. What was the most recent?"

Baldwin thought of Hetta's miracle, the woman in her dream, the orgasm. He glanced at Ernest and then looked down at the table.

"I'm not encouraged to talk about other people's miracles."

"I won't tell anyone."

"I can't."

"Just one."

"He *said* no. Let it go."

Christine's cheeks reddened. She blinked angrily at Ernest.

"You're the one who can't let go."

They were silent a moment. Ernest exhaled wearily and motioned at Baldwin with his chin.

"Are you in a romantic union?"

"Yes."

"How long?"

"Five years."

"I got you by one." Ernest took another sip from his vial. "You love your wife?"

"I did."

"You don't anymore?"

"I don't think so."

"Why not?"

"Mostly because she wants to kill me on the Day of No Consequence."

"Really?"

"So I've been told."

Ernest pushed out his lower lip and nodded reflectively.

"Well, at least you're on her mind," he said. "I wish my wife cared enough about me to want me dead."

"Maybe she does."

It was Christine. The color had drained from her cheeks. She lifted her vial and took a slow drag.

"Okay," Ernest said. "I'm sorry I yelled."

"I'm not. It makes me see you more clearly."

"And how do I look?"

"Ugly."

Baldwin had to agree. Ernest was not a handsome man. Collectively his features made no sense, but individually they were worse.

"Excuse me."

Baldwin looked up. A man was standing over the table. He was of medium height but very thin, neatly dressed in gray slacks and a matching gray-silk vest. He was not wearing a shirt under the vest, and his skinny arms moved as if attached to something other than his shoulders. He was also very bald, with a pink protruding mole on the outside of his right nostril.

"This doesn't sound like anything related to false empathy," the man said, fingering the mole. "And this gentlemen" – he pointed at Nathan– "is clearly not contributing to the conversation."

"He's listening," Ernest said, the corners of his lips curling into a smile. "That's just as important to a conversation as talking you know."

"Are you trying to be funny?"

"Yes."

"Well, you failed."

"Then I retract my answer. I wasn't trying to be funny."

The man held his gaze on Ernest. He gave the mole a final tap and smiled.

"I have a unique idea – why don't you leave on your own now, before I have to encourage you to leave later."

Ernest's face flushed. His lips tightened.

"You sometimes forget how many chits I spend here."

"Your wife's, you mean."

"You take them all the same."

The man sniffed out a mocking laugh.

"I don't have time to play," he said, smoothing down the front of his vest. "This is a last warning. I want to hear false empathy at this table the next time I pass by. And if the older gentleman is not contributing to the topic, you're all out."

After the man moved to the next table, Ernest turned his head and spat on the floor. He wiped his lips with the back of his wrist and looked at Christine.

"Now you believe me about that guy?"

"Well, we really weren't talking about the theme. He's just doing his utility."

Ernest spat again. He looked at Baldwin.

"You saw it, right? The way he treated me."

"It wasn't nice."

"Exactly. He's not nice. Worse, he's not likable. Don't you agree?"

Baldwin nodded.

"I didn't like him."

"Thank you."

Ernest raised his vial, nodded at Baldwin.

"To like minds," he said.

He drank off the remains. Set the vial down carefully. Smiled at Christine.

"Do you still hate me?"

"Doesn't everyone?"

"Not Baldwin. He doesn't hate me. Isn't that right?"

"I don't hate anyone."

Christine grunted.

"You haven't been around Ernest long enough."

Baldwin shook his head.

"It doesn't matter. Even if I wanted to hate him, I can't. I don't know how."

"That's not a bad thing," Ernest injected. "I waste too much time hating."

"You just realize that now?" Christine sighed. "I can't count the number of hours you complained to me about people at work."

"You guys share the same utility?"

Christine nodded.

"We're division counselors."

"Christine excavates, I build."

"Meaning I clear out weeds and brush, while he piles up rocks and stones."

"You make it sound like a child playing with blocks," Ernest said defensively. "Building fences is an art, but better because the end product is useful."

"Then I guess I'm an artist too."

"You are. There's a deadly beauty in the way you swing your sickle." Ernest winked at Baldwin. "You should hear her go through a swath of high grass—whoosh, whoosh, whoosh, it's amazing."

"Keep going," Christine smiled. "I'm starting to hate you less."

"That's because I'm likable."

"Maybe you are."

Baldwin wished they would talk more about their utility. Although he felt himself oddly suited for miracle work, he sometimes longed for a job that offered such a simple objective as clearing weeds, something that tasked the body more than the mind.

"May I ask where you are working now," he asked.

"Me, nowhere," Ernest said, turning the vial over and tapping at its bottom. "I've been on a five-season leave to rest my back. Unfortunately, my back still hurts and I have to go back to work after the Day of No Consequence. At least my wife will be happy I'm out of the unit."

Baldwin hesitated.

"Your wife doesn't have a utility?"

"She does. But she's home a lot."

"What does she do?"

Ernest laughed.

"Other than being mad at me, she's a touch counselor. That's actually how we met: my back hurt and I went to her for relief. But now, when I need her help even more, she won't touch me."

Christine leaned forward, blinked hard at Ernest.

"I'm sure she thinks you take her for granted, that all she's good for is a rub. She probably thinks she means nothing to you."

Ernest widened his eyes with incredulity.

"See how women stick together," he said to Baldwin. "It's just like it says in *The Book of Ash* – he snapped his fingers – "feces prejudice."

"Species prejudice," Baldwin corrected.

"Yeah, that's it. How does that encouragement go?"

"Species are prejudiced, women and men. It's why we fight to be together, only to separate again, again and again."

"See." Ernest smiled broadly. "Men and women are as different as pure and impure water."

"I agree," Christine said, "men are *impure*."

"Impure."

It was Nathan. He had woke and now looked wildly around the table.

"Impure, impure, impure."

In an instant, the man with the mole was back.

"That's it," he said, pushing past Nathan and pointing at Ernest. "You're out."

"What did I do?"

"I warned you."

"But he's the one yelling."

"No matter, I've been listening to your useless talk about your utility and your bad back and your wife not touching you. Not one thing pertaining to tonight's theme."

Ernest stood, pushed his chair back.

"Don't blame me because she won't touch you anymore either."

The man's face grew white.

"I don't know what you're talking about."

"Yes you do. Ramson told me what happened the last time she went to your unit, what you tried to do to her. I would have handled it myself, but I know he's much better at these things."

"It's not true."

Ernest smiled meanly. He moved around the table, came up to the man and faced him.

"At least I accept that she hates me," he said. "Why can't you?"

The man threw a punch with his right hand. But he started it too far back and it was too slow not to be sidestepped by Ernest. But he did it with style, moving to his left and countering with a smooth right cross that cracked open the side of the man's nose with the mole. Blood shot forward onto the table, causing Christine to scream and jump into Baldwin's lap. Nathan was still yelling for impure, and Ernest was sizing up the man for a finishing blow, when he was suddenly lifted high into the air. It was the big man from the door.

Christine was still in Baldwin's lap. There was a splattering of blood on her cleavage. She wiped at it and looked at him.

"I'm encouraged to make a run for it," she said.

"Me too."

And so they did.

ENCOURAGEMENT 29 - EXPLORE YOUR LIMITS

The most difficult question confronted by man, and one that can never be answered correctly, is why are we here? What is our purpose? We cannot possible know the answer. To know would mean we do not exist. It is the uncertainty of our creation that binds us to this star. It is a blindfold saving us from a reality so frightening we would wash away and leave nothing but dust in our wake. Still, many search for an answer, and when they cannot find one, the seeds of resentment and fear and paranoia take root. It is this fermentation of bewilderment and anger that diminishes our humanity, makes us create imagined spiritual institutions, fuels our murderous and genocidal rages, and encourages us to take premature refuge in the one aspect of life that is certain: death.

Reaction Step: The next time you are tempted to explore the 'meaning of life,' explore your body instead. Find an isolated spot and strip away your clothes so you are naked. Then, systematically, and methodically, take close stock of each and every inch of your skin. Check for moles, discolorations, black heads and pimples, scars and stretch marks. Once done, switch attention to your moving parts. Wiggle each toe, bend each finger, flare your nostrils, kick out your feet, and flap your arms. Move everything on your body that will move in any direction it will move. Finally, when you have done all of the above, hold your breath until you subconscious self takes over and forces you to take in air. Then, and only then, consider what life really means.

22 PUSSY FOOT

*B*aldwin woke with the clang of the sunrise gong. He swallowed hard and turned to see if Nadine was beside him. She was not, but in her defense, he was not in their bed. He peered down the sheet. His two feet were sticking out the end. One was bare, the other jammed into a lady's purple pump.

He scanned the room with alarm. The bright green walls looked familiar. The window to his right, too, had a long crack across its middle he recognized. The picture on the nightstand cinched it: a sand drawing of a frowning face with no eyebrows.

"Manu," he called out.

"In the kitchen."

Baldwin fell back onto the mattress. Manu's unit was situated similar to the one he shared with Nadine. In fact, it was the same one he had lived in with Manu years before. Manu had never left, and had never been assigned another roommate.

"Baldwin. Do you want some pure water?"

"Please."

Baldwin reviewed with trepidation the rest of his body. He was still wearing his jeans, but no longer his shirt. He blinked his eyes fast to jumpstart his memory and review what had happened to bring him to Manu's bed. After fleeing The Silo, he and Christine had gone to her building, to the basement, where a running in place contest was being held. It was crowded and hot in the windowless room, and Christine had left him for a moment with her roommate, a taught-bodied woman with a narrow face and stark white hair, while she went looking for impure. She came back with three vials and they downed them and then…Baldwin could remember only images, flashes of action, fast motion and slow motion, whirls of color, faces, feet stomping, bodies colliding, fists connecting. Yes, there had been a fight. The scene played out for him in a burst of clarity: he saw himself stumbling through the crowd, pushing through to the back of the basement, where the two running in place contestants were in heated motion, he losing balance and falling into one of them, the two of them crashing into the wall, wrestling on the floor, others joining in, kicking at him, punching… and then he was free, dragged away by his shoulders, the melee continuing without him, oblivious of his absence, feeding off the energy of the contest, the fuse lit by his clumsiness. And then he was moving again, out the basement and up the stairs, into a unit, it was dark, a candle lit, a bed emerged, and on it Christine's roommate, her narrow face framed by the flickering flame, her taught body softer looking without clothes, her legs spread open in invitation.

Baldwin gasped with panic. He could recall nothing more past that moment. He lifted the sheet, examined his flaccid penis, traced the head with his fingers, gripped and rubbed the shaft. It was not sore, not red, but looked exhausted. He just didn't know.

"Please, Baldwin, not in my bed."

Manu walked into the room. In his right hand was a clear glass of water. He was frowning, but congenially so.

Baldwin let go of his penis. He pulled the sheet up.

"I wasn't doing that. I was just checking."

"To see if it still worked?"

"Something like that."

Manu sat down on the bed and passed Baldwin the glass.

"Thanks."

He finished the water and handed it back.

"Can I have another?"

"Of course, but first you have to tell me where you got that horrible shoe? I know it's not Nadine's. She never wears heels, although with her sleek legs she should."

Baldwin stared at the shoe.

"I'm not sure. Some woman from last night, I think."

"I would have bet you took it off a man. I've seen a few sad gentlemen wearing the same style. I'm sure they found a crate of these atrocities in a timehole. If only someone with a modicum of taste had thought to burn them as fuel."

Baldwin recognized the beginning stages of an impure hangover. It always started with a longing sadness, a feeling of complete emptiness, before turning physical: stabbing pain in his extremities, his fingers and toes, the tips of his ears, followed by a discharge from the eyes, salty, heated tears that reddened the skin. But gratefully, the entire episode, both the melancholy and the body eruptions, was brief.

"Water," he said to Manu, a surge of hopelessness griping his body.

"Okay. But we're going to talk more."

Manu left and Baldwin closed his eyes. He covered his ears with his hands and held his breath, a trick he learned many years ago as a way of short-circuiting an impure-induced emotional drop. It didn't work. He was miserable when Manu returned.

"So what's going on with you that you're acting so crazy?" Manu asked, handing over the refilled glass. "You know I won't judge, although I might criticize."

"I drank too much impure."

"I inferred that. Actually, I smell it. You reek of stagnation."

Baldwin finished the water. This time he held the glass in his hands, looked inside as he spoke.

"I went to The Silo."

Manu shook his head. He was wearing tight red shorts and yellow slippers. It looked as if he had newly shaved off his eyebrows.

"Why would you ever go back to that place?"

Baldwin shrugged. He felt a subtle lifting of his spirits. He braced himself for the next phase of the hangover.

"Can I have a hand towel? You know what happens to my eyes after I drink impure. I don't want to ruin your sheets."

"Trust me, they're already ruined. No offense, but as soon as you get up they go out the door and into the community fire."

"That's wasteful."

"Blame my life counselor. He's never been able to make me slovenly. Life would be much happier if I was."

Baldwin felt the first prick of pain in his toes. He wiggled them under the sheet and gritted his teeth.

"It's a shame I wasn't here when you came in," Manu said, sitting back down on the bed. "I could have gleaned everything out of you then and at least washed you up and rid you of that shoe."

"I'm sorry."

"It's okay. But don't think you're the only one who had a difficult evening. Ramson and I broke up."

Baldwin's toes felt on fire. He set his jaw tighter and exhaled though his nose against the pain.

"I went over to surprise him last night," Manu continued. "And I found him with a woman. Of course I went crazy. I started yelling at her and then Franklin hit me and I guess it triggered a seizure. When I came out of it he was gone."

"Are you okay?"

"Physically, yes."

"Is the woman his girlfriend?"

"I guess not. At least she convinced me after she wasn't. She was actually very nice and concerned about me. She even offered to touch me to help me calm down."

"Touch you?"

Manu nodded.

"She's a touch counselor. That's why she was there with Ramson. At least that's what she said. She told me she was only there because of her utility."

"Did you let her?"

"Touch me? No. My clothes were messy and I wanted to go home."

Manu stood, left the room, came back with a towel that matched his shorts. He traded it for the empty glass.

"I'm very sad about Ramson," he said, sitting down. "Heartbreak is not good. It's like I'm trapped in misery. It's worse than a fit – at least then I don't know what's happening or feel anything."

Baldwin's eyes began to tear. He held the towel to his face, breathing in its scent. It reminded him of when he lived in the unit and Manu would launder their towels, soaking them in water and lye and then hanging them out the window overnight. Manu's theory was that the moon generated a "gentler" dry than the sun.

"Do you think I should go see Ramson this morning and apologize?" he asked.

Baldwin lifted the towel from his face. It was damp.

"Why? You said he hit you."

"Not very hard. More like a slap."

"I don't think you should apologize or see him again."

"But I love him so much," Manu said. "I want him even more."

"Well, sometimes we have to let go of things we want to get them."

"That sounds wise. Where did you hear it?"

"It's what Leonard used tell me whenever he took something away from me."

"Like what?"

"My mother, to start."

Manu sighed.

"Ramson actually reminds me of Leonard. They each have an anger of innocence about them, like their rage comes from this pure place – it's not contrived at all."

"You think that's a good trait?"

"No, but it turns me on."

They were silent a moment. Manu broke the spell with a hard slap to the bed.

"Enough wallowing on men, let's focus on women – meaning, why are you wearing that hideous shoe and why are you not right now with Nadine?"

Baldwin blinked. Images again flashed through his mind: he and the woman on the bed, Christine barging into the room, shouting, clawing, he scrambling to put on anything he could find, stumbling out of the building, out into the night.

"I'd rather not talk about it."

"You have to. You owe it to me for sleeping here last night, unless you want to give me a chit."

"I've not one left. I spent them all at the club."

"Then you better start talking."

23 HIDE AWAY

Manu believed miracles were connected to sadness. He called it the "triumph of tears." He believed miracles were always happening, perhaps even with each breath, but were only experienced consciously by people in pain, be it emotional or physical. "Who wants to see beyond oneself when you're happy," was his standard defense of the position. "But if you're down, if you can't imagine why you should take another breath, then you are ripe for miracles, simply because you need them to keep going."

Baldwin did not disagree with Manu's thinking, but he didn't really give it much thought either. Manu was often espousing new philosophies, new revelations on how to live, sudden insights into the behavior of others, what made people do what people do. Baldwin listened with an amused ear, but not an interested one. But now he saw wisdom in the theory: he longed for a miracle, something profound and life-changing, a sign from something greater than himself that his life held meaning, that his downward spiral over the past few days was not a spiral downward, but instead a curve with an upward slope.

"By the way, you were singing last night."

Baldwin drained another glass dry. He and Manu were sitting at his kitchen table, facing each other.

"I was?"

"Uh huh. I think it was *The Rhyming Reason*."

"How did I sound?"

"Terrible."

Baldwin nodded. *The Rhyming Reason* was his mother's favorite song. She liked to sing it during rust storms, keeping time with the patter of flying metal particles clattering against the windows. Her singing always calmed him, slackened his muscles, sometimes forcing him to fight back drool as he listened to her words:

"If you forget the words, if you forget the lines, if you forget the meaning, it's time to rhyme. If you have no love to recall, if you have no love to assign, if you have no love at all, it's time to rhyme. If death is near, if death is close, if death is your future, it's time to rhyme. But if life is good, if life is fine, then please take heed, and never, not now or ever, open your mouth and rhyme."

"Of course," Manu continued, "I can't get the stupid song out of my head now."

"I'm sorry."

"You should be. Why couldn't you have sung *Me and My Drama*? At least that has a real beat."

"I mean I'm sorry I came here last night and bothered you. I know I drank a lot of impure, but I still should have made it home."

"I have a theory why you didn't."

"Why?"

"You didn't want to."

"You might be right."

"Plus, I imagine the last time you had that much impure was when you still lived here, so your internal navigation system must have assumed you do still live here. "

"But I don't. I'm really sorry."

Manu waved him off with a flip of his hand.

"It's okay. It's actually kind of fun. Reminds me of when we were young."

"That feels like many seasons ago."

"It was."

Baldwin eyed Manu. His friend's skin was very pale.

"It seems like your seizures are more frequent."

Manu flipped his hand again.

"Maybe it's because I'm in love. My brain is overheating."

Baldwin lowered his eyes.

"Can I tell you something?"

"Of course."

"I think the woman you met at Ramson's is the same one who came to the miracle office the day you were sick. Her name is Hetta."

"Why do you think that?"

"Because she works for Ramson; I mean, her utility is at a warm wash, but she touches people on the side for him."

"She told you all that during her claim?"

Baldwin hesitated. He did not like to lie to Manu, but decided to anyway.

"She talked about a lot of things. I guess she thought it was connected to her miracle."

Manu blew out a sigh.

"I didn't think Franklin was so enterprising as to run a touch counselor."

"Everyone likes chits."

"Not you."

"Don't be so sure. I owe you four chits. I took them from your desk the other day; one to pay the messenger you sent, and the rest I spent on my own. But I promise I'll replenish your supply after I get my allotment."

"No need. My chits are your chits."

"Don't be silly."

"I'm not. They're actually yours. I never told you, but your mother came once to the office while you were out and gave me ten chits to hide away for you in case of an emergency. I guess she trusted me."

"That was a mistake."

"Not really. She encouraged me only to give them to you if you were really in a bind. It's been so long, that every now and then I take a few when I'm short, but I always fill it back up. Do you want me to give you the rest?"

Baldwin shook his head.

"It's best to follow my mother's encouragement: only when I'm in a bind."

"Like now."

"My problem isn't chits."

They were silent a moment. Manu broke it with a belch. He wiped at his lips as he spoke.

"What was this Hetta's claim anyway?"

Baldwin' penis stirred. He was not sure if it was connected to his hangover or the mention of Hetta. He cleared his throat and swallowed.

"She had an orgasm."

"That's a miracle?"

"There was a little more to it."

"Like what?"

"She never had one before."

"More."

"It came to her in a dream."

"Stop." Manu held up a hand. "Just say you found her attractive so you approved the claim."

"It wasn't just that. Like you said, she's nice."

"Nice isn't a miracle."

"Sometimes it is."

They were silent again. Baldwin eyed the empty glass in his hands.

"I should go home."

"I imagine Nadine must be wondering where you are."

"She probably didn't come home either. I actually haven't seen her in days."

Manu's eyes widened. He blinked with incredulity.

"You haven't seen your wife in days, you drink so much impure you end up in my bed, you're wearing a woman's shoe, and you approved an orgasm miracle. What happened to my friend Baldwin?"

"He's in hiding."

"Well, when he comes back, tell him to stop by. I miss him."

Baldwin borrowed from Manu a shirt and also sandals as his toes still stung a bit from the hangover. The shirt was much too big for him and the sandals made a flopping sound as he walked, but it was better than the purple pump, which Manu had thrown in a pile with the bed sheets for the community fire.

Manu walked him out.

"What am I going to do about Ramson?" he said, opening the door for Baldwin.

"I told you already. You should stay away from him."

"But I'm so crazy about him," Manu continued, as if not hearing Baldwin. "I can't think of anything else but him."

Baldwin hesitated, wanting to tell Manu about his meeting the morning before with Ramson, about the conflict counselor's request that he kill Leonard. But it seemed a difficult conversation to start, explain or finish, so he said instead:

"I'm sorry, but I just don't like him. I think he's mean, cruel and dangerous."

"That doesn't help at all," Manu said. "You know I'm drawn to men you don't like who are mean, cruel and dangerous."

"Don't joke. I'm worried about you. I don't want you to get hurt."

"It's too late," Manu said. "You know my relationships always end badly. I would just like to extend my time with Franklin a little more before the inevitable destruction."

Baldwin saw that Manu was going to see Ramson again no matter what he said. His idea now was to delay it.

"At least wait until after the Day of No Consequence to visit him. You know how conflict counselors get around this time. They'll snap their learning stick at anything that moves. It's probably why he was so quick to hit you."

"You think so?"

"I do. Give Ramson some time to see what he's missing. Let him come to you."

"And if he doesn't?"

"Then forget about him. It's never good to be needy."

Manu smiled.

"You mean like a friend I used to have named Baldwin?"

"Yes," Baldwin said, stepping into the hallway. "Like him."

24 SECOND HAND

*N*eediness. Ironically, it was he who had once broached the subject with Harold, complaining that Nadine's neediness was causing friction in their union. Harold crunched on a peeled pear while he listed examples of Nadine's insecurities, her constant demands for affirmation, her nagging tests to prove his affection, that he loved her more than any other breathing person in the Circle, including his mother.

Harold waited for him to exhaust his complaints, then plucked the stem from the core and began to clean his front teeth.

"So Nadine's needy," he said, flicking the stem onto the floor. "But you're needy too. Maybe even worse, because you need her neediness to feel needed. The problem is that when two needy people come together, their neediness cancels each other out, and they become the very thing they fear most."

"What's that?"

"Not needy."

That evening he and Nadine had got into a terrible argument. It started with a silly disagreement about what to eat first from the edibles bag, radishes or rose petals, and continued until well past the moonrise gong. For the first time in their union, Nadine insisted they sleep separately – he on the floor, she in the bed. It was an excruciating night. The arguing had spiked his adrenaline and he twitched, moaned and twisted on the hardwood for hours. Finally, he fell to sleep, waking with agony at the sunrise gong, surprised to find Nadine beside him, her head nestled against the fold of his arm.

Walking back to his unit, Baldwin could not help but worry where Nadine might be and if she was okay. It was a logical concern. He had not seen her since their last fight, had heard no word from her, while learning, in that time, that she may or may not be romantically involved with his stepfather and may or may not want to kill him. But any desire to seek out Nadine and resolve these issues had been obliterated by the chaotic events of the past two days. His neediness now centered on fulfilling one desire: to rest, to forget, to curl up in his own bed, and to hide.

The walk began to tire him more. The heat from the sun burned into his flesh, causing him to break out in a sharp sweat, the more stubborn properties of the impure flowing out, smelling of sulfur and stale bread. He wished the cement path he was traveling had tree cover, but it was barren of natural growth on either side, a straight white swatch of false rock. He closed his eyes as he moved, tried to cool himself mentally, visualizing a whipping wind lashing his body with freezing rain. It didn't work. Not only did he feel even hotter, but he veered off the path, caught one of the borrowed sandals on a loop of rusted cable and landed hard on his face. When he looked up a hand was coming toward him. It belonged to Ernest, Hetta's husband.

"Are you okay?" he said, helping Baldwin up.

Baldwin blushed. Sweat teamed into his eyes. He wiped them clean and took in a breath.

"I must have tripped. But I'm alright."

"Are you sure?"

"Yes, I'm good. Just embarrassed."

"I guess that's better than breaking an ankle."

"I guess."

Ernest smiled.

"Anyway, I'm grateful to see you."

"Likewise."

"Baldwin, right?"

Baldwin nodded.

"And you're Ernest?"

"Or Ee-Ee…whatever you prefer."

"Okay."

Ernest pawed at the ground with his big toe. The nail was pointed and yellow. He was barefoot.

"I actually just got back from checking on Christine," he said with some remorse. "She said you two got out of the club fine but then got into some more trouble."

Baldwin blushed deeper. He mopped his forehead with his shirtsleeve.

"I'm not really sure. I don't remember much."

"Something about you getting into a fight with her roommate."

A replay of the bedroom scene, the two women flailing on top of him, flashed in Baldwin's mind. He blew out his lips as he exhaled.

"Maybe I should go apologize."

Ernest flared his nostrils, as if smelling an obnoxious odor.

"I wouldn't. Jessie, that's the roommate, isn't around right now, and Christine doesn't feel well."

"I feel terrible too. I'm not used to so much impure so fast."

"Not me. I can drink it all night and wake up feeling as if I poured nothing down my throat but brewed ginger."

"You're lucky."

"Or cursed. Maybe if it hit me harder at the end I wouldn't take so much in at the beginning."

"It hit me hard all the way through," Baldwin said. "I never even made it home last night. I stayed over at a friend's."

"At least you had someone to talk too." Ernest's eyes drifted up toward a passing cloud. "My wife never came home. I guess my romantic union is doomed."

Baldwin felt a sudden closeness to Ernest. Looking at this man through the shimmering sweat of an impure hangover, he realized they shared not just the pain of marital friction, but an even greater bond – they both loved the same woman.

Ernest snapped his fingers.

"I recall you saying last night you are in a romantic union."

"I am."

"Your wife must not mind you staying out all night."

"I'm not sure," Baldwin said. "I'll see when I get home."

"Well, let me give you some advice," Ernest said. "The key is not to tell her too much. And don't act like you regret what you did: just say you were enjoying yourself, you lost track of time, and because it was so late you stayed at a friend's. If you act like it's not a big deal she will think it's not a big deal. Just do that and you're home free."

"Besides," Ernest continued, "whatever happens you'll have it better than me this morning. I have to go see my life counselor and tell him I screwed up again. And I can't simple it down. He's got a way of knowing when I withhold information, which makes him even madder."

"I guess it's always best to be truthful."

"It's not so easy with my guy. He's a mentor, very high up. So not only do I worry when I lie, I also worry when I'm honest."

"You have a mentor as a life counselor?" Baldwin asked.

"Yeah. I know it's pretty unique. My life counselor passed away, and

I was drinking a lot of impure and having problems at my utility, and they were thinking of sending me to a gratitude farm, but my wife helped me out. She knows a few important people from her utility and it happened that this mentor was willing to take me on."

Ernest stuck out his hand.

"Anyway, I have to get going. I'm at The Silo most nights, so maybe I'll see you there sometime or somewhere else. The Circle's pretty tightly drawn when you think about it."

"Yes," Baldwin said, shaking his hand but not looking in his eye, "it truly is."

25 WINDOW PANE

*B*aldwin felt very down walking to his unit after leaving Ernest. He did not believe the feeling was connected to his hangover. This was different, less kinetic, not fleeting, more pervasive and solid. Perhaps he was just overwhelmed. It was a reasonable assumption: his wife was missing and supposedly wanted to kill him, the woman he had newly fallen in love with did not appear to be as pure of mind and heart as he first thought, his neighbor's head had turned up burning in a pool of incinerated deer, and after a night of swilling impure and fighting half-naked with two strange women, he had woken unexpectedly in a friend's bed. It all pressed down on him; he actually felt heavier with each step, until he had to stop and rest. His body tried to help: igniting its cooling system and sending a wave of perspiration through his pores, a sickening, stagnant-smelling sweat that clung tight to his skin. He wiped hard at his eyes, cleaned them of the sheen, and saw with relief that he was near to his building, fifty paces at the most. He started walking again, slightly revived by the promise of cleansing in pure water and resting in his own bed. He drew closer, glanced up at his unit, saw movement though the kitchen window. He quickened his pace, stared harder at the window, furrowed his brow in puzzlement, and then drew in a fast breath when he was sure of what he was seeing.

Baldwin moved as fast as he could without running, elongating his stride with each stride, until his body was longer in the air than on the ground. He cruised through the entrance, raced up the stairs, got to his door and stopped. He gathered himself and thought what he wanted to say. It didn't sound right so he thought of something else. Then he twisted the knob and pushed open the door with his forearm.

"Nadine."

There was no answer, no sound in the unit save his breathing.

"Nadine."

He closed the door behind him and headed into the kitchen. It was empty, as were the other rooms. Nadine was not home.

Baldwin returned to the kitchen and sat down dejectedly at the table. He was sure he had seen her. But perhaps her image was an illusion, or a delusion – just wishful thinking on his part that she was home. The idea bothered him: he did not want to miss her, did not want to be worried about her. But he did, and he was.

He looked across the table and realized the edibles bag was missing. He went back to the door, opened it, hoping he had overlooked the bag in his haste to get inside. No luck. He glanced down the hall, at Simon's door, saw that his bag, seemingly full, was dangling from the knob. He headed toward it. He did not think it wrong to take the bag: he was hungry and Simon was no longer breathing. Still, he took caution, tried to be stealth as he reached for the bag. But as soon as his fingers touched burlap, the door was flung inward, and so was he.

"Where's Simon?"

Baldwin winced as the hand that pulled him into Simon's unit twisted his right wrist.

"You're hurting me."

"I don't care. Where is he?"

"I don't know."

"Who are you then?"

"His neighbor."

The man let go of his wrist.

"Let's go to the conversation room."

They sat down on a long brown rug, facing each other a few feet apart. The man was very long of leg and it took some time to curl them under his behind.

"You look familiar," he said to Baldwin.

"Like I said, I live down the hall."

"Not that. Now I know. I saw you last night."

"You did?"

The man nodded.

"You were at the running-in-place contest. I was one of the performers."

Baldwin felt the intensity of the man's stare, actual heat from the gaze.

"You're lucky I didn't stomp you," he continued.

"I'm sorry. I had too much impure."

They were silent a moment.

"I'm Morris, by the way."

"Baldwin."

"Funny that I've never seen you before last night," he said.

"I guess it's a big building."

"Not that big."

His angular neck bulged with blue veins.

"Simon owes me more chits than I can count," he said. "That's why I'm waiting for him. What about you?"

"He doesn't owe me."

"I mean, when's the last time you saw him?"

Baldwin thought of the fire pit, of Simon's smoking head, the blue thong melting into the seared dear meat.

"I'm not sure. He was always pretty private."

"Please. He walks around this building and hits everyone up for chits. I saw him just recently talking to a woman outside your door, passing chits back and forth. If that's your wife, you better tell her to get in line to get paid back."

Baldwin studied the room while he considered the idea of Nadine and Simon together. His neighbor's taste in furniture and décor, opposite his clothing, was stark and sober, even tasteful.

He looked at Morris.

"Any idea why he owed so many chits?"

"Not owed...owes. You talk like he's dead."

Baldwin flushed.

"I'm just curious."

"I was too. So I asked him."

"And he told you?"

"He did – but it was a lie. I'm pretty good at reading people. I think it has something to do with my feet. When you live with pain it's easy to spot it in others. When Simon told me he needed chits to pay a vertical counselor to stretch his back I knew he wasn't telling the truth. I never once saw his face twitch with a spasm or even see him stoop or shuffle. His spine was fine."

Morris smiled smugly.

"But I finally got the truth out of him," he continued. "Funny, too, because I don't see him that way."

"Which way?"

"Motivated."

"I don't understand."

"He's bribing people. Conflict counselors, mostly. He thinks he can be a mentor if he gets enough chits into the right people. He told me the last time he borrowed chits he was close to the top, whatever that meant."

Baldwin folded his hands and said, "Never want what you deserve."

"What's that mean?"

"It's from *The Book of Ash*."

"Don't ever tell anyone," Morris said, "but I don't care for the text. Too much advice makes people dull and cautious. It's better to think on your feet."

"Even when it hurts?"

Morris smiled.

"Especially when it hurts."

26 NO BODY

*P*uberty was a bad time for Baldwin. It started late and lasted long. Leonard was particularly impatient with him during this period. Once, after seeing Baldwin emerge naked from a bath, he threw a tirade, thinking that his stepson (at the time 14) was purposely holding back his body's maturation. From that day on, Leonard was determined to make Baldwin feel ashamed of his boyish body, to make it such a burden in his conscious mind that his subconscious would push toward adulthood. To start, he held Baldwin back in school, making him repeat lessons with a group of younger students. He also forced him to wear little or no clothing, sometimes even just a worn dishtowel wrapped around his waist. After a few weeks of this treatment Baldwin began to develop nervous habits related to wildlife, such as spitting twice over his right shoulder when he saw a crow, and twice over his left shoulder when he passed a cat. He also had trouble eating, not able to swallow before chewing his food exactly forty-four times. When Baldwin held onto his nipples as he walked, fearful, or so he told his mother, that they might fall off, she begged Leonard to ease up, explaining that all was well with his stepson's development, as his testicles and underarms were beginning to shadow with pubic hair. Finally, Leonard relented, returning Baldwin to his regular class and allowing him again to wear clothing that covered his body. But despite this return to normalcy, and a cessation of the nervous tics and habits, Baldwin felt shaken and exposed, grotesque, really. He saw himself as hideous, and his skewed body image and low self-esteem caused him to shun mirrors as well as the eyes of others, particularly when they were connected to the female form. This carried into his first year living with Manu, when he endured his newfound freedom and access to women by ingesting copious amounts of impure.

Then he met Nadine.

Baldwin always gave her credit for helping him see himself for what he really was: perfectly average. The fact she found him attractive, and in the beginning of their relationship she pawed and preened over his body with a manic furor, did not sway her sober, somewhat unflattering assessment of his physical composition. "You're a tweener," she told him early in their relationship, "not tall or short, fair skinned or dark, fat or thin. You're almost invisible because you don't stand out in any way." As such, she encouraged him to wear "baggy and brown" outfits. She explained that people with benign body forms should never wear bright colors, wild patterns, tight-hugging clothing, which only served to draw attention to the blandness of the body beneath. Better to match blandness with blandness, was her theory, to dress so boring that the body, by comparison, looked exciting.

Over the years, his clothes, limited as they were, reflected Nadine's vision, something that made her happy but not his mother. She was vocal in this displeasure, many times telling Baldwin, even with Nadine present, that "he looked silly" wearing clothes too big for him, and that his skin tone and features favored whites and blues, perhaps even yellows, rather than brown, which she felt made his nose appear too big for his face and his neck too small for his head. Nadine never once interrupted his mother's critiques, never spoke up that it was her idea for him to dress like that. But later she would erupt, directing her anger at Baldwin, telling him he should have said something to his mother, that he should have defended the clothing choice, that by not doing so he was not defending her.

Baldwin accepted Nadine's rage just as he accepted his mother's critiques, thinking both justified. He initially saw the problem as his being "too empathic," not wanting to challenge his mother, who he felt was merely trying to remain connected and relevant in his life, and not wanting to challenge Nadine, who he felt was merely doing what a wife should do. Harold, in their sessions, intimated that Baldwin was too lenient with both women; that they were exerting an unhealthy control over his life, and that if he did not challenge them, stand up for what he wanted, he might eventually forget what he wanted. But Baldwin had never challenged his mother and, in all honesty, he had never challenged Nadine.

He wondered now – lying in bed, returning to his unit to calm down after the altercation with Morris, to rest and recover from the impure binge – if he had ever challenged himself either? It made sense that he was the person most to blame for his problems, the course his life had taken. It was not his mother, Leonard or Nadine who led him to this point, but him. He was the one responsible, wasn't he? The thought empowered him, gave him a burst of hope, some energy. He slipped of his shorts and underwear, fingered the hanging testicles, and gently squeezed the growing shaft of his penis. He began to rub, thinking of Hetta, her full breasts, blonde hair, the missing ear, the way she rode him on the stone slab.

But soon the image of Nadine punched through the fantasy, took over the action and introduced a different type of sex. With her it was always regimented, first her turn to orgasm, and then his. It was divide and conquer, with each experiencing their release separately and unconnected. He watched his penis swell in his hand, the tip tingling. He arched his back, stroked faster, erotic images of Hetta and Nadine flitting back and forth, each challenging the other for his attention, for his climax. When it happened, both disappeared from view; he was alone, a man grasping a shrinking penis, alone in a bed, alone in a unit, with not even a fantasy left to distract his mind, with nothing to do but close his eyes and think what not to do next.

27 WOMAN KIND

*B*aldwin woke from his nap. His right leg was sticky with ejaculate. His left was being kneaded, from thigh to knee, by strong and sure fingers. Hetta was topless, her midsection covered with a red sash, the rest of her lower body, down just past her knees, by a skirt which looked to be made from the same course material as an edibles bag.

Baldwin flushed with surprise. He diverted his eyes away from Hetta's breasts and focused on her fingers.

"What are you doing?"

"Touching you."

Baldwin tried to focus. Judging by his dry mouth and confusion, the nap had been long and hard.

"When did you come in?"

"Not long ago. The door to your unit was open."

Baldwin wondered if he had forgotten to shut it. He usually was careful about such things.

Hetta leaned over and pressed her lips to his knee. Her kiss was soft and short.

"I missed you."

Baldwin sat up. He drew his knees in, away from her lips. Hetta looked surprised by his retreat.

"Are you mad I'm here?"

"Just surprised."

"Good surprised…or bad surprised?"

"Just surprised."

Hetta ran her hand over her forehead, up the slope of her head and down to the back of her neck.

"Maybe you don't think I'm pretty?"

"You know I do."

"Then penetrate me."

Baldwin took in a breath. He did not feel sexual.

"I think we should talk."

"Talk while you're inside me."

Baldwin pulled his knees closer. He felt disjointed from the nap. He wanted most to drink pure water, to wash up and to feel clean.

"I don't know. It doesn't seem right."

"Because of your union?"

Baldwin hesitated.

"Maybe it's your union. I met your husband last night, at a conversation club. We drank some impure together. He seems like a nice person."

"Ernest isn't nice," Hetta snapped back. She blinked angrily. "Was a woman named Christine with him?"

Baldwin hesitated.

"Don't worry about hurting my feelings. I really don't care if they're together. I just feel sorry for her. She's totally in love with him."

"They acted more like friends."

"Exactly. It's an act. They're not friends – they have sex."

Baldwin eyed Hetta. The flush of anger made her face even more attractive, filled her skin with a pulsing vibrancy.

"I'm sure Ernest said nasty things about me," she continued. "I never touch him anymore. I don't give him enough of my chits. I'm never home. That's his standard complaints."

"Maybe he just misses you."

Hetta laughed derisively.

"Ernest really fooled you. No wonder – he's expert at deception."

Hetta's seemingly casual disdain for Ernest began to anger Baldwin. Perhaps it was remindful of Nadine's attitude toward him.

"I doubt he even knows how to be honest anymore," Hetta continued.

"And you do?"

Hetta looked startled.

"What do you mean?"

Baldwin was sorry he had said anything, but he couldn't hold back.

"I found out some things about you."

"What things?"

"That you work for a conflict counselor named Ramson who sets you up for touch dates."

"Did Ernest tell you this?"

"No."

"Then who?"

Baldwin remembered his vow to Nathan.

"My neighbor, Simon," he lied. "The one who took me to the warm wash."

"Why would he know that or tell you that?"

"Is it true?"

Hetta's gaze turned defiant.

"Touching is my utility, no matter when or where I do it. When I get chits for doing it, the skin means nothing to me. Why does that bother you?"

"Because I heard you touch mentors. Maybe you even touched Leonard Living. He's my stepfather, you know. He's a horrible person. He ruined my life. I can't stand the idea that you touch him with the same hands you touch me."

"Then we have a problem."

"So you admit it."

"Yes."

Baldwin exhaled disgustedly through his nose.

"Does he penetrate you too? Is that how you end all your sessions?"

Hetta's voice grew hard. She wiped at the scar tissue where her left ear once was.

"I touch for chits," she said. "That's all."

"Then why would Leonard help you?"

"Help me how?"

"By being Ernest's life counselor. Your husband told me you helped him get a mentor for a life counselor. It's Leonard, isn't it?"

Hetta paused.

"He only did it as a favor."

"Leonard doesn't do favors unless he owes one or is sure he'll get two in return."

Hetta took in a long breath, held the air until her face reddened, then pursed her lips and let it out in short bursts, her stomach pushing in and out with the effort. When she was done her voice was calm, her stare soft.

"I'm not lying to you. Leonard saw that Ernest was killing my self-esteem. It was right after his wife died...your mother, that is. I think he was more in tune with suffering during that time and he recognized mine. He could feel sadness in my touch. So he asked what was bothering me and I told him about Ernest. That's when he said he would work with him."

"But Leonard hasn't helped Ernest, according to you."

"No, he's worse."

Hetta looked hard at Baldwin.

"That's why his breathing has to come to an end on the Day of No Consequence."

"You're going to kill him?"

"Not me. Ramson."

They were silent a moment.

"What are you thinking?" Hetta asked.

"That's it's not right. As bad as Ernest is, there are other things you can do besides taking his life."

"Like what?"

"Break the union."

"I want to, but Leonard won't encourage it. He thinks it reflects badly on his work with Ernest; that if people in the Circle find out he failed to make him a better husband, then they will lose confidence in him as a mentor. He also thinks it's not the right time to give up on the union because I'm still fertile. He says that's the time when a woman's moods and feelings are most volatile and inexplicable. He thinks women make bad decisions about men when they can make babies… He thinks it's my fault."

Baldwin knew that sounded like Leonard. He often said that older women were more pleasing than younger ones, women who no longer had the instinctual urge to procreate, whose bodies shut down the intricate systems that made baby-making possible, leaving their minds free to focus on the men in their lives. He looked at Hetta, his anger dissipating, compassion creeping in.

"Can't you hold on?"

"What do you mean?"

Baldwin thought about Nadine, how he hoped it would get better between them. How this hope had become in essence the relationship.

"Can't you live with Ernest and not love him?"

Hetta reached out and touched the top of his hand.

"There's no other option for me. If I stay with Ernest any longer I will die. I feel it in my skin. The body knows when the mind is not well, not in balance, not happy. It starts to compensate, to try to correct the problem that the mind can't. Eventually, it shuts down. That's why people end their breathing – the body gives up hope."

"But if Leonard doesn't want Ernest away from you, he won't want him dead either. And he's not someone who lets things go. If you have Ernest killed, he'll find out and have you sent to a gratitude farm."

"That's why I made a deal with Ramson."

"What deal?"

Hetta flushed. She wiped harder at the scar tissue, as if trying to tear it away from her skin.

"I'm very sorry."

"Sorry for what?"

Hetta eyes grew moist.

"I was desperate. And Ramson offered a way out. He said that he would kill Ernest if I could convince you to kill Leonard."

"When did you make this deal?"

Hetta looked down.

"The night before my miracle."

"So it's all a lie."

Hetta looked up. Tears wet her cheeks.

"I did have the dream. The woman did speak to me. Everything that has happened since between us, the way I feel about you, it's true. You have to believe me." She paused. "I love you."

Baldwin grew tense.

"How are you supposed to convince me to kill Leonard?"

"I guess I felt if I could get you to feel about me the way I feel about you, would want to end Leonard's breathing to save mine."

Baldwin hesitated. He looked away from Hetta as he spoke.

"It's not who I am. I'm not capable of having anyone's death on my conscience. I can't hate anyone that much."

Hetta reached out and put her hand over Baldwin's.

"I realize that now. Ramson told me what you said when he asked you. I was wrong to make the deal. It's why I wasn't able to see you last night. I had to see Ramson and tell him that I can't ask you to do such a thing. I told him to let Ernest live. Even if it means I will die."

"What did he say?"

"He said it's too late. That I made a promise and had to keep it."

Baldwin thought a moment.

"Can't you just give Ramson chits to forget the whole thing?"

"I already gave him everything I had – even the chits for the miracle. He needed them to bribe someone who knows where Leonard plans to hide on the Day of No Consequence."

"Then Ramson stole from you," Baldwin returned. "No one knows where Leonard hides that day. He never even told my mother and me when we lived with him. He always left us alone to fend for ourselves."

"He told someone this time."

"Who?"

Hetta blinked with compassion.

"Your wife."

"Nadine."

"Ramson bribed someone to get close to her. Leonard must trust your wife for some reason and told her where he goes. She passed it on to this other person who told Ramson. All I know is it's a timehole. If you agree to kill Leonard, Ramson will give you the exact directions."

Baldwin thought of what Morris said about Simon and Nadine passing chits.

"Do you know who the person is — the one who got close to my wife?"

"I asked but Ramson wouldn't tell me."

Baldwin shook his head.

"This isn't right. We shouldn't have to make these choices. We shouldn't have to kill people, bribe them, do horrible things just to be happy. I'm going to go and talk to Leonard. I'll ask him to let you break your union with Ernest. He owes me that. And I'll tell him that Ramson wants him killed. I might even tell him that Nadine betrayed him. He can do what he wants with the information."

"And what about us?"

Baldwin felt a surge of decisiveness.

"Then we can be free to make a new union."

Hetta paused. Her eyes looked sad.

"It doesn't seem possible. Can people who love each other really end up together?"

Baldwin took Hetta's hand. He pressed it to his lips, kissed the center of her palm. Her skin had the scent and flavor of fresh air.

"Only if they want to," he said.

"And you want to?"

He kissed her palm again.

"Yes," he said. "I do."

28 BAG MAN

It was many paces to Leonard's, and Baldwin performed them with his head up, his gaze forward, his carriage erect, his body propelled forward by a newfound strength. He had made a choice: Hetta over Nadine, Hetta over Leonard, Hetta over the Circle. She was his responsibility now, and he walked with surety and purpose. At least until he reached the trailer. Then the familiar insecurity gripped him, trepidation, haunting from the past, the little boy trapped, the mother in pain, the angry father who was not the father.

Baldwin stopped a few feet from the screen door, tried to quell the reversal of confidence, to regain the fortitude, the conviction he felt when he left Hetta at his unit.

He glanced up to the roof, to the black wind vane shaped like a hairy chicken. Its wings once twirled with the breeze, but the right one had broken off, leaving the left to quiver and sway, pointing directly at him. He steadied himself, swallowed twice, smoothed down his shirt and pulled up his pants, and stepped up onto a plastic foam riser. He knocked twice on screen door and peered inside.

"Leonard."

There was no answer. He knocked some more.

"Leonard."

The latch was off the door. It was also ajar. Baldwin pushed it open some more and slipped inside.

"Leonard."

Baldwin squinted as the screen closed behind him. It was dark in the trailer. This was not unusual. Leonard always covered the windows with thick, red curtains, no matter the time of day.

"Is anyone here?"

Baldwin moved into the kitchen. An edibles bag was on the table. His eye caught on something oozing out of the bag, spreading along the table, dripping onto the floor. Blood.

"I'm grateful to see you."

Baldwin whirled to his right. Christine was standing in the corner, holding a sickle in her right hand. Its blunt handle was wrapped in pink cloth. The blade, curling toward him, leaked red droplets onto the floor.

"I had no choice," she said, her voice flat, deadened. "He pushed me too far."

Baldwin had developed some skills as a miracle counselor on how to interact with someone who was distraught, delusional, or both. He learned the best way to guide them back to lucidity was to listen intently, to affirm everything they said, to back up affirmations with sincere nods, to wipe away all appearances of judgment, to show nothing but empathy and compassion. The look, the stance, the aura, came easy to him; perhaps he had practiced all his life doing it with Leonard.

Christine looked at the sickle, then at Baldwin.

"Why did he have to be that way?"

"Probably only you know."

Christine's face softened.

"You're right. Even he didn't understand himself."

Baldwin nodded.

"He's horrible."

"Yes."

"Thinks he knows what's best for me...for everyone."

He nodded again.

"He never suffered as much as me. He never cared as much as me. Just because he is who he is doesn't give him the right to control me, to ruin my life."

Baldwin could not stop himself from speaking. Perhaps he was swept up in Christine's words, connecting with his own issues, to Hetta's lament. He was certain Leonard's head was in the bag. He was not sad.

"You didn't do wrong," he said. "He pushes everyone to the brink of craziness. He's cruel and self-centered. He ruined my life too."

"Ee-Ee ruined your life?" She raised the sickle. "Did he sleep with your wife? Your girlfriend? Your sister? Your mother? Tell me."

Baldwin inched back.

"You didn't kill Leonard?"

"Who's Leonard?"

"Leonard Living."

"The mentor?"

Baldwin nodded.

"Why would I kill him?"

"You're in his trailer," he said with as little indictment as possible.

Christine blinked with confusion. She loosened her grip on the sick-le.

"I thought this was where another of Ee-Ee's mistresses lived. He told me this morning it was over between us, that he wanted to concentrate on getting back with his wife. I didn't believe him. I had an idea maybe he was just tired of me. So I followed him after he left my unit. I figured he would go home and I could see for sure, maybe even talk with his wife, to both of them, see if they really had a chance to repair the union. I wouldn't get in the way if that's what they wanted. I'm not like that. I love him, but she loved him first, and I'm polite. I never cut in line."

Baldwin eyed the bag. Blood continued to seep through the burlap.

"But he came here. I saw a woman open the door and let him in. I heard them talking inside, laughing. So I broke in and…"

Christine let out a gasp. She laid the sickle on the table.

"I had no choice."

Baldwin's stomach tightened. His toes and fingers tingled. His feet felt leaden, as if bolted to the floor.

"What's in the bag?" he slid out of his mouth.

Christine began to cry.

"I thought I might take it with me," she said. "Rest his head in a nice spot of wild mint."

"*His* head?"

Christine nodded.

"Ee-Ee always liked mint," she continued, her nose running. "I know a patch of it that grows near a fence we worked on. It's where we first kissed."

Baldwin took a gentle step forward. He eyed Christine and the sickle as he reached for the bag. It was heavy and wet to his touch. He shook it from the end so the contents spilled out. Christine's sob greeted the arrival of Ernest's head. He was smiling and his eyes were open. He looked happy.

Christine reached over and smoothed Ernest's hair.

"You can see how much I loved him."

"I do."

"And I had no choice."

"No, you didn't."

Christine wiped at her nose. She smoothed Ernest's hair again, pushed some strands behind his right ear.

Baldwin took in a breath.

"I don't see the rest of Ee-Ee. Is his body still here?"

"In the bedroom."

"And the woman he was with. Did you…is she in the bedroom too?"

Christine shook her head.

"She ran away when she saw me."

"I think we should leave," Baldwin said.

"I can't go without Ee-Ee."

"Then take him."

Baldwin watched Christine gently place the head back in the bag. She cradled it tight to her bosom.

"It's clear how much I love him, isn't it?"

"It is."

Her eyes widened. Baldwin recognized in them a morsel of clarity.

"When is the Day of No Consequence?" she asked.

"Tomorrow, I believe."

"Perhaps it would have been best if I waited."

"Perhaps."

Baldwin let Christine leave the kitchen first, then he followed her, but not before picking up the sickle.

29 BONE HEAD

*L*eonard's trailer ran adjacent to a narrow walkway of white bricks, set so close and so precise to each other that they appeared to be one elongated slab of cement. The walkway extended several hundred paces before connecting at a right angle with a wide gravel path which, given the time of day and season, or an individual's viewpoint, either bisected the Circle vertically or horizontally.

It was at the path that Baldwin and Christine headed in opposite directions: she to place Ernest's severed head in a mint patch; he, sickle in hand, to find a quiet, safe place to sit down and think and plan what to do next. It took less than fifty paces to identify such a spot, a weed meadow on the shadow side of the Stone Tower, the tallest non-living structure in the Circle. Its triangular top held the gong, which provided people in the Circle with the imprecise time.

The tower's shadow was long and wide enough that he was able to walk away from the path in cooling protection, finally finding, encircled by high dandelions, a tree stump to sit. It was not a natural stump; the cut was too fine and too straight to be done by wind, lightning or rot. It was rare to see such handiwork in the Circle, where it was encouraged to let living things die on their own accord. But like many things, an encouragement was, merely, an encouragement, meaning healthy trees did get cut down, healthy animals did get eaten, and healthy people, for various reasons, did get their heads chopped off.

The blood on the sickle's blade, Ernest's blood, looked purple in the shade. Baldwin dropped it next to the stump, sat down, breathed in part of a sudden breeze that bent the dandelions forward and caused the hair on his head to tremble. When the wind subsided he exhaled, thought about Christine, the jealous mania that compelled her to end the life of the man she proposed to love more than any other. He realized he had never felt that level of passion for Nadine – even now, when it was clear she was engaged in romance with Leonard, his own stepfather, he did not have a desire to harm her.

Of course, his reluctance to confront Nadine could be taken as a sign of maturity, even generosity, allowing her the space and freedom in their union to do what she wanted with whoever she wanted, believing, as *The Book Ash* encouraged, 'that the best way to hold onto anything is to let it go.' But Baldwin sensed this was not the truth, that the real reason for his inertia, his unwillingness to confront Nadine over the entirety of their union, was hope. It was not that he hoped she would become the wife he wanted, but that he would become the husband she did not want; that Nadine, as it now seemed to be the case, would leave him. It was a horrible thought for him to cultivate, but he knew it was there, lurking, ready to come out and be embraced.

The breeze kicked up again and with it the shade began to shrink with the setting sun. It was getting toward dusk and Baldwin, who had not eaten the entire day, was growing hungry. He did not want to go back to his unit and get the dinner bag. It was a walk with many paces and in the opposite direction of the warm wash, where he had agreed with Hetta to meet up after talking with Leonard. That hadn't happened, and he wondered how he would tell her about Ernest. He set aside his worry and made a plan. Harold's unit was on the way to the warm wash. He would go there first and see if he had food to share.

While it was never encouraged to "drop in" at one's life counselor, Harold had made it clear to Baldwin early on in their work together that he did not mind such visits, but if they did occur the dynamic of their conversation would not center on problems; Baldwin's, that is. Harold felt that doing so would dilute the time they did appoint each week to such matters, just as he believed that the only thing to do in a bed was sleep in it, suggesting that sex, reading, or any other activity be undertaken elsewhere.

Baldwin hid the sickle in the dandelions and returned to the path. As he walked he felt the diminishing heat of the sun edge down his back. When he arrived at Harold's building, the last tendrils of light licked at his knees. He went to the back, walked down the steps, knocked on the dented door, waited, knocked again, waited some more, gave up and walked around to the front.

"Baldwin."

It was Harold. He was chatting with an attractive older woman.

"Come give your gratitude to this wonderful lady."

Baldwin blushed as he came over.

"I'm grateful to meet you," he said to the woman, "but I'm sorry to interrupt."

The woman smiled. She was thin with white gray hair cut close and folded neatly around her ears. She had a very compact figure, slim yet feminine, flattered by a silken wrap of aqua blue, which rose from the top of her ankles to the bottom of her long neck. She was barefoot, and Baldwin noticed that her toenails were painted the same shade as her dress.

"I'm grateful for your manners," she said, widening her eyes in surprise. "It's so odd to find them in young people anymore."

"Baldwin's not that young," Harold injected. "How old are you now?"

"Thirty-three."

"That's young to me," the woman reinforced.

"Not me," Harold returned. "Then again I'm thirty-four."

The woman patted Harold's forearm playfully as she laughed.

"It's true," Harold continued. "I just look old."

"Do you want me to say you don't?"

"Of course."

The woman shook her head, feigning annoyance at Harold. She smiled at Baldwin.

"I'm Leslie, by the way."

"Forgive my manners," Harold spoke up, taking her hand and shaking it. "I'm Harold."

"I remember," Leslie said. Her eyes, almond-shaped and purple at the center, crinkled at the corners with amusement. "Although I'd like to forget sometimes."

"That's not true."

"Okay, it isn't."

Harold released her hand. He bowed slightly at Baldwin.

"This somewhat young man, by the way, is in my charge. I'm his life counselor."

"Lucky for Baldwin."

"I'm not so bad, am I?" Harold asked.

Baldwin blinked. He was enjoying the light interplay between Harold and Leslie, the humor pushing aside, at least for the moment, the troubling thoughts swirling inside him.

"Do you want me to say you aren't?"

"Good for you, Baldwin," Leslie laughed. "Don't let him bully you into a compliment."

She turned her attention to Harold.

"So you will try it?"

Harold nodded. He turned to Baldwin.

"We were talking before you came about how moon phases affect circulation. Leslie says that if I spend at least one afternoon standing on my head during the crescent phases I'll never have another pain in my joints."

"It's just a suggestion," Leslie said, "but it works for me."

"Well, I'm going to try it, even if I have to wedge my feet into the top of a bookshelf to keep my legs up."

"Just as long as you can get them out," Leslie said. "I'd hate to come by and find you stuck like that."

Harold blinked flirtatiously.

"I've been found in worse positions."

"I don't doubt it."

Leslie turned away from Harold, smiled at Baldwin.

"It's been wonderful to meet you, but I do have to go. But I'll be grateful when I see you again."

"Me too."

"Then it will be so."

She kept the smile going, pointed it at Harold.

"I'll see you later."

"If I'm still breathing."

"Make sure of it."

They watched her walk away, her torso straight as a poplar, her arms swaying incongruently against a stiff-legged gait.

Harold broke the silence.

"Leslie is a very unique and amazing person," he said. "She lives on the other side of the Circle, a good distance to walk, but she does this route each evening, starts at her unit and ends at mine. We've been friendly for some time, but things have changed recently."

"Sounds like you two are close."

"We are when I penetrate her. But we'll see if that continues. When you get to be our age, sex is more about the past than the present. You can't help but compare how it feels now and how it felt when you were younger."

"Is there a difference?"

"Only in contentment. When you're young, good sex is enough to keep you happy and together no matter your problems."

"And when you're older?"

"There's no such thing as good sex if you have problems. Unfortunately, when you get near the age of not counting it, the urge to pro-create isn't as strong and so you have to rely on emotions, not instinct, to love someone."

"I would think that's a good thing."

"It is but it's more complicated; certainly more painful if it goes bad." Harold sighed.

"Anyway, so far so good."

"She seems like a nice person."

"She is nice. But I think I like her more for her problems. For ex-ample, she can hardly bend her knees. It's like her bones are fused together. But it's amazing how she has adapted. She figured out a way to walk, with just the right swing of the arms and positioning of her torso and neck, so that she can move without any discomfort or hitch. It's what attracted me in the first place. Her walk."

Harold grinned mischievously.

"It's made our lovemaking quite interesting, her not being able to move her knees. But she more than makes up for it with other parts of her body that open quite well and wide."

"Okay."

"You didn't want to hear that, did you?"

"I don't mind."

"My point is that sometimes limitations in one area bring out the best in another."

"I get it."

Harold smiled at Baldwin.

"How's your hand?"

Baldwin had not thought of the incision made by the conception counselor since he had last seen Harold. He opened his palm. Only a feint white mark remained.

"I see the jelly worked," Harold said. "Did you eat the scab?"

"I did."

"Good?"

"Delicious."

"I knew it. Blood and sugar always mix well."

Harold shook his head as if amused.

"Back to Leslie. The first time we had sex, a few weeks ago, she asked me to perform all the usual functions under the covers. I mean, I was under the covers, my entire body, while she wasn't, at least not her head. I didn't mind at all, thinking that maybe she was a little shy, perhaps because her knees don't bend or something. But you know me, I had to ask why. It turned out it wasn't shyness at all. She just wanted to imagine I was someone else. She told me she's hot for some other guy and wanted to pretend I was him."

"Didn't that bother you?"

"Why would it? I was pretending she was someone else too."

Baldwin laughed. Harold always had the ability to amuse him.

"At least you're both having fun."

"What else should we be doing? Making each other miserable?"

"Some couples do?"

Harold exhaled.

"Is that why you came by? Problems with Nadine?"

"No, I mean, we're having problems, but I was really hoping I could share your edibles bag."

"I'm sorry," Harold said. "I told Leslie I'd eat with her tonight. We're going to mix bags."

"I understand."

Harold fidgeted.

"I'd invite you to come in and talk, but you know our rule about discussing problems outside of sessions."

"It's just…" Baldwin's voice constricted. "I've had a bad day."

"Maybe you can go see your friend, Manu. Go eat with him. He's fun."

"I don't think so."

"I guess you can eat with me and Leslie. I don't think she'd mind, as long as you leave after dinner. I promised to sleep over. She's nervous about being alone on the Day of No Consequence. She broke up with some old idiot a few months ago and he's threatened her. She has the idea that I'll protect her."

"Won't you?"

"I suppose if he's smaller than me."

Baldwin exhaled.

"So I hope to see you next week."

Concern tightened Harold's face. He spat on the ground and smiled. "Forget it," he said. "Come in for a few moments and tell me what's going on. I made some turnip pudding this morning you can have if you're hungry."

"Are you sure it's okay?"

"The pudding?"

"You know what I mean."

Harold's face softened. He patted Baldwin's arm.

"You know, my life counselor once told me that the only thing wrong with me was everything. I saw him once a week for more seasons than you've been breathing. Nice, smart guy, but he couldn't understand why I never did what he told me to do. Sometimes he would lie to me – give me advice that was contrary to what he was really thinking, hoping I would do the opposite. But I was so in tune with him I knew when he was trying to trick me. So I ended up doing my own thing anyway."

"Are you trying to say I don't listen to you?"

Harold smiled.

"I'm trying to say you shouldn't."

They went inside.

30 TRUE BLUE

*H*arold led them into the conversation room, but this time, reversing roles, he motioned for Baldwin to take the chair, while he sat cross-legged on the floor, his knee joints popping in the process.

"Don't get old," he said, wiggling his butt to settle into the floor.

"According to you I already am."

"You know I was joking. But it's true with me."

Harold gave his spine a twist to the left and right, causing another burst of clicks and pops.

"I'll be past the age of counting soon. It's the only encouragement in the Circle I believe in. No need to keep track after seventy – you either feel good or feel bad, look good or look bad, breathing or dead."

"Sounds grim," Baldwin said.

"Actually, it's freeing: once you give up the fight, there's no more fight."

"I wish that was the case now. I feel like I'm fighting a thousand problems."

Harold bowed his head and sighed.

"Begin at the end. What's the most recent problem?"

"You sound like me with a miracle client. They never know where to start."

"Well, I won't give or take away a chit whatever you say, so no pressure."

Baldwin hesitated. He felt uncomfortable in the chair and with Harold on the floor. He didn't like looking down at him. He looked vulnerable.

"Nadine, but it isn't all about her."

Harold narrowed his eyes into a squint.

"Tell me what *isn't* about Nadine."

Baldwin squirmed in the chair. He folded and unfolded his arms, crossed and re-crossed his legs, leaned forward and then sat back.

"That's enough." Harold got up with a grunt. "Let me sit down," he said, motioning Baldwin to stand. "You get on the floor."

They traded positions. Baldwin felt relief as soon as he touched down on the wood floor. His words spilled out fast and in surprising order. He started with finding Christine and Ernest's severed head in Leonard's trailer and worked backwards, his encounters with Ramson, the night at The Silo, his new intention to leave Nadine and make a union with Hetta.

Harold's fingers drummed lightly against his upper cheek after Baldwin finished. He moved his head back and forth, as if considering his options.

"And you haven't seen Nadine in how long?" he finally said.

"Three nights and two days."

Harold lowered his hand. He clicked his tongue in disgust.

"I hate the Day of No Consequence," he said. "It gives people the idea that they can change their lives by changing other people – namely by killing them. They think everything will be better once 'so and so' is not breathing, that they will be free of their pain, but they don't realize that the surest way to stay connected to the pain is to try and kill it. Listen to what I have to say: you don't take away the soul of the person you murder, you give them yours."

"I don't plan on killing anyone," Baldwin said, defensively.

Harold looked down at his hands.

"I didn't mean to snap, but I know what I'm talking about." He glanced at Baldwin and then looked away. "I hate to break your good feeling toward me, but I'm not the nicest person in the Circle."

"I never thought you were."

"I'm not joking now." Harold exhaled wearily. "The truth is I killed a man on the Day of No Consequence. It was years before we started working together. I didn't even know his name before that day; I'd never even seen him before. He sneaked into my unit at sunrise, came right into my bedroom, and began to strangle me in my sleep. It took me a moment to realize it was not just a bad dream. I wrestled his hands away and we started fighting. I hit him only once, in the face, but he fell forward and hit his head on the bed post and died" – Harold snapped his fingers – "just like that. I sat in the room with him the rest of the day. At sunrise I went and got a conflict counselor and they took him away."

Baldwin was shocked by the story, could not imagine Harold fighting with anyone, being so physical and violent, struggling for survival.

"Who was he? I mean, why did he want to kill you?"

"Like I always say, people are funny. His name was Blanton Paint-er. I love that name. It fit his utility too – he was a color counselor. They don't have the position anymore, but it was an important job at the time. They would go around the Circle and stop people who were wearing colors that did not match well with their body type, skin tex-ture, hair, even their personality. I never went in for it, but I knew lots of people who swore by what a color counselor told them to wear. Of course, this was when people were falling into timeholes every other day and clothes were plentiful. I learned later that Blanton was great at his job, with a particular genius for bringing out a person's eyes and their most subtle features, like the curve of their ears, with the right color. But he was also said to be blunt, even cruel, in his assessments of people's clothing, and even more so if they wore his most hated color, which was light blue. They said he was fine with darker blues, but anything nearing the color of a sunlit sky drove him crazy. I talked once with his sister and she said that Blanton told her that light blue reminded him of the infinite, something he could never define, and thus when draped upon the human form made us look even more in-significant and powerless. She also told me he used to wake up at night as a child screaming and crying that he was being sucked up into the sky, so probably it was just a phobia, but he had it and that was what drove a lot of his work."

Harold took in a breath. He nodded at Baldwin.

"You don't mind me telling you all this?"

"Not at all."

"Maybe I'm being over indulgent to myself, but I think it relates to your situation. You see, Blanton was so obsessive in his hate for light blue that it became, in essence, his favorite color. Favorite in that he thought about it all the time, obviously dreamed about it, and spent his days trying to eradicate it from people's bodies. But of course he could never succeed. For one, some people, no matter what people tell them, will wear what they like. And what about the sky? He must have been tormented each day to look up and see that vast color. So he was frustrated and crazy and it all came to a head on the Day of No Consequence."

"You were wearing light blue that day?"

"No, I was in bed, sleeping. And I always sleep naked."

"Then why?"

Harold tilted his head.

"What's the color of my back door?"

Baldwin suddenly realized.

"Light blue."

"Exactly."

Harold paused.

"Now I'm hungry. Let's go eat something while I tell the rest."

Baldwin followed him to the kitchen. Before sitting down at the table, Harold pulled out of the cupboard a bowl with a plate over its top. He removed the plate and slid the bowl toward Baldwin. He retrieved a spoon and passed that to him as well.

"It's the pudding," he said. "It's good."

It was. Baldwin ate greedily as Harold continued to talk. He had pulled out of the cupboard for himself another bowl, but this one filled with fermented grapes, purple, mushy marbles, which he spooned out with his fingers and ate in clumps.

"This is delicious," he said. "Grapes always taste better if they mature when it's really hot out."

"When is it not hot out?"

"Good point. But it's been extra hot lately, so these are extra good."

Baldwin scraped up the final bit of pudding. He was still hungry, but did not want to ask for any more. He wrinkled his forehead.

"You shouldn't feel bad about what you did," he said. "This Blanton was obviously crazy, trying to kill you just because of the color of your door. You were lucky you woke up."

"You're wrong," Harold said, licking his fingertips. "I wish I never did wake up. It's a terrible thing to live a life after you ended one. Each day I think about it, what I could have done differently."

"What could you do? He tried to strangle you while you were sleeping. You just reacted to save yourself. Your survival instinct kicked in."

"That's the point. I wish it hadn't. Better if I let him continue on and then hope he might change his mind. Or at least I could have gotten free and ran away. I was pretty fast then and I doubt he would have caught me."

"But he was crazy," Baldwin said, not comfortable with Harold's guilt. "He had no right to kill you, no rational reason. It's probably better you got him out of the Circle before he hurt someone else."

Harold shook his head.

"There's no such thing as a *rational* reason. What's rational to one person is irrational to another, and vice versa."

"You shouldn't feel bad."

"But I do. I have. I always will. I'm sad I killed him. I actually admire him. There's something wonderful about someone so passionate about his dislikes that he would kill for it."

"I can't agree. I think passion is a problem. Too much of it makes people do mean things."

"Now I don't agree," Harold said. "It's a horrible thing to suppress passion. Take away a person's passion and you create a mad bore. That was my father the last years of his life: angry all the time without one interesting thing to say."

"What was his passion?"

Harold's eyes widened. He smiled, the wrinkles of his face smoothing out with the spread of his lips.

"My mother."

"Oh."

"He loved her fiercely. She was all he ever talked about. From the time he woke up until he went to bed. He couldn't pass her without grabbing her between the legs or biting at her ears. He used to make up songs about her and sing them at dinner."

"She died?"

"No, she left him. As soon as I moved out and started my utility. She packed up as well and admitted herself into a gratitude farm. When my father tried to admit himself to join her she ended her breathing."

Baldwin looked down at the bowl.

"Leonard liked my mother very much," he said. "I can't say he didn't."

"Do you think it's true – is he having an affair with Nadine?"

"I do."

"And what about Nadine wanting to kill you tomorrow, do you believe Leonard?"

Baldwin paused, before shaking his head.

"I can imagine her not liking me anymore, even hating me, but I can't see her harming me. No matter what, I was always nice to her."

"You're projecting your rationality on her. Better to see her as irrational, or what you believe to be irrational, and imagine what she might do to you tomorrow."

Baldwin inhaled deeply.

"I think she'll try to kill me…or have me killed."

"And if she does, what will you do?"

"I'll try to stop her."

"Let's say she comes at you with a knife, what will you do?"

"Dodge and take it away from her."

"Not retaliate?"

"I don't think so. I don't want to kill her."

"But in the moment, the survival instinct, the blood lust, it's strong." Harold's face congealed. "It takes over."

"I won't let it."

"And what about Leonard? Will you seek vengeance for his dalliance with Nadine, will you do as this conflict counselor asks and kill him?"

"I don't want to kill him either."

Harold smiled.

"Then your problems are solved. You have a plan for the Day of No Consequence: don't kill anyone or get killed."

"What about Hetta?"

"What about her?"

"What should I do? I mean, she needs me to kill Leonard tomorrow. If I don't do it, something bad will happen to her."

"Then it does. You can't throw away your own life to save someone else's. That never works. You end up miserable and so do the people you helped. Trust me, people hate owing someone such a debt."

Harold licked at his lips, wiped them dry with a quick squeeze of his hand.

"Where is Hetta now?"

"At her utility. The warm wash not far from here. I'm supposed to meet her there soon."

"So do it. Like Ash says: 'Always keep old plans before making new ones.'"

He repeated the wetting and drying process with his lips.

"If it was me, I'd take her somewhere safe tonight, and then penetrate her from sunrise to sunset tomorrow. Once the Day of No Consequence is over, sift through the chaos and start fresh."

"It sounds too easy…or too enjoyable."

"Of course," Harold smiled. He gave Baldwin's arm one more tap and then rose from the table. "Everything's easy and enjoyable when you're irrational."

31 TENDER FOOT

It was dark outside. Harold and Baldwin hugged as they departed and went in opposite directions to meet the new women in their lives. The pudding in Baldwin's stomach settled as he walked. It was a still night, hot and humid. Baldwin looked up. He could not locate the moon. Perhaps it was behind a cloud, but he did not spot any.

The path narrowed as he neared the warm wash, his peripheral sightlines cut off by the rise of a thick and tall hedge. It was not a long span of hedge, maybe twenty paces at best, but it gave the effect that one was in a secret passageway, on an isolated journal, totally alone.

But he wasn't. Nathan greeted him when he emerged from the hedgerow.

"Baldwin." He was sitting on the stump. It appeared a struggle for him to lift his head and smile. "I'm grateful to see you," he said weakly.

"Likewise."

Baldwin eyed the entrance to the warm wash.

"Is Hetta inside?"

"She was, but she left."

Baldwin squinted to see Nathan more clearly. It was very dark out.

"Did she say if she was coming back?"

"She didn't say anything." Nathan paused. "Him either."

"Him?"

"It'll cost you a chit."

Baldwin realized he had not taken any chits with him.

"Sorry, I'm chitless."

Nathan shook his head with more resignation than dejection.

"I guess it doesn't matter, seeing how I have no more taste for impure. Hit me this morning. I woke up and said to myself, 'I don't want anymore ever.' And I mean it. The craving is gone. Maybe it means I'm going to die."

"We're all going to die."

"I mean soon. A man loses the desire for the one thing he has desire for, that's a bad sign."

"So you'll tell me his name."

"You could probably guess it anyway. It was Ramson. He came after her and then they both came out. She didn't look happy about it, if it means anything to you. Maybe he booked her for a touch date she doesn't want. He was handling her rough."

"Rough?"

"You know, encouraging her to move with something more than words."

"Do you know which way they went?"

Nathan looked at Baldwin as if he was daft.

"Only way out" – he pointed to the hedge row – "is to go through there. After that I wouldn't have a guess as to their direction."

Baldwin took in a breath. He was trying to think what might be his next move.

"So you gave up impure?"

"More like it gave up me."

Nathan looked down at his hands a moment, then at Baldwin.

"Maybe it was all that trouble last night. You know that was Hetta's husband with us last night. After we got thrown out we both ended up here. I guess he was looking for Hetta. Didn't find her and left. Hope he got home okay. He was really messed up from the impure and being thrown out of the club."

"I ran into him this morning."

"You talked to him?"

Baldwin nodded.

"So he was okay?"

Baldwin didn't answer.

"No matter. If he was up and moving, that's all that counts. Still, it's a terrible thing to be in a romantic union and feel unsettled. It's my opinion that the main advantage of a union is feeling settled, that there's at least one person in the world who you can count on no matter what. Then again, you can count on yourself and feel just as good. But when you don't have a person you can count on, and you can't count on yourself, then you're really in trouble. At least that's what happened to me. I went from my parents to a bad union and when it got really bad and we split I had no clue what to do with myself. So I took up with impure to fill the time. That's why I'll never talk bad about it – whatever bad the drink might have done to me, I could always count on it to clear away the loneliness. Or at least the fear of being alone, which is all the bite that loneliness really has."

Baldwin recognized the wisdom of Nathan's words. With Nadine frequently absent from the unit for long periods, he had been more troubled by the idea of loneliness than loneliness itself. Manu chided him whenever he brought up the subject at the office. As a single entity in the Circle, Manu's life was spent mostly in his own company. He thought it lunacy that Baldwin should be so distressed at having to spend a few hours alone waiting for Nadine. Manu's advice was not to wait, to go out and do something, even if it was nothing. "Go find some recreational grass to stretch out on," he advised. "Some of the most engaging times in my life have been spent in such repose, particularly if there are others around and talking. I just close my eyes and listen. Sometimes I get involved in the conversation in my mind. And if I'm really interested, I'll get up and go over and introduce myself and begin talking too."

But Baldwin had never given in to that sort of communal expression. His mother raised him to be private, and Leonard's controlling influence added to his reluctance to invite the attentions of strangers. And so he sat at night in wait of Nadine with mounting frustration, grinding his teeth until his jaw ached, pacing the unit, sometimes falling onto the bed and groaning in agony, as if her absence was inflicting physical pain

Nathan spat.

"I talk too much when I'm clean," he said. "When I drink impure I'm quiet as this stump."

The sound of footfalls caused them both to turn their heads toward the hedgerow. They were solid, even loud, as if someone was purposely stomping the ground hard to announce an arrival. An image emerged, a tall and lean man. In the darkness, he looked ethereal and kinetic, dressed all in white and walking with pronounced, straight lifts of his knees, so high they kissed his abdomen, before being brought down with a clean and sudden force. So hypnotic and interesting was his gait that Baldwin was surprised by the alacrity of his forward movement. He was on them in a blink.

"Is the girl without the ear here?" he said immediately to Nathan. "I need my feet touched."

"She's gone."

"Is she coming back?"

"I doubt it."

The man shook his head. He turned, seemed surprised to see Baldwin standing there.

"What are you doing here?"

Baldwin realized for the first time that it was Morris, from his building

"I came for the same thing as you."

"You got bad feet?"

"No, a bad wife."

"I don't understand."

"I came to see Hetta."

"Oh."

Nathan cleared his throat to interrupt.

"Best to come back in two days," he said. "No one is doing any utility tomorrow."

Morris spat angrily. "I wasted paces coming." He turned to Baldwin. "You see Simon today?"

"No."

"He still hasn't come back to his unit."

"You mean your neighbor?" Nathan said.

"You know him?"

"Sure. He came in with Baldwin the other day for a touch."

Baldwin flushed.

"I forgot to tell you that," he said to Morris.

"And last night we found his head?"

Baldwin winced at Nathan's words.

"Clear cut off and burning in a pit right behind us."

Morris lifted his right knee and landed his foot between Nathan's legs. His voice was menacing.

"What did you say?"

"I didn't do it. We" – he pointed at Baldwin – "were just going to spear some dear meat."

Morris twisted his head at Baldwin.

"Is this true?"

"Yes. I mean, it looked like Simon's head."

"Why didn't you tell me this earlier?"

"I guess I was scared. Maybe I thought you had something to do with it."

"Why would you think that?"

Baldwin shrugged.

Morris retreated from the old man. He concentrated his gaze on Baldwin.

"I knew something was wrong, and he owing me a mess of chits." He shook his head. "I almost barged into your unit before I came here. I heard your wife talking to someone and thought it might be Simon. But I listened and it wasn't him."

"You heard Nadine?"

"She has a high pitched voice, right?"

"I guess."

"Then it was her."

Baldwin licked at his lips.

"You didn't find out who she was talking to, did you?"

"I'm not rude. I don't go inside units without an invite unless I have a good reason. I listened to hear if it was Simon, and when I was sure it wasn't, I figured it was probably you. But I guess I was wrong." He looked at Baldwin with extra concentration. "You sure Simon's not breathing anymore?"

"Pretty sure."

"Maybe he owed someone not as patient as me."

"Maybe."

Morris paused.

"You going home?" he asked.

"I probably should."

"I'll walk with you. I don't like the way things feel right now. Probably safer to travel in pairs."

Baldwin nodded, although he wasn't worried about being harmed. His concern for the moment was tied up with Hetta. He smiled thinking how selfless he was being, how love was making him courageous, and then fell into step behind Morris, realizing, as they made their way through the hedgerow, that he didn't mind having company at all.

32 STRETCH MARKS

*T*he path they took home was well marked with white birch, so there was no trouble navigating in the darkness. Baldwin also had the brightly clothed Morris to follow, who seemed to fill the whole of the path with his peculiar but effective walking style. He also broke into song several times, short, rhyming verses that warned others coming the opposite way of their approach. One he repeated several times went, "Two men moving fast, far to the right, so stay to the left, and please hug it tight." He had an interesting singing voice, deeper than his speaking tone and more weathered, hinting at a wisdom born from deep and turbulent emotions.

As they neared their building, Morris slowed his pace and then came to a stop. He turned to Baldwin and frowned.

"I need to rest my feet."

"Okay."

Morris removed his sandals, revealing spindly toes that glowed white in the darkness. He leaned over and rubbed the bottom of his right foot, then the left. When he was done he returned the sandals to his feet and exhaled with relief.

"That's better," he said.

"They really hurt you?"

Morris nodded.

"It comes with the utility."

He raised his right arm overhead and grabbed a low hanging birch branch.

"So what did you think of my performance last night?" he asked.

"I don't remember much. I'd drunk a lot of impure. Did you win?"

Morris reached up with his left hand and grabbed the same branch. He arched his back as he pulled himself off the ground, rising all the way up until his chin touched the branch, before lowering himself and letting go of the branch.

"I won, but it means nothing. Well, maybe to some, but not me. I'd rather lose and hit the ground right, than win and hit it wrong. The other night my feet weren't hitting flush. The heel was connecting before the toes on my right, and the arch on my left collapsed altogether. I sounded like a joy drummer – you know the kind that sit outside all night banging sticks on slabs for chits. Not a whiff of rhythm, just noise. That's all I'm making with my feet anymore, noise."

Baldwin looked past Morris. He could see just enough ahead to where the turn in the path led past the rust field. He was as eager to get home as he was fearful. If Nadine was indeed there, there would be much to discuss and confront.

"I sort of remember you now," Morris continued. "I think Simon told me once about his neighbor getting hit by a deer. Was that you?"

"Yes. Near here."

"When did it happen?"

"About a year ago."

Morris whistled.

"That must have hurt?"

"I broke a few bones."

Morris whistled again. He cracked the knuckles on each hand without the aid of the other hand.

"My first utility was as a flight counselor," he said. "Our job was to go through a thicket or heavy woods and stomp our feet and yell and scare all the birds out of their nests and hiding spots and collect their eggs. I guess that's why I was reassigned to running in place exhibitions, given that I was better at stomping than spotting nests. Now and then we'd scare up a deer and they'd go careening around. One nearly rammed me from behind; the point of his antlers skimmed my neck. Another inch closer and they would have punctured my jugular."

"The one that hit me had a big rack."

"Did you see it coming?"

"At the last moment I saw his head, and then I was on the ground."

"You smell him?"

"Smell?"

"The deer. Did its scent get into your nostrils?"

"I'm not sure. I do remember tasting blood when it connected with me."

"Connected?"

"It's how my life counselor wants me to describe it; you know, to make it seem less violent."

"Seems like bad advice to me."

Morris stretched his arms again, but this time he clasped his hands together and bent sideways at the waist, lowering his arms while keeping them straight, looking somewhat like a poplar bent by a strong wind. He rose and repeated the motion on the right side, and then he rotated his shoulders. He saw Baldwin looking at him.

"You don't stretch?" he asked.

"Not often."

"You should, especially if you had injuries like you say. Take me, my feet are shot, so I keep everything else in perfect condition, that way I can compensate for the imperfection of my feet. What I'm saying is I keep the pain concentrated in one place; I give it no place to spread. And pain is like a weed, it wants to move and take root; it wants to take over."

"That woman I wanted to see at the warm wash, she told me my wounds would help my body. That pain gave it a reason to get stronger, you know, to overcome it."

Morris spat. He rolled his long neck in half-circles back and forth.

"I don't come to that conclusion, but maybe it's not wrong. I only know what's right for my body. And I know if I let that pain out of my feet it will take me over."

Baldwin paused a moment.

"So Hetta helped you with your feet?"

"Who?"

"The touch counselor. That's her name."

Morris shook his head.

"Hetta. I don't know why she wouldn't give me her name when I asked. I think sometimes genius comes with craziness, or maybe crazy people are just freer to exhibit their genius. Anyway, she had a genius in the way she touched my feet. It was like she inhabited them with her fingers; her touch went from the inside out, do you understand? But after she was done she treated me like I was the worst enemy she had. She brushed me out and wouldn't answer one question, just took a chit of thanks and got rid of me."

Baldwin exhaled. He thought of what the old man said, about Hetta being led away from the warm wash by Ramson.

"I penetrated her."

"Did you?"

Baldwin did not know why he shared this information. It was not to brag, to show another man his virility, his ability to conquer an attractive woman, but more to make real in his mind what really happened.

"Twice."

"Is that why you're having trouble with your wife?"

"What trouble?"

Morris smiled knowingly.

"Come on – you didn't even know she's home, who she's talking to, and that she was hanging all the time with Simon. I told you I'm perceptive to people in pain."

Baldwin decided to make it even more real.

"I'm going to break our union," he said. "After the Day of No Consequence. "I'm going to put in a claim to end it with Nadine and be with Hetta."

"You think she'll say yes?"

"Hetta, I think so."

"I mean your wife. You can't break a union without both parties agreeing to the break. That's what's encouraged."

"I forgot that."

"A good encouragement, if you ask me," Morris said. "I've never been in a union, but I've been around them enough to know that it's always one person in the union who wants out more than the other. The problem is it's usually the one who wants out that suffers in the end. The one left behind always does better. So if you help the one who wants to leave stay, you're helping them."

"I don't want to help Nadine."

"Then she'll probably suffer."

"Yes", Baldwin said, stretching his own arms and bending backwards, causing a warming release of tension in his back. "She probably will."

33 NOTE BOOK

*T*hey walked the rest of the way in silence. Perhaps thinking about the deer, Morris moved even faster once they came upon the rust field, so fast that Baldwin needed to skip to keep pace. By the time they got to the building's entrance Baldwin was winded, red-faced and gasping. He bent over and grabbed at his knees, spitting several times into the ground as he tried to fill his lungs with replenishing air.

"Don't fight for your breath," Morris advised, patting Baldwin between the shoulder blades. "Let it come back to you when it's ready. All you're doing is scaring your mind into thinking something is wrong with your body. Stand up and pretend you're fine."

"I'm not fine. I can't breathe."

"Of course you can. You just can't breathe well."

Baldwin straightened. He smiled with embarrassment.

"I'm not feeling very strong these days."

"I can see." Morris's flat lips curled into a twist of disgust. "How old are you?"

"Thirty three."

"Really?"

"I look that bad?"

"It's not that. I'm thirty-three too. I was born in the sowing season. What about you?"

"Growing."

"Figures," Morris said. "Grow babies are always soft."

"I'm not soft."

"It's not a criticism. I wish I was soft. Being hard hurts; you're never able to cushion a blow."

"Tell that to my deer."

Morris nodded.

"Maybe you're not so soft after all."

Baldwin's breathing regained normalcy. He eyed the front door of the building.

"I guess I'll head in."

"I'll follow you to your floor," Morris said. "I'm going to Simon's unit; see if I can find any chits hidden about." He paused, looked at Baldwin. "I'm not heartless or greedy, it's just that I don't like anything out of order, and a debt is a debt, dead or alive."

This time Baldwin led the way. His heart beat rapidly as he took the stairs, both from the exertion and the prospect of finally seeing Nadine and whoever Morris heard her speaking with. He waited for Morris to move down the hall and enter Simon's unit before pressing his ear close to the door. He heard nothing, considered knocking, stopped himself, set his shoulders, told himself it was his home, after all, and twisted the knob and pushed open the door with inspired bravado. It was dark and silent. He purposely shut the door behind, loudly, hoping to jar the attention of anyone inside.

"Nadine."

Despite his physical bluster, his voice sounded hollow and weak. He kept calling out her name as he checked each room, checked inside the lone closet, behind the coach, under the chairs, even inside the cabinets, as if she had been able to shrink in size, scattering plates, rustling cups, and opening and slamming shut every drawer.

Baldwin slumped into a chair. Shook his head at his momentary madness. Took in a breath. Exhaled. Wondered if he should go check on Morris, and then saw the edibles bag. It was placed neatly on the table's center. He reached out and parted the burlap opening. It was empty save for *The Book of Ash*. He pulled it out. It was a new copy, its cover shiny and unworn, the rims of the pages crisp and covered in a fine dust. A sprig of mint leaves stuck out from the book's middle. He opened to that page, removed the sprig and sniffed the leaves. They were supple to the touch, green as if still growing, fragrant.

Baldwin's eyes moved to the bottom of the page. In a wavy hand, in red ink, was written: *Don't try to find me.*

"I'm grateful to see you made it home…finally."

Baldwin dropped the sprig and turned.

Ramson entered the kitchen. He was not carrying his learning stick, nor was it attached to his belt. He also was not wearing the purple coloring of a conflict counselor. His lips were bare and pink, the underside of his eyes pale. In his right hand was a sickle, its handle wrapped in pink cloth. He had returned to his black leggings, but now wore a clear white shirt buttoned at the collar.

Baldwin scanned the table, the counter, looking for a knife, a plate, anything to grab and defend himself.

Ramson's eyes sparked with intuition.

"I can't believe you're still frightened of me," he said, resting the sickle on the table and sitting down in the other chair. "The last thing I want to do is harm you before you harm the person I want you to harm."

"I told you I'm not going to kill Leonard."

Ramson pointed at the sickle and smiled.

"Yes, you are."

"You're wrong."

Ramson exhaled wearily.

"I'd admire your resolve more if I wasn't in a hurry. Believe me, I'd much rather end conflict with talk than violence – for example, cutting someone's head off. But sometimes we can't be picky or selective in the method we choose to end a crisis. Am I right?"

Baldwin eyed the sickle. The blade was colored a deep red. Ernest's blood had fused into the metal.

"I didn't cut anyone's head off."

"I didn't say you did."

Ramson reached out, rubbed his right palm gently over the sickle's handle.

"I doubt you would own such an item given your rather cerebral utility," he said. "Or customize it in such a feminine manner."

Baldwin did not answer.

"But let's talk about something else for a moment," Ramson said, dragging his hand over his shirt. "Do you like the look? It's formal, I know, but so light and porous that if I left it on for a week my chest hair would grow right through the fabric. The guy who gave it to me didn't want to part with it, but I made him a fair trade: the clothes or a gratitude farm."

"That doesn't seem fair."

"Have you ever been to a gratitude farm?"

"No."

"Then you don't know what you're talking about."

Baldwin spied the counter again. In arm's reach was a wooden cutting board. It had a handle. He visualized grabbing it and swinging for Ramson's head.

"Where's Hetta?"

Ramson continued to rub the handle.

"Interesting that you ask about Hetta and not your wife. Why is that?"

"None of your business."

"But it is. Hetta works for me, not you."

"She loves me."

Ramson snorted.

"Every man she touches thinks she loves him. That's what makes her so good."

"It's more than that between us."

"Oh, you penetrated her. You think that's unique?"

"You're just trying to make me angry."

"No, I'm trying to test your heart. Because if you love her like you say, then you won't hesitate to do what I say."

"You don't understand," Baldwin replied, "there's no point to all this about Leonard. Even if I agree to kill him, I know I won't be able to go through with it when the time comes. And I don't believe you really know where he is."

"Oh, I see Hetta told you about Nadine. That was wrong of her to disclose."

"I told you, she loves me."

"Regardless," Ramson said, removing his hand from the sickle. "I'm not worried about the information. Nadine just confirmed it all again, and I choose to believe her."

"You spoke with Nadine?"

"I did indeed. Quite a talk we had. Sat right at this table before you came in and shared the edibles bag. Sorry about that if you're hungry. It was good too – dried rabbit ears and cucumbers. Nadine had a stash of mint that we chewed it down with. Wonderful for the digestion."

"Nadine put the book in the bag with the note?"

"Well, I didn't."

"Why would she do that?"

"Who knows with women?" Ramson shrugged. "Maybe she still loves you?"

"That's not a very good love note."

"Maybe she's not very good."

They were silent a moment.

"Where is Nadine now?" Baldwin asked. "Why isn't she here?"

"I guess she got excited when I agreed to kill you tomorrow. She probably ran off to tell Leonard the good news. At least, I hope so."

"So you are going to kill me?"

"Don't be daft, Baldwin. I only said yes to Nadine to protect you. This way she won't hire anyone else for the job." He paused, licked at his lips. "I got to say, if I liked women, I would like her. She's got that erotic madness that's very enticing. She actually wants me to cut off your penis when I'm done and bring it to her. I imagine she's quite evocative in bed. Too bad things didn't work out with your union."

"Yeah, too bad."

"Anyway, you have nothing to worry from me – as long as you do what we planned."

"I've planned nothing."

"Did I say you?" Ramson returned, annoyed. "You don't listen well. I said '*We*,' not you."

Baldwin hesitated.

"So who's this other person?"

"What makes you think it's just one? You don't think there are others who would like Leonard out of the Circle?"

"Don't include me in the group."

"You sound as if you feel sorry for him. He is penetrating *your* wife. Worst of all, he's penetrated your precious Hetta. And I don't doubt this double penetration will continue on as long as he continues on."

"Not Hetta. I don't care about Nadine. But Hetta knows how I feel about Leonard. She won't touch him again."

Ramson's lips flattened to a hard sneer.

"Maybe she will, maybe she won't," he said. "It really doesn't depend on her, but me. If I want her to touch Leonard, she will. If I want her to open her legs for him, she will. If I want her to drink his spit, she will. Do you get it?"

Baldwin twitched his fingers, measured with a glance the distance to the cutting board, the angle he would need to smash Ramson in the face with its hard edge.

"Why can't you just kill Leonard, or get one of the people you mentioned to kill Leonard? You know the place, you have the motivation. Go kill Leonard and leave me and Hetta alone."

"I told you why already. It has to be you."

"Well, find someone else."

"No. We keep to the plan. It all makes sense, don't you see? You kill Leonard because he's penetrating your wife. The people in the Circle will understand your motivation and not think Leonard's death has anything to do with ambition or ideology or my taking over as Mentor of Self Esteem."

"And if I don't kill Leonard?"

Ramson eyed the sickle.

"To start, I'll bring you in for killing Ernest. It's pretty clear, given I watched you leave Leonard's trailer with it in your hand and hide it in the dandelions."

"Then you also saw another person leave the trailer. A woman named Christine. She was Ernest's lover. She did it."

"Perhaps, but poor Christine is no longer breathing herself. It seems she plopped Ernest's head in a patch of mint and then bashed in her own head with a rock. Never saw such self-hatred before. It was very inspiring."

"You killed her."

"Only in that I didn't stop her. But I saw no conflict in the situation. A person has a mind to do something I let them do it, as long as it doesn't impact negatively on another person."

Ramson smiled.

"So you're the only living suspect in Ernest's death. And you have the motivation – you love Hetta and want him out of the way. Pretty simple explanation and judgment, if you ask me. And as you know, murderers, outside the Day of No Consequence, get the worst utilities inside a gratitude farm. No a pleasant way to finish one's time in the Circle."

"I don't care. I'll go to a farm rather than kill someone."

"Well, there's also Hetta," Ramson continued. "You don't kill Leonard, I kill her. It's as simple as that. Kill Leonard, and you and Hetta can enjoy as many sunrises and sunsets as your body will allow, or don't kill him, and spend your time in a gratitude farm while she spends her time in a place without time."

Baldwin made his move for the cutting board. He picked it up cleanly, swung and hit Ramson a glancing blow on his left shoulder. Before he could strike again Ramson pushed the table hard into his chest. He fell back into a cabinet, causing it to fall forward and crash to the floor.

"I told you I won't hurt you," Ramson seethed, rubbing his shoulder.

"You're going to have to."

Baldwin charged, but he was cut off ...not by Ramson, but Morris, who hurtled into the kitchen feet-first and connected with Ramson's chest. The blow knocked him down and seemingly unconscious.

"Are you okay?" Morris shouted to Baldwin.

"I think so."

Morris had his back to Ramson.

"Who is this guy?"

Before Baldwin could answer, Ramson was up. He grabbed the sickle off the table and slashed at Morris, sinking the blade deep into his neck. He yanked it out, swung again, and Morris's head was gone. His body crumpled a second later, his hands resting on Baldwin's feet.

Ramson pushed the dull curve of the blade into Baldwin's breastbone.

"What's your choice?" he said. "Who dies next – Leonard, Hetta… or you?"

Blood poured out of Morris' severed neck. Baldwin did not see where his head had gone.

"I don't want Hetta to die."

"And you?"

"I don't want to either."

"Then Leonard has to."

"Okay."

Ramson lowered the blade.

"We'll meet at sunrise tomorrow," he said, "at Big Birch. We'll go from there to Leonard's hiding spot. That way I can make sure you do as you say, or at least try to. And just for extra motivation, I'll bring Hetta with me. That way you can see what you'll gain if you succeed… or what you'll lose if you fail."

"You don't have to involve Hetta. Leave her out of this. Trust me, I'll do it."

"I don't trust her," Ramson said. "Just to make it clear you know I'm not just having a bit of fun with you, I'll have Hetta close at hand until we meet again. Not that I desire a woman's touch, but it's always nice to have companionship, don't you think?"

Ramson smiled, dropped the sickle on Morris's chest.

"And I'd think about getting rid of this body. One murder is bad enough, but two is the kind of thing that draws all sorts of attention – particularly in a gratitude farm."

Baldwin did not say anything as Ramson walked out of the kitchen. He waited until he heard the door open and shut, and then slumped to the floor. He put his hands over his eyes and held the pose for several minutes, then leaned back against the fallen cabinet, took in a breath, and looked across the kitchen. There, on the floor, propped against the floorboard, was Morris's head. Baldwin began to scream, a long, involuntarily wail that ended with him out of breath and gasping. He looked again at Morris. He knew what he needed to do, what he wanted to do. He picked up the sickle and ran.

34 HOME SPUN

Manu's door was missing. That was odd. Odder was the bed sheet that covered the frame. It was dark blue with red stripes. A circular hole cut out at eye level broke the pattern. Baldwin put his face to the hole and called out Manu's name.

"In here," came back his friend's voice. "I'm in the bedroom."

Baldwin placed the sickle against the doorjamb and pushed through the sheet. He was greeted with a gentle, sucking wind. It was coming from a massive hole gouged out of the wall in the conversation room. Under the hole was a neat pile of debris, splintered wood, plaster chips, and torn strips of pink insulation. He moved into the bedroom. Manu was sitting on the bed, cross-legged, another sheet of the same pattern laid out before him. He did not look up from his work, which appeared to be stabbing holes in the linen.

"What are you doing?"

Manu glanced up at Baldwin and then returned his concentration to the knife. He was working in a crossways pattern, quick thrusts that forced the blade through the sheet and into the bedding below. Tiny puffs of white down rose up whenever he pulled out. Baldwin noticed that Manu's head was white with the material. It gave him the appearance of a much older man.

"I'm ventilating this sheet," he said. "What are you doing?"

"I came to ask you a question."

Manu finished a row, pulled out the knife, set it a few inches below the line he had just completed, and began to stab again, in the opposite direction.

"Did you see the improvements?"

Baldwin narrowed his eyes as he looked over and past Manu. He hadn't noticed it when he first came in, but he saw now that the glass panes in the room's window had been removed, and not neatly, as a low row of shards stuck out like serrated teeth from around the frame.

"I'm making it easier for energy to move in and out of the unit," Manu continued.

"Why?"

Manu made a new stab and let the knife stick. It had a long black handle shaped to conform to a hand. He blew out his cheeks as if exhausted.

"To get Ramson to love me again," he said. "I've been doing what you said: not pushing him, being patient. But nothing is happening. He hasn't come over or contacted me. I can't wait any longer. But what I'm doing will help him come to me."

"I don't understand."

"That's because it's complicated. I just figured it out a few hours ago. You see, I'm blocked up. My mind is a prison. It's why I have seizures. I have all these thoughts and problems that can only get out when I'm having a fit. You see, unlike most people, I evolved emotionally as a child. I became self aware at an early age, and so I didn't need a subconscious to store away for later anything I couldn't handle. As a result my conscious self became strong and dominant. It makes for a pretty stable life, but not an interesting one."

Baldwin tried to follow Manu's words, but his own interests in coming to see his friend filled his thoughts. He worried how he would ask Manu to give him Ramson's building and unit location without letting him know his plan was to go over and kill him and save Hetta.

"You're not listening to me."

Baldwin blinked his eyes fast.

"Yes I am."

"What did I say?"

"Everything is locked inside your brain."

"Okay. You were."

Manu thrust the knife into the sheet and began ripping a line in the linen.

"It doesn't matter," he said. "It's hard to understand if you can't feel it. All I know is there are negative things inside me waiting to get out. And the sooner they leave the more able I'll be to let Ramson in. I realize now I pushed him away because there's no room. My energy is like a wall against love. Ramson's energy felt it. That's why he's not with me right now. Our energies didn't make a connection."

Manu pulled out the knife and looked at the sheet a moment, then cut into it again.

"Since I took out the door and made the holes, I can feel a release," he continued. "It almost feels like a tooth is being pulled out of my head. You watch, any moment my message is going to pop out, all that energy will be released, and Ramson will come running to me and we'll fall in deep love for ever and ever."

"Manu," Baldwin interrupted, "I need some information."

"What?"

"Do you remember the woman you met at Ramson's unit?"

Manu pulled out the knife and looked up at Baldwin.

"Of course."

"I need to find her, but I don't know where she lives, but I'm sure Ramson does. But I don't know where Ramson lives. So I need you to tell me."

Manu shook his head.

"I don't want you going over there until my energy is right. You're my best friend and an extension of me. It will set things back."

"It's really important I see this woman tonight."

"Why?"

Baldwin blinked fast.

"Someone wants to hurt her on the Day of No Consequence and I need to warn her to hide."

"I don't know."

"I need you to give this to me." He paused. "I love her."

Manu's shoulders slumped.

"Promise you'll just ask Ramson where she lives and then leave right away. Don't say anything more and give your energy a chance to connect. Even stand a few feet back away from the door when you talk to him. Promise me."

Baldwin bowed his head. He could not look his friend in the eye.

"I promise."

"He lives in Building Four, Unit 4, Section 4. Isn't it remarkable, given how I feel about the number? Can't you see how perfect we would be together, at least numerically?"

Baldwin watched as bits of down fell from his friend's hair.

"You're a good friend, Manu."

"You say that like you won't see me ever again."

"I'm just grateful for you."

Manu looked up.

"Don't be so dramatic."

Then he began slicing away again at the sheet.

35 NIGHT FALL

*B*aldwin left Manu, stopped outside the door and picked up the sickle, and went down the stairs. He paused a moment outside to gather
his thoughts, chief of which was the location of Ramson's unit. If he
remembered correctly from what Hetta told him during her miracle
claim, Ramson resided in her building, just two floors above. Their living proximity made some sense – perhaps it was the reason Ramson
had latched onto her to perform outside touch sessions. But still he felt
suspicious, even paranoid, that Hetta and Ramson were not entirely at
odds, that they had a long and complex relationship, an intimacy even
he knew nothing about.

   He started to walk. There was no one else on the path he traveled.
This was not odd: most people in the Circle were not inclined to stay
outdoors once the moon had passed its highest point. Only those with
specific duties that encouraged them to be up and moving, such as
nightshade counselors who tended over the plants that grew only in
darkness, or those with a taste of impure and urge for company, who
frequented the conversation clubs, were usually about at such an hour.
Baldwin, himself, was not used to being up so late. Despite the urgency
of his mission, fatigue began to pull at him, his body finally beginning
to come down after the large dose of adrenaline poured into it since
Morris's murder.

   Baldwin estimated it to be a three thousand pace walk to Ramson's
building, at least a half hour if he moved at his normal gait, and counting in his head, stopped at one thousand paces for a break. He found a
flat rock a few feet off the path suitable for sitting. The moon had broken free from some overhead clouds, casing a soft, bluish light around
him. The light was so peaceful-looking and purifying that he thought,
not necessarily morbidly, that this would be a fine place to end one's
breathing – sitting alone, in the focus of the moon, enveloped by quiet.
He thought about what his mother liked to say about a final resting
place: "Where you want to be buried is where you should live. And
I want to be buried in the Circle." It was true, she loved the Circle,

a feeling he envied, since he never felt the same allegiance. Not that he had ever rebuked or made claims against the Circle, but he never shared her passion, her commitment, or her faith in the governing system of encouragement or the reliance on recycled, found goods. The one thing he did find time to reflect on and admire in the Circle was the dirt, the reclaimed soil, which, to his eyes, glistened with appreciation after being freed from its blanket of smothering, choking debris. Perhaps it was also why he so disliked rust fields, which had no hope of reclamation, the dirt, every particle of it, infected with the orange, metal silt, its ability to spark life taken, lost without utility, impotent and angry.

His weariness took stronger hold. Baldwin massaged the back of his neck to relieve its stiffness. Feeling his own touch reminded him of what he had to gain or lose if he didn't continue on, if he didn't kill Ramson and take Hetta away. He gave his neck a last squeeze and stood. The air had cooled and he took in a long breath, stretching his arms and arching his back. A soft cracking in his spine brought added relief. He straightened and took in another deep pull of air. It was time to move.

He remembered not long ago being fearful of the dark, a childhood phobia carried into adulthood. It was never a paralyzing fear; as a child he did not cry or carry on whenever darkness fell upon the Circle, although he made sure each night to wrap tight in his sheet, mummifying his entire body in linen, except for a small air hole he created with help from his mother's scissors. Logic told him, even at an early age, that the sheet was a useless defense against whatever horrible person or thing might be inclined to attack him, but still he could not bear to close his eyes and relax into sleep without having at least one layer between him and the unknown. By his teen years, he had gained some control of the fear and no longer slept in such a self-suffocating environment, but he still suffered with unease each night, fidgeting fitfully in his cot against a windowless wall, while Leonard and his mother, behind a closed door on the trailer's other end, seemingly slept peacefully.

The fear, at least the sleeping part of it, fell away once he moved out of the trailer and into the unit with Manu. Perhaps it was due to a newfound freedom that made him bold, or the idea that another male was in the house to protect him, although having Leonard about all those years had not given him any comfort. Or it could have been as simple as having other things on his mind, like meeting women and making new friends and learning about his utility, which were infinitely more interesting and exciting to him than what might be lurking in the darkness. And then Nadine swept into his emotions with a force that forced out all others, invading his phobias, nascent as they were, with an attacking claw. She dug through his psyche in fast motion, dredging out his fears, all his feelings, really, in all-night talks and fumbling sexual encounters, stomping them to bits with tales of her own tortures growing up, until his travails inside Leonard's trailer seemed trivial, even pleasant in comparison to her experiences.

In short, he replaced his problems for Nadine's. For a time he felt himself healed, having released his own pain by taking on Nadine's. But it was a short-lived solution, and the novelty of the experiment wore off at about the same time his subconscious caught wind of the deal and rebelled against it. The result was a crushing anxiety, punctuated by unwanted thoughts of life and death and what it all meant, and a return, each night, of the fear he had felt certain to have excised for good.

This anxiety, after its initial burst into bloom, gratefully abated over time, but it never totally dissipated, becoming almost like a low-grade fever, a constant tug at his adrenals, and a dampening cloth on his enjoyment, his ability to be present, to enjoy the little and wonderful things he knew he should be enjoying. He never thought to blame Nadine for this discomfort, this nagging cough of emotion, perhaps because he never thought it could be removed, or go away, or be returned to its original home in his psyche. He accepted the anxiety as he accepted every unwelcome thing in his life: with solace, some sulking, and a voiceless, simmering, anger.

But here he was, at a breaking point, a desperate time, with an absent wife engaged in unfaithful acts with his dreaded stepfather, a man who stole his mother from his life, drove her away from his heart, divided their love, leaving him alone and powerless, a victim by his teen years, defenseless as an adult. He blamed Leonard for this past, but it was Ramson who governed his present.

Baldwin tracked his thoughts away from the dark, from his fears, his laments, his frustrations, his life, and raised a more practical question: how to cut Ramson's head off? The two options, as he saw it, were to knock on Ramson's door, and when he opened it deliver a deadly blow. Or he could wait until he was sure Ramson was sleeping, gain entry into the unit, and do what he needed to do to ensure the conflict counselor never woke up. He considered this to be the more prudent choice, as it relied more on stealth and cunning and less on skill and strength. Basically, he'd prefer to kill Ramson with his eyes closed than open.

Set on his plan, he moved closer. When the building came into view, he stopped again, squatted down and studied it. It did not take much deduction to locate the position of Ramson's unit. The structure was narrow and compact with a line of evenly spaced windows, ten, to be exact, starting a few feet from the ground and ending a few feet from the roof. The window at eye level was framed in candlelight. Baldwin kept to a hunch, staying below the window ledge, so that he came up to it unseen. He sneaked a glance. The unit was tiny, a box-like space, with kitchen, conversation room, and sleeping area open to each other. He quickly pulled his head back when he spied a woman sitting cross-legged on a middle spot on the floor. He did not wait to see if she noticed him, darting away and walking the rest of the building's perimeter in the same hunched over fashion. There were no windows on any of the other sides, just the front, and he determined that each floor most likely contained a similar, singular unit.

He retreated, finding a safe spot to stand and study the front of the building behind a thicket of bamboo. He counted his way up the windows until he reached the fourth floor. There was light from inside and Baldwin watched nervously as a shape passed by the window.

"I'm coming for you," he said, surprised by the viciousness in his voice. He squeezed tight the pink felt around the sickle's handle. "I'm coming."

And with his words passing through the shielding bamboo and into the night air, the light in the window vanished.

36 WAX WORKS

*B*aldwin parted the bamboo and made his way to the building's entrance. The door had no knob, just a hole where the knob should be, and a loop of wire stuck out. Baldwin pulled on the wire and the door swung open grudgingly, grating against the tiled floor, noise he did not want to make. He decided not to close the door and risk more sound. The lobby was narrow enough that he could, if he wanted to, touch both sides with his arms outstretched. But he didn't want to and so moved with quiet care to the stairwell.

He no longer felt fatigue. He hardly felt anything; even the sickle in his hand ceased to make an impression on his senses, just another part of this body in motion. The stairway was made of a clean white marble that matched the walls. It was cool and smooth to the touch, without the faintest sign of dust. This maintenance extended to the lighting; someone had taken time to place new candles at the entrance to each floor. They were set on attractive wooden stools adorned with a prim doily to catch the wax. Next to the candles was placed a glass goblet filled with shiny-colored stones. Baldwin remembered the same adornment in Hetta's room at the warm wash, remembered how he thought it a simple yet elegant aesthetic. He liked the style.

Thinking of Hetta quickened his steps. It propelled his resolve, imagining what would happen to her if he did not carry out his plan to end Ramson's breathing. Still, it was quite an undertaking, killing a man, taking his life, ending his thoughts. Harold had warned him of the consequence on his own thoughts, on his soul, his ability to function without guilt, without worry, without feeling.

But he was done worrying about his future, or at least his future as it might be if he did nothing. Doing nothing had taken him to this point, or at least to the point before Hetta came into his miracle office. He was moving without moving before that, following the beat of another's heart, first his mother's, who he adored, and then Leonard's, who he despised, and on to Nadine, who he adored and despised. He had no mixed feelings about Hetta, at least for the moment. Logic told him that there was much to be suspicious of regarding her sudden involvement in his life, in her dealings with Ramson, her hatred for Ernest. But it meant nothing to Baldwin, not while climbing the stairs with the intent to commit murder, to render a man breathless, all in the name of capturing a woman's heart and keeping it close to his. It meant nothing – any real doubts he had about her, any doubts he had in his ability to take such a decisive action, to risk unending guilt, horrifying lament, a blackened soul – because Hetta had gotten inside. She had penetrated him. It was as simple as that; she had replaced Nadine, perhaps the moment he saw her sitting in his office, her eyes tearing, her missing ear breathing scar tissue, the slope of her breasts, the gentle blond color of her hair. It was something no one could ever describe, this immediate hold that develops with a look, with a smile, a sniff. Harold credited it to instinct, survival, the ability to spot a partner, a like-minded soul, a friend, a lover, a champion who will follow you wherever you will follow them. He often said it was a great emptiness in his life not to have such a person by his side, which always hurt Baldwin, because he would be there, was there, at least once a week. Baldwin knew that about himself: he was fiercely loyal, stubbornly so; it was probably what kept him silent and suffering with Nadine; certainly with his mother. He could not abandon her to Leonard, even though the desire to run away from life in the trailer, flee its oppression, suppression, the cruelty and coldness, he could not. Only when he was forced out of the home by the Circle, encouraged, that is, to leave and take on a utility did he finally break free, at least physically, since his thoughts, his emotions, his heart was still with her, his beloved mother, in that trailer, alone with Leonard.

He stopped to gather himself on the third floor. He could not rid himself from thinking about his mother, about how pretty she was when she was young. He remembered how proud he was when people would comment about their similar appearances; that he had his mother's skin, her gentle eyes, the common blackness of their hair. But she had grayed quickly, her skin losing its vitality, her hair becoming brittle, her eyes suspicious. He blamed Leonard for this deterioration; he did not think it a product of years adding up, but of the stress he inflicted upon her, the stress of placing a barrier between her and her son. That was Leonard's true crime, Baldwin thought, coming between a mother and her son. That was evil, that was heartless, that was against nature, against instinct, against survival. Or perhaps it was nature, instinct, survival, driving Leonard to beat down his foe, the threat to his security, his need for love. Because his mother did love Leonard, adored him, something Baldwin did not understand, or agree with, but accepted as true.

But he knew that his mother's admiration for Leonard paled to what she felt for her son. Even if she did not show it, even if she shirked from exhibiting love, affection, maternal care for him as the years progressed under the ever-watchful eye of Leonard, Baldwin knew, or at least he believed, his mother to be zealous in her devotion to her son. Often he was tempted to ask her to decide, to make a choice, to pick either Leonard or he to love, but he never could muster the courage, or perhaps he did not want to make life any harder for her than it was, and so he contented himself to believe in her as he wanted to believe in her, which was without doubt, without animosity, and without regret.

He was about to move when the door on the floor opened. A woman stepped out. Her face and bare breasts were covered in black mud. A thin belt was looped around her waist. He red hair was tied up tight atop her head in a ball. She blinked hard at Baldwin, her green eyes shining out of the dark mask.

"I'm sorry," she said, hugging her arms over her bosom. "I didn't think anyone was out here. I came to blow out the candle."

Baldwin blushed. She had an excellent figure.

"I'm just visiting someone," he said.

"Let me guess, you came to see Hetta?" her voice dripped with disgust.

Baldwin hesitated.

"Yes"

"Well, you have the wrong floor."

Baldwin thought fast.

"This isn't number two."

"No. It's three. But she's on four. The next level up."

"Oh."

"Besides, she's not home."

"How do you know?

"Trust me, I know when she's home."

"I imagine her husband is loud?"

"What husband?"

"You must know Ernest?"

She shook her head.

"I'm not sure you have the right person. These are all single units. The Hetta that lives here isn't in a union. And if she was, I don't think her husband would appreciate her having so many visitors each night, if you know what I mean."

Baldwin felt a stab of panic.

"The Hetta I know is missing an ear."

"That's her then, I guess."

"Maybe I was mistaken about her having a husband."

She shrugged again.

"Can I ask if a conflict counselor named Ramson lives in the building?"

He thought he saw a flash of fear in her eyes. She looked at the floor as she spoke.

"I'm not encouraged to answer questions like that."

"I don't understand."

She pushed past, snuffed out the candle, and returned to the doorway. She let her breasts hang free. Her eyes, for the first time, seemed to take in the sickle in his hand.

"You know," she said, stepping back inside the unit, "tomorrow is the Day of No Consequence, not tonight."

She closed the door with a hard snap.

Baldwin waited a moment, thinking what to do. Logic grabbed at him, imploring him to leave, to abandon his plan to kill Ramson, to forget about Hetta, that she was not who she seemed to be, or perhaps she was exactly what she seemed to be, and it was merely his unwillingness, or the desperation of his desires, to see the reality of her character. But a more powerful force pushed him up the stairs, a far stronger pull than logic: anger. He hated Ramson, that was true, but now he was angry with him. Hetta, too – he felt betrayed, although he was not sure what exactly her betrayal constituted. He decided to go to the unit.

Baldwin climbed the flight of stairs. Light inched out from under the doorframe. He decided not to wait, not to be stealth. He opened the door and rushed inside, the sickle held high overhead. The woman below was right: there was no one inside. There was nothing, really, inside – no bed, no table to eat, no chairs, nothing that indicated a place of living. But despite its bareness of furniture, it did not feel barren. He walked the room, saw now that the floor held various rugs of different sizes and shapes and textures. They were laid out in a ragged pattern, fat and squatty shags, matted sheets of bamboo, ropey knots of fabric, each rug placed, seemingly, next to their opposite extreme, so that each, in a way, stood out uniquely, although the conglomerate, oddly, was not displeasing to the eye. Baldwin thought he had never seen such a magnificent floor covering in his life. The walls, too, particularly in the candlelight, were warm with color, each painted a different hue, so that he saw, moving in a circle from left to right, red, white, blue, and, directly opposite the door, the wall with the lone window in the unit, a startling black.

He did see now that there was one table, small and low like a children's desk, and under that an equally tiny chair. He strode to the desk and rested the candle upon it. There was already another candle there, nearly disintegrated from use, its edges curled downward in falling positions, in a beautiful, still surrender. It sat upon a translucent square of wax, its edges clearly defined, made so with care. There were matches next to the candle and he lit it. He eyed the mound of wax. It was molded over an object within. He used the butt of his hand to nudge it free from the desk, lifted it to his eyes. *The Book of Ash* was trapped inside.

Baldwin cracked the wax on the desk corner. The cover came off and fell to the floor. So did a piece of paper behind it. He picked it up. Written in large black letters was *The New Book of Ash*. He set it down on the desk and turned the page. The first encouragement —'A penis is only sated when limp'— was crossed out. Under was written a new sentence, in small caps, a beautiful and precise script, with words alternating in color, the same red, white, blue and black order as the four walls surrounding him. It read: 'A penis is never limp unless sated.'

Baldwin squeezed himself into the chair and poured through the book. Like the first, the remaining encouragements were crossed out and replaced with a new entry, written in the same exquisite hand, in the same color pattern. The rest of the wording for each encouragement and reaction step were intact, but there were marks and edits in the margin, made in a light pencil, indicating someone was at work to change these as well.

He did not know how long he had been reading, had not heard the moonrise gong if it had been struck, but was sure it was late. The light outside, the darkness, that is, was different than when he sat down, as if being tapped on the shoulder by the sun, which Baldwin always thought of as a bully, begrudging allowing the night and its patrons, the moon and stars, to show themselves, but really only as a sideshow, an intermission, before it rose again and dominated the stage. He thought suddenly of Leonard. He was like the sun – always there, even when he wasn't. He had not thought about Leonard in some time, fixated on Ramson and Nadine as villains. But perhaps they were just moon and stars, bit players behind the ultimate ruler. He shirked the thought. It was no time to think. He needed to move.

He wormed his way out of the chair. Headed to the door. Stopped. Heard a man's breathing coming from the other side. The knob twisted, the door pushed open, he stepped back, raised the sickle…

It was Nathan. The old man screamed at the sight of Baldwin, and then fainted, landing with a thud on the floor, the vial in his hand rolling free, leaking a line of dirty liquid as it made its way across the room.

37 FLOP HOUSE

*N*athan came back to life with a cough. He followed with a belch, spit up some yellow bile, and then struggled to sit up. His eyes looked confused as he looked around the unit. Baldwin had lit some more candles while the old man was passed out.

"You scared me," he said, finding Baldwin's eyes, his own still unsteady. "What are you doing here?"

"I came to find someone. What about you?"

"To hide out for the day."

"Why here? Why not your own unit?"

"This is my unit…I mean sometimes. I loan it out for chits now and then."

"To who?"

Nathan looked away.

"That same guy we talked about."

"Ramson."

"You said it, not me. All I know is that he gives me a vial of impure three times a week to stay away from the unit until after the moonrise gong…sometimes even later."

Baldwin eyed the fallen vial.

"I thought you gave it up," he said.

"I guess I reconsidered the idea."

Nathan eyed the sickle.

"Who you were planning to whack with that thing?"

"I thought Ramson lived here."

The old man scratched hard at the end of his nose.

"I could use some impure," he said.

"I'm sorry I made you drop it."

"Forget it. Maybe it's a sign I should stick to my plan and not take in another drop." He pointed at the vial. "That was going to be my first sip since my last one."

He paused.

"What you want to mess with Ramson anyway? That's a dangerous person to be playing with. What's your point – other than that blade?"

"I want to stop him from hurting someone."

"Who?"

"Hetta."

"Oh."

Nathan managed to get on his feet. He took in a long breath and exhaled.

"I'm going to sleep," he said. "You look tired too. I don't know how far your unit is, but you're welcome to stay here and sleep to sunrise. You can stay longer if you want. I'm not ashamed to say I don't mind company tomorrow. There's nothing worse than staying home alone on the Day of No Consequence – except maybe staying home alone and having someone come after you. Anyway, you were kind to me the other night, lending me chits and all, the least I can do is give you shelter."

The old man's tenderness unwound him. He had been moving atop a tide of anger and rage at Ramson and worry for Hetta, but that fuel was nearly spent. An urge to cry overtook him, and so he did, first a leaking from the eyes, and then a full on sob, strong enough that he struggled to catch his breath. He finally bent over and laid down on the floor, weeping with all his might, his face a mess of mucus and tears, his body shaking in spasms, a seizure of emotion. He did not remember when he stopped crying, but he remembered the soft sheet being stretched over him, the pillow being inserted under his head, and, shortly after, Nathan's gentle snoring not far from where he lay, a sound that took him away from this pain, away from thought, away from everything but the floor, the night, and the powerful pull that is sleep.

ENCOURAGEMENT 100-PLAN TO LOSE CONTROL

Human are animals of the highest order. Like animals, our instincts, our desires, are pure and healthy; in fact, they ensure our survival. If we obey them we will not poison the things that keep us alive. We will kill, but we will not wipe out. We will maim, but we will not obliterate. We will have sex, but we will not rape. Wild we will be reborn. Our minds will expand. We will become stronger. We will love greater. We will feel better. We are dying now. It is not far away – our total extinction. Instinct and desire will save us.

Reaction Step: One day a year, follow all of your instincts and sate all of your desires, no matter how destructive and damaging the resulting actions may be to yourself or to others. After, if you are still alive, start making plans for the following year.

38 BACK STRETCH

*B*aldwin woke with the clang of the sunrise gong. His back was stiff from the floor. His shoulder ached. Nathan, a few feet away, snored loudly.

Baldwin ran his hand through his hair, thought it felt brittle, and rolled his neck, wincing at the cracking noise it produced. A hard light was already streaming in through the window. It made the room appear even smaller than it was. He cleared his throat, coughed, groaned as he stood and stretched, stomped his right foot, then his left, then both. Still the old man snored.

Baldwin walked stiffly to the sink. A basin below held a thin layer of yellowish water. He didn't trust its look to drink, but braved a splash on his face. He also wet his hair, slicked it back with his hands. The light from the window began to dominate the room. It reached where Nathan slept, crept up his legs, past his waist and chest, until hitting his face. Baldwin watched as the old man's eyes fluttered under the energy. Then they opened.

"What are you doing here?" Nathan flared his nostrils. His eyes held nothing but confusion. His lips seemed to have trouble forming words. "We went to a conversation club together?"

"No. I mean, we did, but not last night. I was here when you came home. I was waiting for Ramson."

"Now I remember, you made me knock over my impure."

"Yes. I'm sorry."

"Don't be. I'm glad it happened. One sip I would have been right back at it. But now I'm dedicated again to a clean life."

"That's good."

"I suppose so, except it won't be easy. The thing I'll miss about impure is it helped me not to think about all the bad things I've done. But I guess the bad things I've done are because of the impure. I don't know, I just hate to think about all that thinking."

"I understand," Baldwin said. "But you'll make it."

Nathan exhaled. His eyes began to gain some level of comprehension. They hit on the sickle on the floor and widened.

"You really meant to hit Ramson with that thing?"

"Yes."

"Tell me why again."

"Because he wants to kill someone I love."

"The touch counselor?"

Baldwin nodded.

"Hetta."

Nathan pushed his lips out in disbelief.

"It doesn't make sense," he said. "I mean, she works for him, makes him chits, seems funny he would want to end her breathing."

"It's complicated."

"And I'm not?" Nathan smiled. "Indulge me with something complicated. It might take my mind off impure."

Baldwin exhaled through his nose.

"Basically, Ramson wants me to kill my stepfather. And he thinks he can use Hetta's life as barter to get me to do it."

"Who's your stepfather?"

"Leonard Living."

Nathan's eyes narrowed. He spat hard to the floor, took in a breath, and shook his index finger at Baldwin.

"Now that's a good man," he said. "Always planning for the future."

"You like him?"

"Not at all. I hate all good people. That is, I hate people who care about the future. Maybe that makes me a hypocrite, since I'm giving up impure to live a clean life, but I'm not worried about tomorrow, or the next minute, just this one, this clean moment. You see how nice I am now. That's what you become when you live moment to moment."

"Regardless," Baldwin said, "I need to meet Ramson at Big Birch this morning and kill him."

"You say it like it will be easy."

"I know it won't."

"For sure. He's not the type of person to die because you want him to."

Nathan eyed the sickle again.

"You sure Hetta's worth it?" he asked.

"I told you I love her."

"Well, I guess you have the motivation."

Baldwin took in a breath. He walked over and picked up the sickle.

"I guess it's time I go."

Nathan held up a hand.

"Maybe I can come with you and help."

"Why would you do that?"

"I'm not sure. Maybe with my head clear of impure I want to do something good…or bad, whatever way you see it."

"I appreciate it," Baldwin said. "But I don't see how you can help with this."

"At least I can help you make a plan." Nathan said. "Ramson's not someone to be taken down easily. How were you thinking of doing it?"

"I thought I might sneak up on him and chop his head off."

"That won't work. Ramson's not the type to get sneaked up on. Especially today."

Baldwin looked at the sickle.

"What other way is there?"

Nathan reached under a rug and pulled out a knife. It had a thin black handle and a thinner blade. It did not look like much of a weapon.

"Carry this in your pocket," he said, twirling the knife. "When you see Ramson you go up to him like nothing's wrong, like you're happy to see him. Then when his guard's down, pull the knife out and stick it into his gut."

"I'm not sure."

"Don't worry," Nathan said, as if intuiting Baldwin's doubt about the knife. "This will do the job. I've cut meat, bark, plenty of hard things with it."

He handed Baldwin the knife.

"That's a lucky blade," Nathan continued. "I don't even know how I got it. I was drinking impure for about two straight days and when I came out of the whole thing I was lying in bed with that in my hand."

"Why is it lucky?"

The old man paused.

"Like I said, I've done some bad things in the past."

Baldwin did not like the idea of stabbing Ramson. Slicing his head off with the sickle, while horrifically violent, still seemed less daunting a task, at least less intimate. Stabbing Ramson required a closeness of contact, a pressing together, a moment when he would have to face the reality of the work that made the whole thing seem untenable.

"Actually," Nathan said, frowning. "It would be best to get him in the back. Punch it in right between the shoulder blades. Then pull it out, and if you can, stretch him back a bit, and then shove it into his neck. So maybe we should try to figure out a way to sneak up on him."

Nathan studied Baldwin's face.

"You sure Hetta is someone you want to do all this for? I don't mean to put anyone down, but she's touched a lot of men, and maybe not all of them for chits."

Baldwin smoothed his fingers over the knife's handle, over the subtle grooves made near the base.

"I won't say it again: I love her."

"But do you like her? I haven't thought about this in some time, and I certainly haven't been with a woman in a romantic way longer than that, but I do recall thinking when I did that it was more important to like someone you want to be with forever than to love them. I actually remember getting some advice from my life counselor on it. He wasn't a bad sort but he wasn't very good at the job. His problem was staying focused; he could never sit still when we met, jumping up and pacing the room, moving furniture, cleaning things, even punching walls, he was quite erratic. But every now and then he gave me something to use, like the thing on like and love."

"What did he say about it?"

"If I recall, he said that love was like a fever, flaming up and cooling down. He compared it to having an infection, you know, something that gets into you and stays, something you can't get out just by waiting for it to leave. He said like is lighter but more consistent, I remember that's how he described it. That you seldom like who you hate, or hate who you like, but you often love who you hate, and hate who you love."

"I never hated anyone until Ramson. He's the first person I can openly say I hate and not feel bad about it."

"Ramson's someone to hate for sure. But be careful with that. Hate, I mean. Too much hate and you're liable to lose your head. You need to be calm and calculating if you want to stab him right." He smiled shyly. "I think need is a better motivation to do desperate things, at least in my experience."

"Is that why you let Ramson use your unit?"

"Sure," Nathan said. "I needed him to give me chits and not beat me up with his learning stick every time I saw him. That's a good need."

"You never wanted to get back at him?"

"That's the nice thing about impure. It takes away any desire for revenge, any desire for anything, really, other than consuming it. But now I think I wouldn't mind, as you say, 'to get back at him.' I guess that's why I gave you the knife. And the advice."

"Maybe you'd like to help me more?"

"How so?"

Baldwin lowered his eyes and spoke, somewhat ashamed.

"I distract him from the front, while you come in from the back."

"You want me to stab him?"

Baldwin continued to look at the floor.

"I don't think I can do it," he said.

Nathan lowered his hand. His lower lip sagged. He took in a breath.

"I suppose I could do it, but I don't know exactly if I want to. I mean, I don't like Ramson and how he's treated me, but killing him seems a bit much. I would agree to hitting him over the head with something hard, like a rock, knock him out for a while."

"I'm sorry I asked."

"Nathan took in a loud breath. He tapped his foot on the floor a few times and then clapped his hands decisively.

"Tell you what," he said. "I'll distract him. At least that way you have a better chance of poking him right where you need to get him."

Baldwin raised his head. He was surprised by the old man's eyes – the new energy they held. He suddenly looked vibrant. Somehow, it made Baldwin feel guiltier for involving him in the plot.

"I appreciate your offer, but if I don't kill him, say he overpowers me or gets away, he'll come after you too."

Nathan flipped a hand in the air.

"I don't care," he said. "The point is I need something to do. I don't think sitting here all day without utility will make me crave impure less. Better I get out in the Circle and make something of myself. And I certainly wouldn't mind seeing Ramson's eyes go blank. I like the idea of me being the last thing he ever saw. It makes me feel special."

Nathan jutted out his chin, blinked with toughness.

"Sun's up. So let's go."

They walked to the door. Nathan opened it, but stepped aside to let Baldwin go through first.

"You take the lead now," he said. "But once we spot Ramson, it's my show. I'll distract him, and then you come up and give it to him good. Think you can do it?"

"I'll try."

"Try hard."

Baldwin shoved the knife into his pocket. He stepped through the door, waited for Nathan to do the same, and then led him down the stairs. This time he didn't count floors.

39 AIR BRUSH

It was a beautiful day. The sun was bright, there were no clouds, but the snarling humidity, normal in the Circle, was missing. It made Baldwin feel suspicious, as if he was being coerced into feeling grateful, if not for the lack of heat than the refreshing breeze in his face as he walked. Nathan clearly did not have the same trepidations: he walked with chin up, his upper and lower teeth snapping against each other as he gulped air greedily.

"Have you ever breathed anything like it?" he asked Baldwin after they had traveled a good 200 paces. The old man's chest heaved with pleasure. "This might be the best feeling I ever had not connected to a vial."

Baldwin might have agreed, but he was startled to see a little man with a black cooking pot emerge from a side path and approach them. He was wearing a yellow jump suit with a red sash around his neck. He banged the pot as he drew near, then set it down and pointed at both of them.

"The Day of No Consequence is finally here. Much to look forward to and much to fear. So go get to it, don't hide from strife. The sooner you defeat it, the sooner you begin life."

The little man's eyes locked on Baldwin's.

"Good luck," he said, and then walked away.

"What was that about?" Nathan asked.

"Just someone passionate about the day, I suppose."

Nathan shook his head. "Fellow like that won't last an hour. Someone will brain him for sure."

Baldwin took in a breath and exhaled. He patted the knife in his pocket for assurance. He did not know if he would be successful in killing Ramson; most likely he would not, as he knew, deep down, he lacked the mind for murder. But he was determined to try, willing to risk failure, and possibly his life. Baldwin forced himself not to visualize that consequence. Instead he focused on Nathan, imitated the old man's gleeful breathing. It did taste good. He flared his nostrils, flexed his arms, lifted his chin to the sun. It was a great day, a day to kill or die. He felt alive. He turned to Nathan, stretched out a smile, almost believed he looked courageous.

"If I die today," he said, his throat catching with emotion. "I want you to know I'm grateful for you coming with me."

"Let's not plan on you dying," Nathan said. "You die and I might, too. And I don't want to die, not with this air about."

"I just wanted you to know how I feel."

"It's not that I don't appreciate it, I just think we should focus on killing, not on feelings."

"Okay."

Nathan held his hand up to Baldwin, motioned for him to stop.

"So let's go over this again," he said. "When we get in sight of Big Birch break off. I know the area pretty well. There's a patch of green wheat grass to the left that's high enough for you to scurry through and get around them. Just wait to see me coming up on Ramson. I'll get him in a conversation. Maybe ask him where I can go get some impure. When you think he looks relaxed enough, come up fast from behind. Like I said, hit him hard once right between the shoulders, yank the blade out fast, pull him backwards, and then finish him off. Got it?"

"I think so."

"Don't think," Nathan's voice rose. "Especially when you make your move. Just get the feet going toward him and your arm will follow. Once you get the blade in, instinct will take over. It always does."

Baldwin nodded.

"Just make sure he's distracted," Nathan continued. "That's the key to this whole thing. Distraction. That's the only way…"

The sharp crack caused Baldwin to jump involuntarily. When he landed, so did Nathan, face first in the dust. The old man quivered once and then went still. The back of his head leaked blood. Baldwin could see bone

"There you go," Ramson, said pushing the end of his learning stick into the wound. He probed a bit and then pulled it away. He pointed it at Baldwin and smiled.

"I'm grateful to see you. What a beautiful day, don't you think?"

Baldwin dove his hand in his pocket, pulled out the knife, thrust it at Ramson. But it wasn't the knife. It was The *New Book of Ash*. He had forgotten he had also taken it from Hetta's unit and was carrying it.

"What are you going to do, read to me?" Ramson sneered. He slipped the learning stick into its holder and eyed Baldwin's other pocket. "You can pull that out too, whatever it is. I don't mind."

Baldwin turned. Hetta was coming toward him. Her blonde hair shone golden in the sunlight. The rest of her body was coated in paint: even bands of blue, red, and black rolling up her body, the same pattern on the walls of her unit, stopping only at her neck. She raised her hand and waved.

"I'm grateful to see you're unharmed," she said.

Baldwin took a step back.

"Don't be scared," she soothed. "Nothing is going to happen to you."

Ramson snorted. He nudged his boot under Nathan's chest and flipped him over. The old man's face was smeared with dust. His eyes were open. So was his mouth.

"Let's see if Baldwin's going to do what we want him to before we promise anything," he said.

Hetta reached out, laid her hand on Baldwin's shoulder, on the old wound made by the deer.

"Look at me," she said. "Look at my body. Do you understand?"

Baldwin blinked. He wanted to run, but his feet felt leaden.

Hetta leaned forward, kissed the tip of his nose.

"I think you're perfect," she said. "Perfect for me."

"Please," Ramson snorted again. "He's perfect for one thing: to kill Leonard. Other than that he's got no utility."

"Stop that," Hetta snapped. "You're encouraged to do what I encourage you to do, and not voice opinions."

She took in a breath, began to rub Baldwin's shoulder, sliding her fingers along the muscle until she found the split in his collarbone. Her eyes trailed down to his hand.

"How did you get my book?" she asked.

Baldwin blinked harder. Feeling was returning to his feet, to his hands, to his mind.

"I found it in your unit...or whoever owns it."

"What took you there?"

"I thought he lived there." Baldwin darted his eyes at Ramson. "I was going to kill him and save you. No one was there and I found the book."

Hetta looked suddenly shy.

"Do you like it? I mean, did you read any of it?"

Baldwin nodded. He flexed his fingers, inched his arm toward his pocket, to where the knife still sat.

"Tell me what you think?"

"It's good."

"Don't just say that because I'm asking you. Be brutal. Did it move you?"

"Yes."

She licked at her lips.

"I believe you. That's why you're perfect for me. You get me. I knew it the moment I saw you…the moment I touched you."

Baldwin moved his fingers into his pocket. He glanced at Ramson. He was absently scratching the top of his learning stick, seemingly bored.

"The thing is I have some ideas about the future," Hetta continued. "I guess more than ideas, like a vision. You're part of my vision. I see now that you're the miracle, not the orgasm."

Ramson clicked his tongue with disgust.

"Just tell him what we really want," he said flatly. "Before the sun sets and we lose the day."

Hetta's eyes flashed angrily at the conflict counselor.

"You don't understand that the moment needs nourishing," she snapped again. "You only care about your chits."

"What else is there?"

"Love. Dignity. Freedom."

Ramson spat on his palm, wiped it off on his learning stick.

"You get more of that with chits in your pocket," he said. "It's easier to feel high-minded when you can bribe someone for an extra turnip or a shoelace. But a chitless life is a narrow life, trust me."

Hetta shook her head. She lowered her hand to Baldwin's wrist, took back the book, held it close between her breasts.

"You see I'm not wearing clothes," she said. "I've painted myself. Like a wall. I'm still blank below the surface, but to everyone else I'm alive, vibrant, flowing with color. The way things are now in the Circle, we're just the opposite – our feelings are hidden inside, stuck behind a blank wall. It's what people like Leonard want to continue. It's what Ash wanted. But it's the wrong path. I know the right path."

She reached out and pressed the book to Baldwin's heart.

"Will you follow me?"

Baldwin resisted the sensation caused by the book's touch, a warming feeling, a safe feeling, a feeling counter to the rage and shock and confusion that screamed at him to do something. He pushed the book away, reached into his pocket and pulled out the knife. He waived it at Hetta, then at Ramson.

"I should kill you both," he said.

"That's more like it." Ramson gave the learning stick a last wipe. "You're going to need that kind of mindlessness when you take on your father."

Baldwin waved the knife in a semi-circle.

"I won't tell you again: he's not my father."

"That's getting old," Ramson said. "Will you tell him the truth so we can get moving. We're lucky there's no one about right now, but soon everyone will be up and fighting and looking for a conflict counselor."

"What truth?" Baldwin turned to Hetta. "The only truth I see is that you're a liar."

Hetta did not appear worried about the knife, but she did not try to get nearer than the reach of the blade.

"The thing is that..." She narrowed her eyes to connote compassion. "The thing is that Leonard *is* your father. I guess, in a way, this is what this is all about."

Baldwin pushed the knife toward her throat.

"Stop trying to trick me."

"I'm not trying to trick you," Hetta said. "I never was. I just need you to do what I want."

"Why should I care anymore what you want? What anyone wants?"

"I understand," Hetta said. "But just listen. I promise this is the truth."

She breathed in deep, exhaled, the color bands across her body undulating in beautiful rhythm.

"It started after Leonard began working with Ernest. He was not improving and Leonard came to see me one night in the unit you found, where I do my outside touch sessions. He wanted to see if I had any insight on what Ernest might be withholding, what pain was causing him to act out, to drink impure, to cheat with other women, to be mean to me. Leonard was sincerely concerned. He liked Ernest. He thought he had potential; that he could be fixed. I tried to help, but my mind was already made up. I didn't want to be in a union with Ernest anymore, and so I didn't want him to improve. That would make the issue of leaving him even harder. Plus, by then, I had found out what I was meant to do" – she brought the book back into her bosom – "create a new path for people to follow."

Hetta took in another breath, waited longer to exhale, then continued.

"Around the same time I decided to read through *The Book of Ash*. It never really meant much to me before, but I was fed up with my life and was looking for answers. For one, the chits I was getting were no longer worth what I had to put in to get them. At least at the warm wash I was doing the utility I was encouraged to do; what I had no choice to do. But on my own, touching people I wasn't encouraged to touch, made me feel too powerful. It made me feel like I was taking advantage of my clients, getting them to pay me extra chits for the privacy, that I was no longer the victim. I realized I liked being the victim. So it was a struggle."

"Please," Ramson said, stepping forward. "What struggle is it to get ten more chits a month, even twenty more chits. The only struggle is not getting enough for what you do, like me. All day, every day, listening to people complain about the Circle, getting angry for doing what they're encouraged to do, breaking up fights between husbands and wives, children and parents, lovers. All for five chits a month. While a miracle counselor or some other indoor brain" – he nudged his chin angrily at Baldwin – "gets ten."

"Chits are not the point of this," Hetta said. "I'm just saying that it led me to the truth—about myself, about what I needed to do, about what I'm doing."

"You mean what we're doing," Ramson said. He pulled out the learning stick and pointed it at Baldwin. "Don't forget you need me more than I need you."

"Put that down," Hetta said. "We're not here to hurt Baldwin. We're here to help him. To help everybody."

Baldwin shook his head. He felt more nauseous than scared.

"I don't want help," he said. "I just want to go home."

"To what?" Ramson asked incredulously. "Your wife isn't there. About the only thing left waiting for you is a headless body."

"I don't care."

"You should." Hetta smiled softly. "You should care."

"I don't. I don't care about Nadine. I don't care about you. And I really don't care about him." He pointed the knife at Ramson. "I was going to kill him for you. I thought we would be together. I thought you loved me."

JOHN A. MCCAFFREY

"I do."

"You don't. If you did this would make sense, and it doesn't. The only thing that makes sense is that my life means nothing. Ramson's right: I have no wife. I have no home. I have nothing."

"Let me finish what I was saying," Hetta said, her voice pleading. "About *The Book of Ash*. Then you'll understand."

"I don't want to understand. I just want to go home. I want to be alone."

"I don't blame you," Hetta said. "But you have to listen to me. Please."

"I'll make him listen."

Hetta turned angrily to Ramson.

"Please go away," she said. "Take twenty steps back and turn around. Face the sun and think about how small you are. Just go away and let me talk."

Ramson's glare was hard and mean. He chewed on his lower lip a moment, then released it and spat.

"Okay," he said to Hetta. "Twenty paces and look at the sun. But I'm counting. If things aren't right by 1,000, I'm coming with my stick swinging."

Hetta waited until Ramson stepped away.

"Can you put down the knife?" she asked Baldwin. "It will help me say what I have to say if I know you trust me."

Baldwin looked at the blade, then he lowered it, but he did not place it back into his pocket.

"Thank you," she said. "Can I touch you? It helps me think more clearly."

She did not wait for Baldwin's answer. She reached out and took his right hand into her own. She caressed his fingers, then pulled his hand close to her, pressed his palm to her right breast, breathed into his touch.

"So I read *The Book of Ash*," she said. "Really read it. I tried to do what was encouraged, tried to apply it to my life, but it just wasn't happening. I found myself just getting angrier, feeling more distant and dissatisfied, more useless, more selfish, narrower. I felt completely alone. And I felt this more and more as I read."

Hetta smiled at Baldwin, moved his hand lower, so that it rested under the breast.

"And then Leonard came by, like I said, to talk about Ernest. He saw that I was reading *The Book of Ash* and we started talking about that.

I told him how it wasn't helping me; that the more I read the worse I felt. He got angry. He said it was my fault if I didn't gain inspiration from the words. He said that if reading the book made me feel bad about myself it was because I was bad. He said the book doesn't build character, it reveals it." Hetta paused. "And then he brought up you."

Baldwin blinked.

"Me."

"He said he had a son who also got nothing from the book. That he had tried his best to help him understand its power, but the boy was helpless, flawed, someone who would never reach his potential, mainly because he had no potential. Leonard was brutal and I said so. I asked him how he could be so cruel talking about his own son? And he said it was easy because he never had truly accepted him as a son. He said that although the child was his, biologically, the conception had been achieved without encouragement, and so he and the mother bribed the right people to make it appear the result of a stranger's insemination." She paused. "When I asked his son's name, he told me, 'Baldwin.'"

"You're lying."

"I'm not. This is what Leonard told me."

"Then Leonard's lying."

"Five hundred." Ramson's voice carried over to where they stood.

Hetta looked at Baldwin, lowered her voice.

"I can't tell you if he is or isn't, but what he said inspired me. I mean, after he left that night I decided that the Circle was just like him: cruel and mean. And I thought that men like Leonard are cruel and mean because they can get away with being cruel and mean; that they have a cloak of purity to hide their horrible selves. I saw *The Book of Ash* as that cloak, each encouragement a dagger into the heart of goodness. It might sound high-minded and trite, but that was how I thought about it, how I still think about it. So I started to change it. Each night in the unit, after my clients left, I would stay and write my own encouragements, a rebuttal to each one. I never thought I would show it to anyone, or that I would want to, I never even put my name to it, but I began to invest more and more of myself in the words, in what the book was becoming, and seeing that it might break the cloak, take away the hiding place for the cruel and the mean, put an end to people like Leonard and give room for people" – she swallowed – "like his son."

"Six hundred."

Hetta ignored Ramson's warning. "So I worked and worked, wrote and wrote, and my days got better, my nights filled. I no longer cared about Ernest. I no longer cared about how I felt. I only cared about the book. And then I finished. I wrote the last encouragement. I felt horrible and happy. Empty and full. It sounds confusing, but I was pulled each way, my mind was split. And I suddenly had a void. I had nothing to consume me. No book to write. Just time to think about Ernest, the clients I was touching, the same problems I had before I began."

"Seven hundred."

"So I went back to Leonard. I don't know why, but I needed to tell him about my book. Maybe I wanted to challenge him. Maybe I wanted him to punish me, to put me in a gratitude farm, even end my breathing. But on the way to his trailer something happened." She pressed Baldwin's hand harder to her flesh. "I saw you come out. And I followed you. The son who moved me. I fell in love with you by watching you. But I saw you were in a union – I did not want to add more cruelty into the Circle, did not want to impose my desire on the lives of two others. I considered you might be happy with your wife, might be fulfilled. So I did nothing. But then the miracle. The message. And I was in your office. I saw you were hurting. That you were not happy. That you needed my touch. Needed my love."

She pressed the book back into his hand.

"But mostly you need this. Everyone does. But it's not possible while Leonard is alive. He loves *The Book of Ash* too much, needs *The Book of Ash* too much, and worships it too much, to let anything else take its place. And he is powerful, the most powerful person in the Circle, but even greater than his power is the love and admiration he engenders from the people. They adore him as he does *The Book of Ash*. They don't see cruelty, they don't see meanness, only goodness, strength; he's their leader."

"Eight hundred."

"But you see it," Hetta speeded her words. "You've always seen it. He's wronged you. Not even accepting you as a *real* son. Belittling you. Sleeping with your wife. Degrading you. You have a right to challenge him."

"You mean, to kill him." Baldwin said.

"Yes," Hetta lowered her voice. "It's the only way. The people will understand that. No one else can kill him but you. If you kill him, the *New Book of Ash* lives. If you don't it dies. And if it dies, I die."

Baldwin hesitated. Hetta's words moved him, but he was still uncertain, still untrusting.

"Why did you tell me Ramson wanted to kill you?" he asked. "Why did you lie about the deal you made? Why didn't you tell me about the book? About everything?"

"I'm not sure myself. It seemed horrible to ask you to kill your father." She exhaled. "Plus, you brought that person with you to the warm wash, your neighbor."

"Simon."

"I knew he did something for Leonard, but I wasn't sure. I used to see him hanging about sometimes outside after I touched Leonard. I figured when he was with you that time that he was keeping a close look on you; that maybe Leonard knew something, guessed what I was thinking. I'm a believer in that sort of thing; maybe not mind reading, precisely, but getting a feeling from someone else that they mean to do you harm. You have to remember I touched Leonard; I assumed he sensed my malice."

"Simon's dead."

Her eyes narrowed.

"I know. I killed him."

"You?"

"I'm not ashamed or sorry. He meant to harm you, or at least trap you. I saw him let go of the rope that night. I was there. I followed you from the warm wash to the timehole. I saw what he did. I waited until he left and then tried to pull you out, but the rope came off. So I did the next best thing: I lured Simon back to the warm wash and killed him."

"You cut his head off and threw it into a pit."

"I was mad."

"Nine hundred."

Hetta pressed close to Baldwin.

"Will you do it?" she breathed. "Will you kill Leonard for me?"

Baldwin gripped the knife.

"I don't know."

Hetta turned her head. Ramson was coming forward, the learning stick gripped tight in his hand.

"Perhaps this will be healing," she said. "For you and the Circle. Sometimes the son has to let go of the father to be one himself." She patted her stomach. "Do you remember what happened to us? You left something inside when you penetrated me. I still feel it. We have approval. We can be a family. You can be a father."

Ramson drew close. He raised the learning stick over his head.

"Well," he said to Baldwin. "Kill or be killed. What will it be?"

Baldwin did not flinch. He slipped the knife back into his pocket, leaned forward, and kissed Hetta soft on the lips

"Both," he whispered.

40 MOTHER LAND

*B*aldwin's mother explained to him the ways of the Circle. He was seven when she sat him down at the kitchen table, after they had finished the evening meal, a surprising favorite, moldy plums and wheat grass, surprising because it hardly ever appeared in edible bags, and surprising because it was a food mostly coveted by older members of the Circle, individuals who knew the value of bacteria in their stomachs, people who craved digestive regularity more than taste.

Plum juice dripped from his chin while his mother spoke, explaining some of the basic encouragements for him to follow, such as never to interrupt a person when they are talking, unless what they are talking about needs to be interrupted. Baldwin listened with attention, as he was always very obedient and respectful of his mother, but he really was not much interested in these or other encouragements. At the end of the talk, his mother had left the table and returned with a book. She explained that this was *The Book of Ash*, and that it was the most important possession she or any other person in the Circle received from the Circle. She told him that one day he would get his own copy and the words and messages inside would help guide his life in a good direction. She said that many times she had turned to the book for support when she felt conflicted, and it had always helped her make a choice – perhaps not the best choice, but a choice nonetheless, which, she said with some force, was better than making no choice at all. She then said something curious, something that did not register with Baldwin at the time, or any time for that matter, until this moment, as he walked beside Hetta and behind Ramson, on a side path in pursuit of Leonard. "Your father knows more of Ash than anyone in the Circle. More than anyone will ever know."

His father. He tried not to think about what Hetta had said, tried not to remember more what his mother had said, tried not to think that Leonard might share his genetic material, might be linked to him by more than just marriage to his mother, that he might indeed be his father, his real father, and not a man who just happened to ruin his life by chance.

Hetta's touch was comforting. She held his hand while she walked, matching his stride, so that their legs moved in unison. For a while he concentrated only on her feet, which were bare, the right painted blue, the left red, and each toe an alternating black and white. It was still pleasant outside, but the breeze had ceased and heat began to creep around them, that and the bustling of people, men and women and children moving with extra purpose, some shouting angry insults at passersby, some weeping, some laughing, and some just staring blankly. Baldwin could sense the collective energy, like the boiling of water over a flame, the people in the Circle were beginning to bubble up, readying themselves for the Day of No Consequence, preparing themselves for what they might do or what might be done to them.

Ramson turned, pointed to his right.

"Time to get off the path."

They followed him through a clearing, past a community garden boasting pebble green tomatoes, cucumbers so fat they dragged down their branches, and orange peppers shaped like smiles. Ramson plucked one of the peppers as he passed, took a bite, then spit it out.

"Awful," he said, hurling the pepper to the side. "This is what you get when you reclaim soil that can't be reclaimed."

Hetta pulled Baldwin toward the discarded pepper. She reached down in stride and plucked it from the ground. She did not wipe it but took a bite. She chewed slowly, closed her eyes and swallowed.

"The problem's not the soil," she said, softly. "It's how they grow things now. They give the plants too much water, too much manure, too much food. They give the plant so much of what it needs it doesn't need to search for it, doesn't need to be innovative, desperate, strong. The roots don't need to grow deep. They stay at the surface where the nutrients are. That leaves the plant vulnerable to wind, to hard rain, anything that might cause it to bend or break. A soft plant has no pride, no purpose, no resolve. It grows lazy and fat and what it produces is lazy and fat. This pepper tastes lazy and fat."

Baldwin had never given such thought to a plant, never before thought it possessed any intelligence, direction in life, other than what was set for it as a seed.

"But I don't blame the grower anymore I blame the plant," Hetta continued. "I blame the Circle, *The Book of Ash*, people like Leonard. This is what happens when you live in a place that is bent on making things better, when you follow a doctrine designed to make things better, when you're led by a person who wants to make things better; things eventually get worse."

They continued for a few moments in silence. Baldwin turned his attention to the landscape, to another community garden, this one filled with speckled pumpkins, a variety eaten only for their seeds, dried and salted, while the husks and flesh were mashed and given to the women in jars to be used for face cream. They neared and entered a rust field and Baldwin now realized where they were going.

"Leonard's hiding in the timehole Simon took me?"

Hetta nodded.

"Do you think Leonard asked Simon to kill me?"

"I'm not sure. Ramson thinks Simon was on the take from your wife, in addition to working with Leonard. You know she wanted you dead. Maybe she asked Simon to kill you and leave you where Leonard would find you. That way he would have no excuse *not* to be with her. And since it would reflect badly on him, draw unwanted attention on him, to have his stepson found dead in his timehole, he would probably never let you out. Just plug the hole and leave you inside forever. That makes some sense: that Nadine was that desperate, Simon that greedy, and each counting on Leonard being that protective of his power."

Baldwin exhaled. "It seems like so much effort to do something to me that they just might have asked nicely for. I would have let Nadine out of the union to be with Leonard. I would have been hurt, but I would have let her go."

"Nice doesn't come into people's minds when they are in love. Especially when they are in love with someone they shouldn't be in love with. And even more so when the person they are in love with, who they shouldn't be in love with, doesn't love them as much as they love them. I think that's what Nadine was facing, so she decided to force Leonard to make a choice."

Baldwin thought of his mother. Her axiom about choices, right or wrong, bad or good, making a choice was always better than not making one.

"I'm not sure how I'll get close to Leonard, if he's in the hole." Baldwin hesitated. "I mean, how will I kill him?"

Hetta squeezed his hand.

"We have a plan. He has to think you're not here to kill him, or be suspicious you want to harm him, which is going to be hard considering that you are going to a place he thinks no one knows he's at. So for you to not arouse his suspicion will take a very plausible reason for you being there."

"Which is?"

"Love." Hetta nodded, as if approving the notion. "You followed Nadine to the timehole and came to take her home."

"Are you sure she's there?"

"Yes, both of them." She paused. "I'm sorry if this is painful, but Ramson trailed them to the timehole last night. He heard them coupling inside."

"I don't care. What's your idea – about how I can kill Leonard?"

"We thought you would go up to the timehole, call down for Nadine and Leonard to come out. When they do, you engage Leonard in an argument, get him distracted, and then Ramson will come up from behind with his stick and hit him hard, knock him to the ground. Then you can take time to stab him in the heart, in the neck, around the stomach, enough that he won't ever breathe again."

"Why doesn't Ramson just kill him with his stick? Why do I have to stab him?"

"Because it only works if the son kills the father, the story, you see, what we tell the Circle, what they will understand and empathize with. We can't let them think we killed Leonard for our gain, for the benefit of my book. They will never accept it as the true message if they think it rose from ambition and not inspiration. That's what's so powerful and enticing about *The Book of Ash* – no one has ever met Ash, or knows what he looks like, or who his family and friends were. The unknown is interesting and flexible, it takes the shape of whatever people want it to, it fills whatever void is open, it becomes what it is needed to become."

"But we could just lie. I will say I killed him, even if Ramson does the work."

Hetta stopped. She gripped Baldwin's hand tighter.

"No one believes what people say, only what they see. We need a witness to the act, someone who has no reason to lie, someone who will spread the word, who is involved in the matter, who validates the vengeance."

"You mean Nadine?"

Hetta nodded.

"We need her to see you stab him. We need her to spread the word."

"What if she sees Ramson club Leonard first, or you?"

"It's okay if she sees Ramson. You can just say you hired him to help. No one will care. They will only remember hearing about you stabbing the man who slept with your wife." She paused. "I will be near, but not seen, trust me."

They began to walk again. Baldwin glanced ahead. He recognized the thicket of brush set about to obscure the timehole's entrance.

"There it is."

Hetta stopped. Ramson stopped. They looked at each other. With a nod, Ramson set out to the side, in an arcing circle, crouched low, moving back and away, setting himself up to come from behind the timehole. Hetta squeezed Baldwin's hand one more time. She leaned forward, pressed her body to his, and kissed him tight on the lips. She pulled away in sections.

"I love you," she said.

Baldwin shuddered when they parted. He watched her walk away, the colors on her body radiating against the light bouncing off the dry and cracked rust field. She turned and waved, then slid behind a giant slab of cement. He was suddenly alone. He was still scared. But he made his choice. He moved toward the timehole.

41 CUT THROAT

*M*ovement is the result of a decision to lead, but a decision to lead does not always result in movement."

It was Leonard's favorite phrase when discussing the building of one's self esteem, which, being the mentor of this emotion in the Circle, he was considered to know a thing or two about. Baldwin did not deny Leonard's acumen in this area, or doubt his record of inspiring people to think better of themselves, but he did not think this work ever helped him become a better person, or a worthy one, certainly not someone who deserved the lofty status in the Circle he currently enjoyed. Baldwin, simply, thought Leonard a failure, someone beholden to his urges and desires, someone who could not let go of a moment's control, someone who winked and smiled in public and sneered and raged at home. Basically, Baldwin blamed Leonard, as stepfather, for his unhappy life. And now, having made the decision to move, to walk to the timehole and confront Leonard and kill him, he felt shame.

Perhaps it was the thought that Leonard was his father, that they shared genetic material. But that did not seem to be the problem – no matter the truth, his dislike for Leonard was too great, too long cultivated, too rooted in his thinking to be overshadowed by mere blood. The shame he felt was springing up from a different source, a deeper well, the part of him that always ruled his behavior no matter how hard he tried to overrule it. Not his subconscious, but his mother. Her voice called out to him, ringing in his ears as if boxed by a punch, crunching against his nerves with each step forward in the orange silt. Her anger began to bind him, constricting his ribs, tightening his forehead, strangling against his neck. Breathing became difficult, he thought he might faint, fall into the silt, die right there, but he moved on, shaking his head against her voice, her begging screams for him to stop, to turn around, to end this madness, explaining that she had not raised him to do such a thing, to hate at such a level. That was it. His subconscious mother was not upset that he aimed to kill Leonard, but that he *felt* enough to kill Leonard. He winced as he took in a breath, his chest aching with the effort. The entrance to the timehole was close. He exhaled. Took a few more steps. Inhaled. Took a few more. His mother's voice grew louder, hurt as much as the breathing. Finally he had enough.

"Stop it," he screamed.

He had not planned the outburst. The words spun past his lips and zipped into the clear air. He watched them go, two black specks rising up and away, vanishing into the growing sunlight. And with their departure his body went slack and he took an easy breath. He suddenly felt calm.

"Who's up there?"

It was Leonard's voice. Baldwin peeled back the bushes and sticks until he got to the opening. He peered down inside. A ladder had been fixed leading down into the hole. Candles were lit and it was bright. Leonard was looking up at him.

"Baldwin? Is that you?"

"Yes."

"What are you doing here?"

"I came to get Nadine?"

"Are you alone?"

Baldwin glanced past the timehole. As planned, Ramson was crouched a few feet behind on the other side of the entrance, half his body obscured by a jagged slab of cement. Baldwin saw the tip of his learning stick swirl like a serpent's head low to the ground.

"Yes."

"How did you find us?"

"I followed Nadine last night. She's in there with you, I know it."

Leonard blinked. His face was bright pink and sweaty.

"Yes. But she's hiding in the corner. I imagine she's a bit ashamed for her actions of late. She hasn't been the best wife to you. It's what we've been talking about all this time; how she can do better in your union."

"Tell her I don't want her to do better. I don't want her to do anything."

Leonard clicked his tongue.

"You don't mean that. Nadine is a perfect wife for you, just like your mother was for me."

"Don't talk about my mother."

"Okay. What should we talk about?"

"You and I."

"Okay."

Baldwin locked eyes with Leonard.

"I can't talk looking down at you. Come up where we'll be even."

"I doubt that would make us even."

"Please."

Leonard clapped his hands.

"You know politeness always works with me, but I don't think it's enough in this case."

"Why not?"

"Because intuition tells me the only reason you want me to come out of this hole is to do me harm."

"Do you deserve to be harmed?"

"Well, I can see where you might jump to a wrong conclusion about me and Nadine."

"I told you I don't care. You can have Nadine if you want."

"That's decent of you," Leonard laughed. "But why would I want your wife, when I already had my own? Tell you what: you come down here and we'll talk it all out. The three of us haven't been together as a family in some time, maybe since your mother ended her breathing. I think it would be nice, even healing."

"No. You have to come out."

"I don't have to do anything," he said. "I'm the Mentor of Self Esteem in this Circle, remember. And even though your mother is gone, I'm still the head of your life."

Baldwin turned his head to the spot he last saw Hetta.

"You're right," he said. "I want to do you harm. I always have. But now I'm finally going to do it."

"And why's that?"

"Because I found out you're my real father."

"Who told you that?"

"You."

"That's ridiculous. I never would say such a thing to you."

"But maybe you did to someone else."

Leonard set his mouth in a hard line.

"So you want to kill me because I'm your father?"

"Is it true?"

Leonard's smile curled with arrogance.

"Do you really think I would make a union with your mother if she had already been penetrated?"

Baldwin inhaled through his nose. He patted the blade in his pocket. "So come up and let's settle this."

"Settle what? There's nothing to settle. Maybe if you were just more forthright. Just tell me what you want to do to me, and then maybe I'll give you the chance."

"I want to stab you."

"Good answer." Leonard held up his hands. "And why?"

"For revenge."

"That sounds a bit contrived. Try again."

"Because I hate you."

"Now you got it. I guess I can see motive: longing as a boy for a *real* father, thinking this person would love and understand you and make all your troubles disappear, and then you finally accept that this real father won't be in your life, will never be in your life, and your stuck with the fake father, so you harden your mind and body against the fake father, who is real, while you save the love and softness for the real father, who is fake. And now you find out that your fake father is your real father and that none of them measure up to what you need. Must be confusing."

Leonard nodded his head, cleared his throat and continued.

"And here I sit in a timehole with your wife. Okay, I'll accept your hate and wanting to kill me. And I'll even come out and give you the chance to stab me. But I doubt you'll do it."

Leonard began to climb up the ladder.

"One thing I learned in my time as Mentor of Self Esteem," he said, his voice strained with effort, "is that blood is thicker than confusion."

Baldwin slipped his hand into his pocket, fingered the knife handle. At the same time he eyed Ramson. The conflict counselor nodded back. He rose but remained in a crouch, inched forward toward the hole.

Leonard's hand reached the top rung. He stopped climbing. Looked up.

"At least give me a fighting chance," he said. "Let me gather myself before you try to stab me."

"I won't do anything to you until you're ready," Baldwin said.

"Promise."

"I promise."

"That's good for me. I know you well enough that you don't lie unless you want to make some one feel better about themselves. Since you most likely don't care what I feel, you must be telling the truth."

Baldwin watched as Leonard emerged from the hole. He sprang quick to his feet and smiled.

"Now we're on equal footing, so to speak."

Ramson had stretched up to his full height. He was only a few feet behind Leonard. The learning stick was in position to bring him down.

"So where's this knife," Leonard said. "Let me see what you think might do the job on me."

Baldwin pulled out the knife. The blade appeared small and thin and not at all dangerous.

"That's not much of a knife," Leonard laughed. "I don't think you could cut a stalk of spinach with that, lest a human heart. Are you serious?"

Baldwin blushed. He did not know why Ramson was not striking.

"It will do the job."

Leonard clicked his tongue in dismay. "I imagine it's my fault this time, and not your mother's. A real father would have taught his son to be more ruthless, certainly more realistic. Then again, I should think you never had much chance to practice either in your utility. A miracle counselor is quite a flimsy position. There really is no need to develop backbone when you're dealing with people's fantasies. Patience, for sure, but not persistence." He smiled. "Well, get on with it."

Baldwin glanced furtively at Ramson. He wanted to yell out at the conflict counselor to attack.

"See," Leonard said, mockingly. "You can't do it. I knew you couldn't. And I don't even think it has anything to do with you loving me down deep, just that you're soft and led by fear. I see your mother all in you right now; your eyes give off the same light. She was soft too, but then again she was a woman. It's horrible to see that trait in a man. I imagine that's one reason Nadine favors me over you."

Baldwin decided not to wait anymore. He closed his eyes and lunged forward, the knife leading the way, aimed at Leonard's stomach. He felt the blade dig in, deep enough so that his hand rested against flesh. He release his grip, opened his eyes. Blood began to stain his victim's shirt at the waistline.

"Nice try," Ramson said, pulling out the knife from his stomach.

Baldwin squinted with disbelief into the conflict counselor's eyes.

"But if you want to kill someone right off," Ramson continued, raising his learning stick, "it's best to split their head open."

Baldwin did not move. He made an instantaneous decision to accept the blow. Not that he could avoid it even if he wanted, but it was better this way, not fighting, not hoping, not trying to understand, but just accepting.

Ramson smiled.

"Any last words of gratitude?"

"Yes. I'm grateful for your loyalty."

It was Leonard. He took the knife from Ramson. He wiped away the blood on the conflict counselor's shirtsleeve.

"You have been perfect in every way. A true servant of the Circle, of Ash. But I'm sorry. There's no way to end this day with you breathing. Perhaps you always knew it would end this way, but still it must be a shock. Anyway, I have to kill you."

Baldwin watched Ramson swallow meekly.

"Are you sure?" his voice cracked.

"Oh yes," Leonard said. "I never joke about taking a life. It's something I've always lived by: never joke about killing people unless you want enemies. And I don't want enemies."

"I'm not your enemy."

"No. But you were going to kill my son."

"Because you encouraged me to."

"You always do everything you're encouraged to do?"

"You know I do."

"Well, now I encourage you to die."

Leonard brought the blade up to Ramson's chin. He lifted the conflict counselor's free hand and wrapped it around the knife's handle.

"I encourage you to cut your own throat."

"Is this really what you encourage me to do?"

Leonard looked bored.

"I already told you I don't joke about these things."

"I guess I'm grateful for that."

Ramson took in a breath, and then dragged the blade across his throat, back and forth, causing blood to rush out from the wounds, splashing onto the silt below. Finally, the conflict counselor's legs buckled, he choked, spat blood several times, made a grunting sound, and then fell forward, like a tree sawed off at its base.

42 STRAIGHT FORWARD

*I*s everything alright?"

Baldwin recognized Nadine's voice from inside the timehole.

"Yes, no problem." Leonard returned.

"What happened?"

"Nothing, dear. Just having a chat with Baldwin. I'll be down soon."

"She's not such a bad person, your wife," Leonard continued. "Just a bit confused about her likes and dislikes, but we'll clear it all up today and you two can get back to being in a normal union. But first we have to take care of one more thing." He cupped his hands to his mouth. "You can come out now, dear," his voice carried across the rust field. "It's all over."

Baldwin turned. Hetta, as if hiding flat in the silt, rose up. She was less than twenty paces away and began to move toward them, her eyes set on the ground as she walked.

Baldwin turned back to Leonard, scanned the ground by his feet. Ramson had dropped the knife after cutting himself. It lay in a neat puddle of blood near his head. Baldwin made a move to pick it up, but Leonard beat him to it, reaching down and carefully picking it up by the handle with his index finger and thumb of his right hand. He held it out and wrinkled his nose as blood dripped from the blade point.

"Perhaps I'll keep this," he said. "I'm in need of a good meat knife now that deer season is coming."

Baldwin turned his head again. Hetta was closing in.

"I imagine this all needs some explaining, but perhaps it's best if Hetta tells you herself."

Leonard smiled broadly as she approached.

"I'm grateful for your wonderful decorations," he said. "The colors on your body absorb my attention, so much so that I hardly notice your ripe breasts and fertile regions."

Hetta stopped. She kept her eyes on the ground.

"I'm not grateful," she said. "I'm ashamed."

"Of what?" Leonard said. "Everything is working out. It's turning into an excellent Day of No Consequence."

"You didn't have to kill Ramson."

"I didn't kill him. He ended his own breathing. Isn't that right, Baldwin?"

"You encouraged him to do it."

Leonard shrugged.

"But he didn't have to obey me. It wasn't a command, just a suggestion. He died by choice. A good choice, if you ask me."

"You should leave, Baldwin," Hetta said. "Your father and I have things to work out."

"Perhaps so," Leonard said. "But I think my son – gosh I like saying that – deserves some explanation. I mean, the poor lad has experienced much these past few days. And given that he is clearly smitten with you and the idea he might spend the rest of his breathing days in the Circle by your side, I think it would be nice to tell him why this will never be so."

Hetta looked up at Baldwin.

"It's simple, really. Your father tempted me and I did not resist."

Leonard snorted. He waved the knife at Hetta.

"You make it sound so trite, as if there is not psychology to the whole thing, no suppressed urges, sexual cravings, twisted paternal passions, no craziness. This is not a logical situation, not something that makes sense. Nothing of genius ever is. This is mania on a scale without measure."

Hetta shook her head. "It's not complicated. You make it seem so because you don't want to face the truth of who you are, what the Circle is, what we all are. We're simple and base and our needs dominate. You tempted me and I conceded to the temptation, that's all."

Leonard exhaled. "I see that I'll have to tell him." He lowered the knife. "Look at me, Baldwin."

Baldwin blinked at Hetta, and then turned to Leonard.

"As you know, my utility is to build self esteem, to make people feel better about themselves, to make them feel better about the Circle. Because you can't feel good about yourself if you don't feel good about where you live. And the only way to feel good about where you live is to root out dissent, the critics, people who have the opinion that things aren't that good and they would like to make it better. Those are the ones who bring everyone else down: the skeptics, the complainers, the idealists. They put into people's minds the idea that things are not all they should be in their life, and once that seeps in, penetrates, it's hard to get it out. The result is dissatisfaction, regret and remorse, and, eventually, hate. That's the one thing I loved more than anything else about your mother: she hated hate. Maybe her aversion to the feeling was a bit excessive, or more obsessive, but her thinking was pure and her reasoning right. The problem is that hate can only be stamped out with hate. It's too strong an emotion to be beaten back with goodness. And while forgiving a hateful person for their hate might help that person hate less at the moment, it certainly doesn't stop them from hating more in the future. So the thing to do is to hate the haters, and to do that you have to identify them, find them, bring them out in the open." Leonard pointed the knife at Hetta. "And so that's what I do."

"He doesn't care for my book," Hetta said.

"A most revolting perversion of a good mind's work." Leonard said viciously. "I don't mind the act of writing, you should know, although it does seem a useless enterprise given that no one in the Circle is encouraged to read any more than the encouragement in front of them that day. But to have the mind to create something with the hope of it usurping something already created that is perfect, that is truly audacious, truly wasteful, and utterly unacceptable."

"So why not just get rid of it and me?" Hetta snapped. "Why put me through all this – put your *son* through all this?"

Leonard wrinkled his nose as if detecting a bad smell.

"Somehow 'son' doesn't sound right when you say it," he said. "Makes me feel as if he's my fault entirely."

"There's nothing wrong with Baldwin."

"Maybe not, but I doubt there's much right either. This is to say he is evenly balanced, which is not such a bad thing to be." He pointed the blade at Baldwin. "You look to be in shock. You do comprehend this, don't you?"

Baldwin did not answer.

"Well, even if you don't, I'll feel better about myself if I get it all out. And it's most important for me to feel good about myself, given my status, then anyone else in the Circle."

Leonard closed his eyes a moment, waved the knife.

"Okay, where was I – yes, Hetta's book." He said the two words with mocking disdain. "So my loyal and dearly missed subject, the not-breathing conflict counselor Ramson, alerted me to this young lady's efforts. As it was, she was already engaged in the process of touching me and while her fingers were soothing to my skin, even replenishing, I detected some feeling of sedition in her strokes, a subtle brush of disdain for the life she was leading. In particular, her kneading of my lower back produced in me a feeling not unlike constipation, but perhaps her beauty discouraged me from probing deeper; and, of course, I was making great headway as a life counselor with her husband."

"It would have been better for both of us if we never met you," Hetta said.

Leonard clicked his tongue.

"Don't be silly. It all worked out to your satisfaction, and his, I imagine. Ernest was just not someone who wanted to get better, and although he did not think of himself as wounded, psychically, that is, he was indeed not whole emotionally. Ramson told me he's dead and I am not sorry. Perhaps having his head removed from his body is a fitting end to someone so disconnected from their true self."

Hetta's eyes hardened.

"I didn't have any part of it."

"Of course you did. You made a deal with Ramson to kill him, didn't you? What's the difference if it came as a result of a different hand?"

"I changed my mind. I asked Ramson to leave Ernest alone."

"But that's not what you wanted. Once infected with the passion of an idea, the idea that you can make things better, you can never get rid of it. Ernest was a block to this idea coming true, so you wanted him dead and now he's dead and, I guess, your idea is dead. Your book, to stretch the metaphor, will never breathe."

"But you said if I tempted Baldwin, encouraged him to kill you, you would replace *The Book of Ash* with my book. Give it to everyone in the Circle. Encourage they read it."

"I did say all that."

Hetta stepped forward.

"Well I did it. I shamed myself. I lied. I did everything horrible to Baldwin I could. And here he is, ready to kill you. So you got what you wanted. You owe me."

"What I wanted was to see what Baldwin would do if pushed to the edge," Leonard said, smirking. "You see, other than Baldwin, no one in the Circle is any threat to me. But because he is my *son*, because I made a mistake of telling you this, because I knew it would come back to me someday, might ruin me, I needed to test his resolve now, see if he cared at all, make sure I was right to think him deadened inside, devoid of passion or independent thought. I needed to see that I still scare him, that I can still control him."

"And what do you think?" Hetta asked.

Leonard took in a long breath.

"Even though he did come with a knife, and did thrust in my general direction, I believe him not to be a threat. In fact, I think we might even have a good relationship moving forward. I'm willing to forget this incident, these past few days, and start anew. It's rather exciting to me even to think how we might get along now that we have both accepted our blood connection." He smiled. "What do you think, Baldwin?"

Baldwin blinked. He didn't need to answer, probably wouldn't be able to get Leonard's attention if he did, given that Manu had rushed up between them and fell upon Ramson's body.

"What happened?" Manu said, his voice inflamed.

Leonard took a step back, edged toward the timehole. Manu looked up and saw the knife in his hand.

"You killed him."

"No. He did it himself. He cut his own throat."

Manu stood. He looked wildly at Baldwin.

"Is that true?"

Baldwin shook his head.

"Leonard ended Ramson's breathing. He was in love with him, but Ramson said he loved you. So he killed him."

Manu rose up and moved toward Leonard.

"I waited all night for him," he said. "I made holes in my sheets, in my walls. I opened my unit. I opened my heart. He was my true love. And you ended it."

Leonard took another careful step back. He held up the knife with a shaky hand.

"I encourage you to stop right there, young man. We can talk about your feelings, but not here. I encourage you to think about your loss and come to my trailer tomorrow. I'll give you a whole morning to express yourself. How's that sound?"

"Ramson was my love," Manu said. "He was the message. The seizures. They meant nothing. But they meant everything, because they brought Ramson to me. Now you took him away."

"He took himself away," Leonard thundered

"You lie."

Manu lunged at the same moment Leonard thrust out with the knife. For a moment they stood connected, Manu's arms wrapped tight around Leonard, then they parted. Manu staggered back a step, the knife lodged in his chest. Leonard gasped.

"He's trying to kill me. Baldwin, get him away from me."

Baldwin did as he was encouraged. He gripped Manu under his arms, helped his friend to the ground, kissed his forehead.

"For love," he said. He pulled the knife free. Eyed Leonard. Then charged.

43 FREE FALL

The fall into the timehole felt familiar to Baldwin. The feeling of falling and not connecting, drifting down to a certain demise, weightless, helpless, hopeless. It was a constant dream, a recurring dream, a frightening dream, a dream experienced long before his connection with the deer, a real connection, but one that caused unreal connections at night. Those dreams, his "deer dreams," Harold labeled them, were never as horrid as the falling dreams, the dreams where he floated downward, swallowed up into blackness, waiting and waiting for the bottom which never came.

This time, however, he did connect. He met the bottom, the dream fulfilled, his subconscious fear pulled out into a realistic pain. But it wasn't that bad. Leonard had cushioned the blow, saved him really, given that Leonard himself was no longer moving, or breathing, but merely looking up into his eyes, his son's eyes, a crease of a smile on his face, his arms spread apart, a sign of submission, aided, perhaps, by the knife in his heart.

Baldwin rolled off. Made a fast inventory of his body, checking if every limb worked, moved the way they were intended to move, felt the way they were intended to feel. He was not hurt. He would live. Leonard would not. It was over. He moved to the ladder. A hand stopped him. It held him by the shoulder. He turned. It was Nadine. Her eyes shone blue and bright behind a candle.

"I'm grateful to see you, Baldwin," she said, her voice small, tiny, a girl's voice in a woman's body. It was the voice he married, and the voice he no longer wanted.

"Hello, Nadine."

"Are you alright?"

"I'm fine."

"Is he dead?"

Baldwin looked at Leonard.

"Yes."

"You killed him."

"I did."

Nadine let go of her grip. She lowered the candle, placed it on the floor.

"I guess we should go home," she said.

Baldwin blinked. Nadine looked vulnerable, sweet, needy.

"No."

"Then what do we do?"

Baldwin looked up to the top of the timehole. Hetta was looking down at him, smiling softly.

"Who's that?" Nadine asked.

"The future," he said, moving to the ladder

44 END LESS

They walked with Manu between them, holding him up by wrapping his arms over their shoulders. He was in pain, but the bleeding had stopped with Hetta's help. She had touched the wound, massaged the skin, stopped the flow with her hands, her will. Baldwin was certain his friend would live. He was not meant to end his breathing today, perhaps not for some time. He considered the same held for him, and for Hetta. They were all alive, all breathing, all touching.

They left Manu at a healing center, made certain he had a good mat to rest on, a safe place to heal, to give his mind a chance to take care of its body. They promised they would be back at sunrise, that they would bring with them water and food. Manu craved blueberries and bamboo leaves, and Baldwin assured him he would bring back both. Outside, the sun was setting. It had been a long day, a violent day, a transformative day. Perhaps it was mean of him to take up the ladder from the timehole after he climbed out, leaving Nadine behind yelling for help. But getting out would be her challenge. He had confronted his own and knew there would be more ahead. The thought excited him. He twined his arm through Hetta's. Kissed her absent ear.

"What a nice couple."

The conception counselor they had met with came toward them.

"Don't tell me," she said. "The female is Hetta, the man, Ernest."

"That's right."

"I tell you, I've never seen a better matched couple." She smiled shyly. "Can I ask how the conception is going?"

Baldwin smiled back.

"I think we might have already succeeded. But if not, we'll keep trying."

"That's the spirit. Remember what it says in *The Book of Ash* – 'never give up until you want to try again.'" She made a face. "That doesn't really make much sense does it, but you get the idea, don't you?"

Baldwin held Hetta close. He kissed her again.

"Yes," he said. "We do."

CPSIA information can be obtained at www.ICGtesting.com
Printed in the USA
BVOW08s1925281013

334865BV00002B/8/P